THE TRAIN TO IMPOSSIBLE PLACES

A Cursed Delivery

THE TRAIN TO IMPOSSIBLE PLACES

A CURSED DELIVERY

P. G. BELL

illustrations by Matt Sharack

FEIWEL AND FRIENDS
NEW YORK

A Feiwel and Friends Book

An imprint of Macmillan Publishing Group, LLC
175 Fifth Avenue, New York, NY 10010

The Train to Impossible Places: A Cursed Delivery.
Text copyright © 2018 by Ty Gloch Limited. Illustrations copyright © 2018 by Matt Sharack.
All rights reserved.

Printed in the United States of America
by LSC Communications, Harrisonburg, Virginia.

Our books may be purchased in bulk for promotional, educational, or business use.
Please contact your local bookseller or the Macmillan Corporate and
Premium Sales Department at (800) 221-7945 ext. 5442 or by e-mail at
MacmillanSpecialMarkets@macmillan.com.

Library of Congress Cataloging-in-Publication Data is available.
ISBN 978-1-250-18950-9 (hardcover) / ISBN 978-1-250-18951-6 (ebook)

BOOK DESIGN BY KATIE KLIMOWICZ

Feiwel and Friends logo designed by Filomena Tuosto
First edition, 2018

1   3   5   7   9   10   8   6   4   2

mackids.com

For Aurelien, who heard this story first

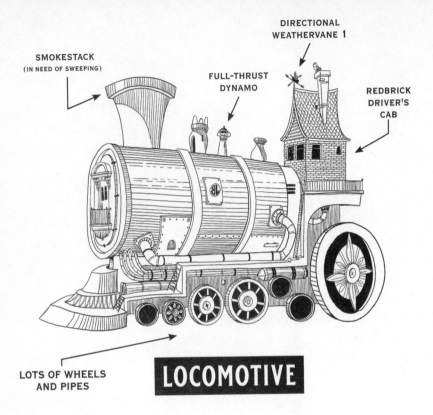

SMOKESTACK
(IN NEED OF SWEEPING)

DIRECTIONAL
WEATHERVANE 1

FULL-THRUST
DYNAMO

REDBRICK
DRIVER'S
CAB

LOTS OF WHEELS
AND PIPES

LOCOMOTIVE

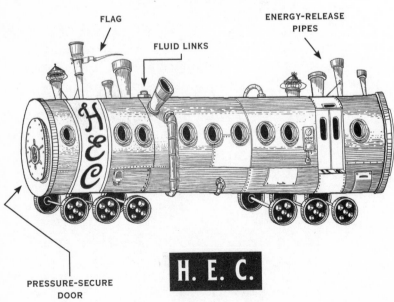

FLAG

FLUID LINKS

ENERGY-RELEASE
PIPES

PRESSURE-SECURE
DOOR

H. E. C.

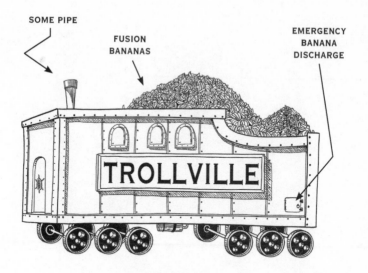

SOME PIPE

FUSION BANANAS

EMERGENCY BANANA DISCHARGE

TROLLVILLE

TENDER

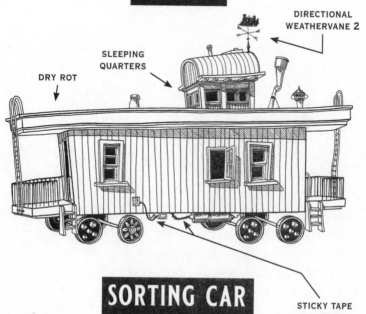

DIRECTIONAL WEATHERVANE 2

SLEEPING QUARTERS

DRY ROT

SORTING CAR

STICKY TAPE AND STRING

THE TRAIN TO IMPOSSIBLE PLACES

A Cursed Delivery

1

LIGHTNING IN THE LIVING ROOM

It started with a flash.

A green flash, as bright and quick as lightning, there and then gone again. It happened so quickly that Suzy wasn't sure she had seen anything at all, although she raised her head from her homework and looked around.

"What was that?" she asked.

"What was what, darling?" said her mother from the sofa, where she and Suzy's father both sprawled in a heap, still in their work clothes.

Suzy frowned. "Did you see it, Dad?"

Her father was hunched over his tablet, reading the news and muttering to himself about the state of the government. "See what, sweetheart?"

"That green flash. Didn't either of you see it?"

"Hmmmm," said her mother, shaking her braids loose while trying to stifle an enormous yawn.

Her father looked around the room in bleary-eyed confusion. "I didn't notice anything."

Suzy set her lips into a hard line. Perhaps it had been the TV? She peered over her mother's shoulder at the screen, but she was watching another costume drama— men with tall hats riding on horses in the countryside. No green flashes there.

"You've been overdoing the homework again," said her father, scratching at his unruly mop of ginger hair. "Give your eyes a rest and come and sit with us for a bit."

"I'm almost finished," Suzy said, and turned back to her workbook.

It was physics homework, and Suzy was good at physics. Actually, she was good at math, but she preferred physics because it made the math useful; it turned the numbers into real things that moved and made a difference. She couldn't understand why anyone would want to do plain old math all by itself—solving equations was fun for a while, but all you ever ended up with was more numbers, and what were you supposed to do with them then? No, math was just another way of filling up pieces of paper. Physics was where the action was.

But lately it had started to make her feel a bit unusual,

which wasn't a feeling she liked much. None of her friends shared her enthusiasm, and they had started to sneak little sideways looks at her in class whenever she gave the right answer or got her experiments to work properly. They never said anything, of course, and they weren't being rude, exactly, but she had seen it in their eyes—it was the same look they sometimes gave Reginald, the class nerd with the dinosaur obsession, who, on the rare occasion when someone engaged him in conversation, would talk about nothing else. It was a look that mixed pity with suspicion, as though she were the victim of some terrible affliction and they were afraid it might be catching.

The thought made her pause and lift her pen from the paper. The homework was pretty simple. Mr. Marchwood, her teacher, had assigned ten questions on Newton's laws of motion. Suzy had actually finished them an hour ago, but her imagination had been sparked and she had carried on, testing herself to see how she could put the knowledge to use. How fast would a rocket need to fly to escape Earth's gravity? How long would it take at that speed to reach the moon? How much force would she need to get back?

She had taken up three extra pages of her book with her own questions, her workings-out spilling into the margins. She was fairly confident she had the answers right, but would need Mr. Marchwood to confirm them.

She hoped he would; he had given a long, weary sigh the last time she had handed in her homework. "Suzy," he had said. "As if I didn't have enough work to do."

Her pen hovered above the page, the next question already forming in her mind. She looked back over her shoulder at her parents, who were now propped against each other, snoring gently. Tomorrow was Saturday—she had the whole weekend to work out the final question, she decided. Perhaps her dad was right; if she was seeing green flashes that weren't there, her eyes probably needed a rest.

Suzy replaced the top on her pen, shut her homework book, and stuffed them both back into her schoolbag.

"Good night," she whispered, deciding not to disturb her parents as she padded across the room to the hall.

Her footsteps had faded upstairs before another green flash filled the living room. Then another. And another. Ribbons of green energy curled out of the air around the table where she had been working, probing down across her chair, as though searching for something. When they didn't find it, they flickered uncertainly for a few seconds before fizzling away into nothing. The green light faded.

Upstairs, Suzy brushed her teeth and prepared for bed, oblivious.

2

An Unexpected Visitor

Suzy wasn't sure, at first, what woke her. She was just awake, in that sudden, surprising way that catches your brain unawares, as though nobody had told it that it had been asleep to begin with.

The clock on her bedside table read two a.m. She sat up, waiting for her eyes to adjust to the dark and tell her what was wrong.

After almost a minute the answer seemed to be: nothing. But she was wide awake, and a troubling little itch at the back of her mind told her there was a good reason.

She swung her feet out of bed and into her slippers, then crept to the window, easing the curtain aside to peer out. The street was deserted, the houses dark and sleeping. No traffic hummed, no people spoke. Even the clouds, vague and shadowy in the overcast night, were still.

She was just getting back into bed when she heard it: a sharp, hard noise from somewhere inside the house. She jumped in shock.

It came again: a *clank!* of metal on metal, like heavy saucepans being smashed together. Her parents wouldn't be up in the middle of the night, banging pots and pans together, which meant only one thing—there was someone else in the house!

The sound drew Suzy toward the door, her chest tight with apprehension.

Burglars!

The thought came crashing into her mind, huge and urgent and dangerous, and it froze Suzy to the spot. She tried to shift it, to send it away somewhere, but it refused to budge.

What if they come upstairs?

Her heart beat a stuttering rhythm in her chest, and she realized she was beginning to panic.

This wouldn't do. If the burglars, or whoever they were, burst into the room at any second, she didn't want them to find her just standing there in her pajamas. (And not even her nice pajamas—the dark blue ones with the lightning bolts on them. These were her spare set: the pink-and-yellow ones with the lacy cuffs that Aunt Belinda had given her for Christmas last year.) If they found her like this, they wouldn't have to hurt her—she'd probably drop dead of embarrassment.

She clearly needed to do something. *But what?*

Despite her fear, Suzy closed her eyes and forced herself to breathe deeply. It was a simple trick, but it calmed the storm inside her mind just enough to let her hear the thought that had been there all along, calling for her attention: Burglars don't make noise. At least, not this much noise, and never on purpose. You couldn't expect to steal anything if you woke everyone up.

So, probably not burglars, then.

This reassured her a little, but she was still tense as she crossed to her bedroom door and eased it open, taking her bathrobe down from its hook as she did so. The noise was deafening, even out here on the landing. Definitely not burglars, she decided. If she didn't know any better, she would say it was builders, but what would builders be doing in her house in the middle of the night?

No, it was her mom and dad—it had to be. But what on earth were they up to?

The light in the hallway was on, but looking down the stairs from the landing, Suzy couldn't see much. The noise was getting louder—too loud for pots and pans, although it was definitely the sound of metal striking metal. She crept down the first few steps and was about to peer through the banisters into the hall when a cascade of orange sparks leaped into the air from somewhere below her, ricocheting off the ceiling and walls. She flinched and almost toppled over, but grabbed the banister just in time.

"Mom?" Her voice shook. "Dad? Is that you?"

The hammering sounds stopped immediately, and she heard someone gasp. There was the sound of something heavy being dropped and a sudden scuffle of feet on the hall carpet. Then a rustle and a flap, like bedsheets being folded. Then silence.

"Hello?" Suzy leaned over the banister, wary of another eruption of sparks, and looked down into the hall. At first everything seemed normal, but then a glint of metal caught her eye. Two long silver strips winked up at her from the carpet. They lay side by side, several feet apart, and seemed to run into the house from underneath the front door. Suzy frowned in confusion, her fear momentarily forgotten as she descended the stairs, trying to understand what she was seeing.

They were train tracks.

She knew they couldn't be, but she prodded the nearest track with her toe, then knelt down and rapped her knuckles against it. It was cold and hard and very, very real. A railway line, set into the floor of the hall. Someone had even cut strips of carpet away to make room for them. She could see the frayed edges.

"But that doesn't make sense," she said to herself, stepping back and giving them a hard look. They glinted back at her, indifferent. Suzy turned and followed their path with her eyes, past the door to the living room and down the whole length of the hall, toward the kitchen. Before she got there, though, her attention fell on the object sitting to one side of the kitchen door.

It was a workman's tent, made of grubby red-and-white-striped tarpaulin—the sort she had seen erected over holes in the road when people had to dig up gas mains or water pipes. They were usually small, but this one was minute. Even though it sagged a bit in the middle, it barely reached her shoulder.

Light spilled from between the canvas flaps.

"Mom? Dad?" she called, taking a cautious step forward. Something shifted within the tent, and a vague shadow played across the inside of the fabric. "Who's in there?"

"Nobody!" replied a hoarse voice that she did not recognize. "There's nobody in 'ere. Go back to bed."

There was a stranger in her house!

Where were her mom and dad? Why hadn't the noise woken them up, too? She took a step back, ready to turn and run. She should call the police, or go get help.

But...

Whoever this person was, why were they hiding in a tent? And what were those train tracks doing here? Her mind started to prickle, searching for an answer that didn't seem to be there.

Very carefully, she reached out to the house phone, which stood on a small table beside the front door, and lifted it from its cradle.

"Tell me who you are or I'll call the police," she said, trying to keep her voice steady.

For a moment there was no response. Then the voice said, "I'm no one."

"Well, you must be someone," she said. "You're talking to me."

The voice grunted in obvious annoyance. "No, I'm not. You're dreamin'. Go back to bed."

Without realizing it, Suzy took a few steps toward the tent. "If I'm dreaming," she said, "then I'm already in bed."

Another grunt, even more annoyed than the last.

"Well?" she said, creeping closer.

"Aha! You could be sleepwalkin'." The voice sounded rather pleased with itself.

"Maybe," said Suzy. "That would certainly explain a lot."

"There you are, then," the voice concluded. "Sleep-walkin'. Now, off to bed with you."

Suzy took another step, but her toe struck something hard. "Ouch!" She hopped onto one foot and looked down. A squat hammer lay on the floor between the rails.

"What 'appened?" snapped the voice. "What's goin' on?"

"I've just proved to myself I'm not asleep," said Suzy, reaching down to rub her throbbing toe. "That hurt."

"Serves you right."

Suzy thought the voice was starting to sound a little scared, which gave her a bit more confidence. Then she glanced over to the living room door, which stood open. There, slumped on the sofa where she had left them, were her parents, still snoring.

"Mom! Dad!" She ran into the living room and shook them. Neither of them woke, but her dad snorted and gave a big, slightly dribbly grin.

"More cake?" he muttered. "Just one slice."

"Wake up!" she shouted.

"You're wastin' your breath," said the voice from the tent. "They're out for the count."

"What have you done to them?" she said, marching back into the hall, her anger rising.

"Me? Absolutely nothin'. Anyway, they're happy. Best just leave 'em dreamin' for a bit."

Suzy threw the phone down. "Come out!" she said, stamping her foot for emphasis.

There was a pause. "No."

"I'm not asking," she said in her best imitation of her mother. She didn't feel half as fearless as she sounded, but the owner of the voice didn't seem to realize that. "Come out here right now!"

"Have it your way," muttered the voice. There was more movement inside the tent, and then something poked its way out between the canvas flaps. It was a nose: the longest, strangest nose that Suzy had ever seen— almost a foot long, aquiline, with a pair of enormous nostrils filled with thick, bristly gray hair. A broad mouth, as wide as a toad's, was set in a sneer beneath it, while two small yellow eyes squinted at her over the top. This strange face was set in a round, bald head, with skin as thick and knotted as old tree bark. A huge pair of pointed ears stuck out on either side.

"Well?" said the creature, stepping into full view. "Here I am. Take a good look, why don't you?"

Suzy realized her mouth was hanging open and shut it with a snap.

The creature, whatever it was, stood almost a head

shorter than Suzy and wore orange overalls over its squat body. A name tag pinned to its chest read FLETCH.

"What, I mean . . . who? I mean, what are you?" stammered Suzy.

"I'm behind schedule, that's what," said Fletch, elbowing her aside and snatching up the tools from the floor. "They'll have my ears for slippers if I don't get this connection finished. Out of my way." He slouched past her to the kitchen door, where he stooped and gave the nearest rail an experimental tap with his hammer.

"You put these here?" she asked, coming up behind him.

" 'Course I did," he snapped. "An' in record time, I'll have you know." He pulled a tuning fork from the pocket of his overalls, flicked it, and set the stem down on the rail. The fork emitted a high keening note, and Fletch nodded, apparently satisfied. "Back in the day, I'd have had a whole crew with me, and we'd have been in an' out in five minutes flat. Blinkin' cutbacks. This job gets harder every year."

Suzy listened without really understanding. "But what are they for?"

Fletch looked as though he was about to reply, but paused with his mouth open. "Never you mind. You've already seen too much. You're not even s'posed to be here."

"Excuse me?" She stamped her foot again and meant it this time. "I live here."

"Which is why you're supposed to be fast asleep and leavin' me in peace," he said, getting to his feet. "I don't know how the prep team missed you. They got those other two." He waved a hand in the direction of Suzy's sleeping parents in the living room. "They're normally very thorough."

"What are you talking about?" she said. "What prep team?"

But Fletch just spun on his heels and marched past her, heading for the tent. "I'd make meself scarce, if I was you," he said. "Just go upstairs and pretend you didn't see anythin'. This'll all be gone by mornin'." And before she could say anything, he had ducked inside the tent and disappeared.

She stood there until her anger finally overcame her confusion. "Listen," she said. "You can't just turn up in my house in the middle of the night and start telling me what to do. I don't even know what you are! And what about my parents? I demand you wake them up!" But if he'd heard her, he ignored her. She could see his shadow moving back and forth across the inside of the tent and heard the sound of rummaging.

She considered following him into the tent, but she was still cautious enough not to want to be stuck in a confined space with a . . . whatever Fletch was. A gnome? A pixie? Maybe an elf? But that was ridiculous. Those things didn't—*couldn't*—exist, and she shook the thought off as quickly as she could. All she knew for certain was that Fletch was an intruder, which meant he had to be up to no good.

This thought drew her eyes back to the tracks. She made her way to the kitchen door and pulled it open, wanting to see how far they reached. She was a little surprised to see that they stopped dead, right on the threshold to the room. The kitchen floor was untouched.

"'Scuse me."

She was elbowed roughly to one side by Fletch, who had reappeared carrying a black cylindrical rod, about the length of a pencil but much thicker. He swung the door shut again with a crash and began tapping the end of the rod against the doorframe.

"What are you doing now?" she demanded.

"Concentratin'," he said. He pressed an ear to the wood. "Not my finest work, but it'll have to do."

Her patience finally at an end, Suzy leaned over his shoulder and plucked the rod from his fingers.

"Oi!" he shouted, jumping to snatch it back. Suzy held it over her head, out of reach.

"I'm not giving this back until you tell me who you are and what you're doing here," she said.

"That's not a toy!" he said, still jumping and waving his arms. "You're stealing. Thief!"

"Intruder!" she countered, and raised herself up on tip-toes.

"That's not fair," Fletch whined, finally coming to a breathless halt. "It's size-ist."

"It's perfectly fair," said Suzy, trying to maintain some composure. "Just tell me, and you can have it back. I promise."

Fletch shut one eye and peered at her sideways. "Really?"

"Really. But neither of us is going anywhere until you cooperate."

Fletch sighed, and his shoulders sagged in defeat. "All right, you win. But I hope you realize how much trouble I could get into for this."

"You're already in trouble," she said. "With me."

He gave her a resentful look and scuffed a foot back and forth on the carpet. "I'm an engineer," he muttered. "I maintains the lines, and builds new ones when they're needed."

"What lines?"

"What lines d'you think?" He indicated the tracks. "These lines. The railway lines."

Suzy blinked. "But the nearest railway line is miles away. And anyway, this is a house. You don't get railway lines in houses."

16

"Well, not normally, no," said Fletch in a tone of voice that Suzy had only ever heard used on other people. It made her feel a bit stupid, and her skin prickled with embarrassment. "But we're in a bit of a pickle, y'see. The Express got held up at those new border controls in the Western Fenlands, and we've got to make up the time before our next delivery. Going by the normal route would take an age, so this is a shortcut." He tapped the side of his great nose. "Strictly unofficial, of course. We're not really allowed to set foot in human territory, but here we are, for a one-night-only sort of thing."

Suzy didn't grasp most of what Fletch had said, which only made her more frustrated, and she seized on the one nugget that she felt sure she'd understood. "Railways can't just appear and disappear overnight," she said hotly.

"They can when I'm around," said Fletch with a proud smile. "Fastest in the business me, although, at my age, I'm starting to feel it a bit."

"Why? How old are you?"

Fletch puffed his chest out and affected an air of great dignity. "A thousand and ten," he said. "And still two centuries from retirement."

"Don't be silly," she said. "Nobody's that old."

"Really? And how old are you, exactly?"

"Eleven," said Suzy.

17

"Ha!" Fletch's laugh was so explosive that it rocked him back on his heels. "So I s'pose you know everything, then?"

Suzy felt a fresh rush of embarrassment and, hot on its heels, a surge of anger. She was so angry that she could hear her blood singing in her ears. Perhaps her feelings showed on her face, because Fletch began backing away from her toward the safety of the tent, his eyes widening.

"Don't walk away from me," she demanded, but he plunged a hand into his overalls and pulled out an old-fashioned pocket watch. He flipped it open. "Crikey, where's the time gone? They're here!"

Only then did she feel the tremor beneath her feet and realize that the singing sound she heard wasn't coming from her ears at all—it was coming from the rails.

A rush of cold air barreled down the hall, and she turned, thinking the front door had opened. Instead, it had vanished, and in its place stood an archway of old stone bricks. She just had time to realize that the world that should have been visible outside it—the street, the houses, the neat little gardens—was missing, replaced by an echoing black void, before she was blinded by the glare of a huge light, racing toward her through the darkness. The scream of a whistle filled the hall, metal ground on metal, and Suzy threw herself backward as the train bore down upon her.

3

THE IMPOSSIBLE POSTAL EXPRESS

The last thing Suzy saw before she hit the ground was a train erupting in a whirling mass of wheels, rods, and pistons from the tunnel mouth. Then she screwed her eyes shut, and for a second, the world was dark and full of noise. Hot steam gusted over her hands and face, metal screeched and clashed, a whistle howled. She gritted her teeth and clapped her hands over her ears.

The scream of brakes reached a crescendo and died suddenly away. There was a last outrush of steam, like a sigh of relief, and everything went quiet.

Suzy risked opening one eye.

She had fallen at the foot of Fletch's tent, her feet just

inches from the track. Rough hands grasped her shoulders, and she looked up to see Fletch standing over her, pulling her into a sitting position. She was too shocked to resist.

"What were you thinkin'?" he said, hopping from foot to foot with agitation. "You almost became an Incident!"

"A what?" she said, her ears still ringing.

"An Incident on the Line! The worst type of Incident it's possible to be."

Suzy looked at him blankly and wondered what to say. His tone made her want to apologize, but she wasn't sure he deserved it. In fact, didn't he still owe *her* an apology? She was just gathering her thoughts to say so when a new voice called out from somewhere high above them.

"Fletch? Is that you, old chap? What the dickens is going on down there?"

They both looked up toward the source of the voice, and Suzy almost fell backward in surprise. A mighty old steam locomotive towered over her, hissing and shuddering and belching yellowish steam from its chimney. It was bigger than any Suzy had seen before—at least, bits of it were. To her eyes, it looked like a large train had smashed into several smaller ones, and maybe a few buildings along the way, and the parts had all got mixed up and stuck together; its chimney was too wide, none of the drive wheels quite matched, and the cylindrical belly of its boiler was too fat at the front and too narrow at the back. The driver's cab was nothing less than a neat little redbrick cottage, complete with tiled roof, window boxes, and a bright red front door, which stood open on the near side of the boiler.

It was from here that the voice had come, and as Suzy watched, a small figure scampered out of it and onto a narrow gangway that ran along the length of the locomotive's flank, a few feet above the wheels. The figure carried a lantern and, when they were directly above Fletch, shone the light down over the gangway's safety railing, like a spotlight. "Fletch? We didn't just have an Incident, did we?"

Suzy tried to make out the figure's face, but it was just a black patch of shadow behind the glare of the lantern.

"It's worse than that, Stonker," said Fletch. "Look." He hooked a thumb in Suzy's direction, and the light swung over to cover her.

"Good grief, a local! And it's awake."

"Looks like someone on the prep team messed up," said Fletch. "Who was on shift tonight?"

"Not a soul, old chap," said Stonker. "Didn't you get the memo? They did it all remotely."

"Pah!" Fletch spat. "No wonder. What do I keep telling 'em? This remote spell business is all well and good, but you need people on the ground if you want the job done properly. I mean, it's just a sleeping spell. A common tooth fairy could do it."

"Quite right, old boy, quite right," said Stonker, clearly distracted. "But given that it's here, what do you suggest we do with it? We're still behind schedule."

Fletch scratched his scalp and looked Suzy up and down. "I should put a call in to HQ, I s'pose. See if they can send someone to reset 'er memory."

"Don't you dare!" Suzy said, jumping back. "You can't go poking around inside my mind. It doesn't belong to you."

"It's probably for the best," Stonker told her. "We're not really supposed to be here, you see. Outside our jurisdiction and all that, and it won't do to have you giving us away. Although having said that, it might take HQ a while to get somebody out here. Couldn't you do it yourself, Fletch?"

Fletch sucked his breath in through his teeth. "I dunno, Stonks. Memories are fiddly, like unknotting spiderwebs. You never know which bit's connected to what. Maybe I could do a confusion spell instead."

"No, you won't," said Suzy, backing away. "I'm confused enough as it is." She squinted into the circle of light hiding Stonker. "And I am not an *it*, I'm a *she*, thank you very much."

"Female of the species, eh?" said Stonker. "Afraid I'm

not really well versed on the fauna in these parts. Do you have a name?"

"I'm Suzy," said Suzy. "Suzy Smith. And I'd like to know who you are and what you're doing here, please."

"I suppose we do owe you the courtesy." The light bobbed and weaved as Stonker grappled with the lantern, then it flickered out entirely. It took Suzy a few seconds to blink away the red-and-green smudge it left on her vision, and then she saw him.

He was the same sort of creature as Fletch, though his skin was a flinty gray, and less warty and wrinkled. He wore a smart blue uniform, with a coat that fell to his waist and a peaked cap with silver piping. He looked down at her past both his enormous nose and an equally impressive salt-and-pepper mustache, as thick and lustrous as a badger, which hung down almost to his knees before the tips curled back up into rigid little spirals. His blue eyes twinkled as he spoke.

"J. F. Stonker," he said. "Driver of the Impossible Postal Express. The finest troll train on the rails." He reached up and gave the locomotive's boiler an affectionate pat.

"You're trolls?" she said. "How is that possible?"

"We hadn't intended to stop," said Stonker, clearly misunderstanding her, "but I'm afraid you wandered onto the tracks. You're jolly lucky the brakes have just been serviced."

"But that wasn't my fault," said Suzy, feeling the temperature rise in her cheeks. "The tracks aren't supposed to be here. None of this is supposed to be here. Including you!" This was all starting to feel terribly unfair.

"Fear not," said Stonker. "We'll be on our way again momentarily, and Fletch will have the tracks up and everything back to its normal proportions in no time. You'd never know the difference."

"*Normal proportions?*" For the first time, Suzy realized there was a question she hadn't asked herself: How could such an enormous steam locomotive even fit inside the house? She looked up and saw the hall ceiling impossibly high above her head, the purple light shade like a distant hot-air balloon. The hall had grown to the size of a cathedral without her even noticing.

"What happened?" she said, wide-eyed. "What did you do?"

"Not really my department, I'm afraid," said Stonker. "Fletch here is the technical genius."

Fletch sniffed. "I try my best."

Suzy hardly heard them. She was running back and forth, trying to take it all in. The living room door was as tall as a cliff now, and she would have to stand on tiptoes if she wanted to reach the top of the baseboard. The kitchen door had vanished altogether, replaced by another enormous stone arch. The tracks didn't end there anymore, but ran on into the blank darkness beyond. Her voice echoed in the cavernous space as she cried, "You shrank us!"

"Nah," said Fletch, cocking his head to one side and plucking at the hair in his ears. "I just gave the hall a bit of a stretch, that's all."

"You mean you made everything *bigger*?" Suzy gaped at him, horrified. "But that's worse! How big's the house now? It must take up half the street."

"What sort of a fly-by-night merchant do you take me for?" said Fletch. "I didn't make the outside any bigger, and I haven't touched any of the other rooms. What would be the point in that?"

"Wait a minute." Suzy fought to digest this new information. "You mean the house is still its normal size, even though the hall is bigger than the house?"

"That's right." Fletch grinned, warming to his topic. "It's pretty standard stuff, really, your basic metadimensional engineerin', a dash of magic, and a few bits of double-sided sticky tape. Job done."

Suzy looked again at the living room doorway. She could still see her parents beyond it, fast asleep and normal sized, but the doorway itself seemed to flicker and stretch when she focused on it. It only took her a few seconds to realize she was seeing it in both sizes at the same time, but by then it had started to make her feel seasick and she had to look away. "No," she said, shaking her head. "I'm sorry, but that's impossible."

"Is it?" said Fletch, feigning surprise.

"You can't just make something bigger on the inside than the outside."

"'Course you can. It's simple fuzzics."

Suzy frowned. "You mean *physics.*"

"No," said Fletch. "Fuzzics. Like physics, only fuzzier."

"Physics can't be fuzzy," said Suzy, indignant that something so precious to her should be treated like a bit of a joke. "It's either right or wrong. It won't let you break the rules."

"That's why fuzzics kind of saunters past 'em," said Fletch. "It's easier than doing everything by the book." He gave her an infuriating grin, and she was drawing breath to argue her case further when Stonker cleared his throat.

"This is all jolly nice," he said, "but I'm afraid we really must be leaving. We're already late, and I want to get under way before—"

"Mr. Stonker! Mr. Stonker!" The voice came from the direction of the carriages.

"Too late," sighed Stonker, pinching the bridge of his enormous nose. "Here he comes."

&⁊℃

The train's locomotive pulled a large tender behind it, which Suzy assumed must be full of coal, or whatever fuel the engine burned. Behind that were two carriages; the first was big, bulky, and cylindrical, like an armored gasoline tanker, but with a row of small portholes in the side and a knot of tubes and chimneys sprouting from the top. The letters H. E. C. were stenciled down the side in large white script. The carriage at the rear was smaller and looked like an antique goods coach, the red paint peeling from its wooden panels.

It was from this rear coach that another troll had emerged and was now hurrying toward them, waving frantically. He looked quite different from both Stonker and Fletch; his arms were long and bent in strange directions, and he seemed to have no legs at all, just a pair of large feet attached directly to his body. Only when he tripped and landed flat on his face did Suzy realize why he looked particularly

strange—he was wearing a uniform that was several sizes too big for him.

"Aren't either of you going to help him?" she asked as the new arrival floundered in a confusion of sleeves and coattails, trying to get back on his feet.

"I suppose we ought to," said Stonker. "Fletch, be a good chap and help the Postmaster up, would you?"

"Not in my job description," muttered Fletch. "Why don't you do it?"

"Because I'm all the way up here," Stonker said. "Besides, I helped him up last time."

Suzy shook her head and hurried over to the flailing bundle of clothes. It was hard to tell which part of the troll was which, so she just reached out, hauled him up, and deposited him on what she hoped were his feet. His uniform wasn't the same as Stonker's, she saw—it was red instead of blue, and it looked older, more ornate. A tarnished gold medal dangled from the chest, and an old-fashioned horn or bugle was embroidered on both the shoulders, although the thread was badly frayed.

The bundle shook itself, and another huge nose, followed by a small, wide-eyed face, poked out from above the collar of the coat. This troll's skin was a pale lichen green and hardly wrinkled at all. Suzy guessed he was much younger than the others.

"Thank you," said the troll, and then, "Oh no! A local!"

He leaped into the air in fright, but his feet were already moving by the time he touched down, and he took off like a bullet, swerving around Suzy and heading for Fletch and Stonker, where he promptly tripped over the hem of his coat and went sprawling once again.

"It's all right, Postmaster," called Stonker. "We think she's harmless."

The fallen troll said something in response, but his words were muffled by several layers of cloth. Neither of the others made a move to help him, so with a weary sigh, Suzy retraced her steps and set him back on his feet. He shrugged the uniform away from his face and gave her a suspicious look. "Are you sure, Mr. Stonker? She looks like she might bite."

"I promise I won't," said Suzy.

"She'd have to chew her way through all that uniform first, Wilmot," said Fletch. "You know they come in smaller sizes, right?"

The Postmaster sniffed and turned his nose up. "I've told you before, Fletch—this was my father's uniform, and his father's before him. I have a legacy to uphold."

"The legacy needs longer legs, boy," said Fletch with a sly grin. Wilmot flared his nostrils in response.

"What exactly did you want, Postmaster?" said Stonker. "As you can see, we're a trifle busy."

"I came to see what was causing the delay," said Wilmot. "Our next customer is waiting for us."

"I'm aware of that," said Stonker.

"And I can't just leave the package on her doorstep and run," Wilmot went on, jiggling from foot to foot inside his uniform. "It needs to be signed for! I don't want to be the one who rings her doorbell if we're late."

"We'll get there as quickly as possible," said Stonker. "I'm just waiting for . . . Aha! Here we are."

A second figure had emerged from the driver's cab and was hurrying along the gangway; Suzy could tell imme-

diately that it was not like the others—it was bigger than she was, loping along on all fours in a powerful run. It wore faded blue overalls but was otherwise covered from top to bottom in vivid yellow fur. Only when it came to a halt beside Stonker and reared up onto its hind legs did Suzy realize what she was looking at.

"Is that a *bear?*" she exclaimed. The creature spared her a curious glance.

"A brown bear, to be precise," said Stonker. "*Ursus arctos.* A bit of a departure for a troll train, I'll admit, but she scored top marks in all her entrance exams. Ursel here keeps the firebox stoked and the wheels turning."

Ursel flashed a set of startlingly white fangs at Suzy, who wasn't sure if the gesture was meant as a greeting or a threat. She tried not to show her discomfort.

"How are we looking, Ursel?" said Stonker.

"Growlf," said the bear with a voice so deep that Suzy felt it as a shiver in her bones.

"Jolly good. Well, stand by the valves and be ready to give it plenty of pep. I want to get out of here before anything else goes wrong."

"Grunf." With a last glance down at the assembled audience, Ursel turned and began loping back toward the cab.

Suzy felt the question well up in her throat before she had time to stop it. "If it's a brown bear, why is it bright yellow?"

Everything stopped.

Stonker and Wilmot stared at her, mortified, and even the train seemed to have quieted its hissing and clanking. Fletch winced. Then, very slowly, all eyes turned to Ursel.

Suzy clapped her hands over her mouth, as though she

could stuff the question back inside it. She could tell from everyone's reaction that it had been the wrong thing to say, but it *shouldn't* have been. This whole situation—trolls and bears and trains and just *all of it*—was starting to upset her. Because, while she never would have admitted it, she had always been secretly proud of her ability to understand the nuts and bolts of reality. Now, though, it felt as if that reality was tilting underneath her, threatening to throw her off. She just wanted to make sense of it again.

Ursel turned and padded back toward them, dark eyes fixed on Suzy, who was now too terrified to move. *It's going to eat me*, she thought. *Eaten by a bear, in my own house.* But the thought that made her saddest was this: *Now I'll never get to understand what's happening.*

Ursel reared up and leaned over the railing. A string of saliva hung from a large incisor. "Growlf," Ursel grunted. "Grrrrunf orf nnngrowlf!"

Suzy stood to polite attention, not daring to take her eyes off those fangs. "What did it say?" she said with a pleading look toward Stonker.

The driver gave a knowing smile, and his eyes twinkled again. "She said she's not an *it*, she's a *she*, thank you very much. And it's none of your business if she happens to prefer being blond."

Suzy looked again at Ursel with a mixture of shock and relief. "You mean you're a girl?"

This was met with a guttural roar that made everyone jump back.

"What!" said Suzy, trembling with shock. "What did I do wrong this time?"

"It's a common mistake," said Stonker, rubbing his ringing ears. "She prefers the term *woman*. Something to do with being a responsible adult who pays her taxes."

Ursel flexed her shoulders and gave a decisive nod before turning and lumbering back toward the cab. Suzy wasn't sure it was possible for bears to wink, but she was sure Ursel gave her one as she went.

A few seconds later, steam hissed from between the driving wheels. The boiler rattled and the whole train lurched forward an inch, straining against the brakes. Wilmot turned and dashed back toward the rear coach, his coattails flapping behind him.

"I'm sorry there's no more time for pleasantries," Stonker called over the rising noise. "I'll leave you in Fletch's capable hands."

Fletch grunted.

"But I still don't understand what all this means," Suzy protested. "Where did it all come from? Where are you going?"

Stonker drew himself up, eyes twinkling. "From Trollville to the five corners of reality, my dear. No package too big, no postcard too small. Come rain, shine, or meteor shower, the Impossible Postal Express will deliver." He whipped off his cap and gave a theatrical bow as the locomotive strained forward again, its carriages rattling. "Farewell," he called, steadying himself against the handrail, "and try not to worry. Fletch really is jolly skilled." He turned and hurried back along the gangway to the cab, slamming the door shut behind him. A second later, the brakes unlocked with an almighty *clunk*, and the huge driving wheels ground slowly forward.

"I s'pose we'd better get on with it," said Fletch, cracking his knuckles. He reached to his tool belt and paused. "Where is it?"

Suzy had no idea what he was talking about, but some nervous instinct told her to start backing away as the train lumbered into motion beside them.

"I can't do the job without it," said Fletch. He patted his pockets and looked around in confusion. Then his head snapped up and his eyes fixed on Suzy. "You!" he exclaimed. "You took it from me."

Suzy started retreating slowly as Fletch advanced on her. "What?"

"Where is it? I need it!"

Before Suzy could answer, her foot came down on something hard and narrow, and it rolled out from under her, taking her foot with it. She felt a moment of weightlessness before she landed flat on her back.

She sat up, nursing her head with one hand, and looked down to see what she had stepped on. It was Fletch's metal rod. She must have dropped it when she threw herself clear of the train.

He saw it at the same instant she did, and pounced for it. He was fast, but she was faster—she snatched it up and sprang away.

"Give it back!" he shouted.

"No," she said. "Whatever it is, you'll use it on me. You just said so."

Fletch crept toward her, his hands up as though she were pointing a gun at him. "I know how to use it properly. You don't."

"I don't want to use it," she said. "And I don't want you to, either."

The locomotive slid into the archway. The huffing of its chimney, the clank of its wheels, the hiss and gush of steam echoed back out of the darkness as it continued to gather speed, drawing the carriages ever closer to the tunnel mouth. Suzy felt a sudden tug—a fear that something very important was right in front of her, but was slipping away.

"Are there really five corners of reality?" she asked.

Fletch stopped, surprised. "'Course there are. Don't they teach you anything useful at school?" The tender slipped through the tunnel mouth and out of sight.

"Now give back what's not yours." He started forward again.

Suzy didn't realize she had made her mind up until she started running—not away from Fletch, but toward him. She saw the startled look on his face as he spread his arms wide to catch her, but she was too quick. She heard his little yelp of shock as she rushed past him and felt the slight tug on her bathrobe as he tried to snatch at her.

She was running level with the train now, but it was still gathering speed and steadily outpacing her. The tug of anxiety felt stronger, but clearer as well; the world made no sense anymore because of this train and the things that were on it. If she ever wanted to understand the world again, she couldn't afford to let the train go without her. If she did, they would make her forget she'd ever seen it, and she'd live out the rest of her life in blissful ignorance, never knowing any better, and that scared her. That scared her so badly she put her head down and ran until she could feel her heartbeat in her throat.

The strange cylindrical tanker that bore the letters H. E. C. entered the tunnel, leaving only the old red coach at the rear. It was close enough to touch, but the tunnel mouth was fast approaching and she was running out of ground. She had no idea what would happen to her if she ran on into the tunnel, and she wasn't keen to find out.

"Stop!" bellowed Fletch.

The carriage slid past her, the leading wheels vanishing over the threshold. The door through which Wilmot had disappeared was gaining on her fast. Last chance. She put on a final burst of speed, swerved toward the coach, and jumped.

Her hand closed around the coach's door handle in the same second that the world around her went dark. The deep echoes of the hall were swept away by the noisy rush of the tunnel. Cold wind tugged at her hair and clothes, and she planted her feet as securely as she could on the narrow metal step below the door. Looking back, she was just in time to see the tunnel mouth shrinking away into the distance. Framed inside it was the tiny figure of Fletch, standing in the hallway, shaking his fist in anger.

4

THE INTERDIMENSIONAL POST OFFICE

Suzy pressed herself flat against the door to the coach. The train was still accelerating, and the pull of the wind was getting stronger. If she stayed out here much longer, it would simply pluck her from the side of the train and cast her off into the darkness.

For the first time, she realized how impulsive and unplanned this all was and began to feel scared. She was clinging to the outside of a train—a magic train, if such a thing were possible—hurtling through a tunnel that shouldn't exist, on its way to who knew where? Her parents couldn't help her. She was alone, and already in danger.

She was also still holding Fletch's metal rod, she

realized, and stuffed it into her bathrobe pocket for safekeeping. She had meant to throw it back to him before she jumped, but there hadn't been time to think.

Nor was there time to feel guilty now. She made sure her grip on the handle was secure, then raised her free hand and knocked as hard as she could on the door.

Nothing happened.

The door had a small window set in it, but a blind had been folded closed behind it, so she couldn't see in. She knocked again, hard enough it hurt her knuckles. "Hello?" she shouted. "Is anyone there? Wilmot? Please!"

Nobody answered, and her imagination taunted her with a horrible idea—what if Wilmot couldn't hear her over the noise of the locomotive? She would be stuck out here, alone, until—

The door swung open, knocking her back on her heels. She tried to regain her grip on the handle, but her fingers slipped, and she windmilled her arms. Right in front of her was Wilmot, his eyes wide with shock in the small gap between his collar and his cap.

"You!" he yelped.

"Help!" she cried as she started to tip backward.

He darted forward and caught her bathrobe cord, stopping her midfall. "Got you!" he said, but then his eyes widened again as her weight began dragging him steadily out the door.

"Pull!" she cried.

"I *am* pulling!" He braced first one foot, then the other against the inside of the doorframe, leaning back almost horizontally in his effort to stop them both from falling. "Help!" he shouted.

Their tug-of-war stretched the bathrobe cord taut. Suzy reached out and grabbed it, pulling herself up hand over hand until she was standing upright again, at which point, without her weight as a counterbalance, Wilmot dropped backward onto the floor with a thud, yanking her in through the door. She tripped over him and went sprawling on her front.

They both lay there for a moment, catching their breath.

"Thank you," said Suzy. "I think you just saved my life."

"Really?" Wilmot gave an embarrassed little smile. "Well, I'm happy to be of service, and I—" He broke off, and his face went pale. "What am I saying?" He sprang to his feet. "This isn't allowed! You're not supposed to be here." He ran in a little circle, flapping his hands in panic. "I need to call Mr. Stonker. I need to call HQ."

"Please don't," said Suzy, getting up. "I don't want them to send me back."

"But they have to! You're in breach of regulations. Only authorized personnel are allowed in here. And you're *unauthorized*!"

"I'm not going to cause any trouble," she said. "I just wanted to see where this train was going. And to get away from Fletch." As if to underline her point, she pulled the door shut, muffling the scream of the wind in the tunnel.

Wilmot paused. "Oh, well, that much I can quite understand. I've always found him thoroughly disagreeable. He doesn't have an ounce of respect for the work I do here." He spread his arms to encompass the whole carriage.

Suzy looked around. It was cramped but cozy, stuffed from floor to ceiling with bundles of letters, parcels, and other, more strangely shaped objects, most of them wrapped in brown paper and string. A small wooden desk had been squeezed in among it all, and the lamp that stood on it cast a warm, reassuring glow. It all had the sense of well-ordered business. Not a scrap of space had been wasted.

"It looks like a little post office," she said.

"That's exactly what it is," Wilmot said, brightening. Suzy guessed he liked talking about his work. "We receive, sort, and distribute mail from throughout the Impossible Places. No package too big, no postcard too small. Come rain, shine, or—"

"Or meteor shower," she chipped in. "Yes, Stonker told me. But what are the Impossible Places?"

The question appeared to surprise him. "You mean you don't know?" He frowned. He seemed to be constructing his answer in his head, and Suzy guessed he was trying to find words for something so self-evident he had never dreamed he would ever have to explain it to anyone. It made her feel a little foolish.

"They're home," he said with a little shrug. "The Union of Impossible Places, or sometimes just 'the Union' for short. All the weird and magical places that don't quite fit anywhere else."

"Yes, but what *are* they?" she said. "Are they different countries? Different planets?"

"They're a bit of everything, really," he said. "Cities, realms, worlds, and dimensions, plus a few spaces no one can quite agree on a name for. All different shapes, sizes, and types, threaded all throughout reality."

Suzy blinked. Her brain was so busy trying to process such a huge concept that it wasn't able to provide her with a better reply than, "It all sounds very interesting."

"Interesting?" Wilmot lifted his cap and scratched his head in thought. "Yes, I suppose it is, really. And I'm quite lucky that my job lets me see a lot of places, even if it's never for very long. I'm usually too busy in here."

Suzy looked around and, for the first time, realized what was missing from the sorting car. "Do you do all this by yourself? There's no one to help you?"

"In an ideal world, I'd have a sorting team and a squad of posties to handle the deliveries," he said. "My grandfather was in charge of a dozen sorting cars like this one and a staff of a hundred trolls. My father had a staff of fifty. Of course, things were very different in those days, but I do my best."

Suzy looked again at the towers of letters and boxes. "But there's so much of it."

"Yes, I suppose there is." He gave a nervous little laugh, as though only just realizing this fact himself. He soon rallied. "But it's nothing a little hard work can't fix. The Union has relied on the Impossible Postal Service for generations, and it's still as reliable as the day it was founded."

The train jolted, and he fell over sideways. Suzy helped him up again.

"That was the end of the tunnel," he said, his anxiety returning. "We're almost there."

"Almost where?" She hurried to the little window in the door and pushed the blind aside.

The land outside was featureless—a desert of frosty blue sand stretching to the horizon, broken only by the skeletons of a few dead trees. But the sky... Suzy stared in wonder. She had never seen so many stars, not even in her astronomy textbooks. They pulsed and flared like fireworks, strobing yellow, purple, and green against the neon ink stain of a huge nebula. Whatever sky this was, it was a long way from her own.

"It's beautiful," she exclaimed. "Where are we?" When Wilmot didn't answer, she tore her eyes away from the window to see him pacing in circles around the desk, clutching a small, square parcel in one hand and an antique fob watch in the other.

"She'll turn me to stone," he fretted. "Or file a complaint. Or both!"

"Who will?" said Suzy.

Wilmot jumped, as though he had forgotten she was there. "This is a priority package," he said, holding it up for her to see. "That means five hours' delivery, doorstep to doorstep, guaranteed."

Suzy looked at the address on the parcel. It read simply:

THE LADY CREPUSCULA
THE OBSIDIAN TOWER
THE CREPUSCULAN WASTES

And below that, in red ink:

FRAGILE

"Who's the Lady Crepuscula?" she asked.

"It's been five and a half hours already!" he said, recommencing his pacing. "We're thirty minutes late!"

"I see." Suzy couldn't understand why he was getting

so worked up about a simple parcel, when the wonders of the cosmos lay right outside his door, but realized it wouldn't help his mood to say so. Instead, she said, "She might be a bit annoyed, but I'm sure she'll understand if you just explain why you're late."

"Explain?" he said. "Nobody *explains* things to the Lady Crepuscula. She's the most powerful sorceress in the Union! One of its highest authorities. She explains things to *you*!" The color was draining from his face again. "Oh, what am I going to do? I can't face her like this. She'll blast me into next Tuesday."

"She's not really that bad, is she?" said Suzy.

"She's worse. She's perfectly horrid."

Suzy looked at the quivering little figure in the oversized uniform, and two things happened at once. The first was that she realized she felt sorry for him. He must spend so much of his time shut up in this little carriage, she reasoned, doing the work of a hundred trolls, all alone. And she supposed she was at least partly responsible for the delay that now had him so worried, even if it hadn't exactly been her fault.

The second was an idea that lit her mind up as bright and clear as the strange constellations outside.

"Would you like me to deliver the parcel?" she asked.

Wilmot looked up sharply. "What do you mean?"

"I mean, you don't have to ring her doorbell and get shouted at. I could do it for you."

"But you can't!" he said. "Only I'm allowed to make deliveries."

"Your father and grandfather had people to do it for them," she said. "And you said you'd like to have your own team."

Wilmot rolled his cap around his head. He seemed caught somewhere between confusion and excitement. "But that was different," he said. "They were all professional postal trolls. They'd had years of training."

"What if I just ring the doorbell, give her the parcel, and get her to sign for it?"

Wilmot's face lit up. "So you *are* qualified!"

She smiled and held out a hand for the parcel. He was about to pass it over when she pulled the hand away. "There's just one condition," she said.

"What's that?"

"If I help you, you won't call HQ or Stonker or anyone else. I get to ride along for a bit, see a few of these Impossible Places of yours, and then you take me home before my parents miss me. Plus, I get to remember it all afterward. None of Fletch's brain surgery. Do we have a deal?"

He licked his lips and turned the parcel over and over in his hands. "I'm not sure. It's highly irregular."

Suzy said nothing, but put her hand back out, ready to accept the package. She did her best to look calm, but inside she was as nervous as he looked. She was gambling everything on his decision.

The Postmaster dithered, clutching the parcel tight to his chest, looking from Suzy to the old-fashioned rotary phone on his desk and back again. His nostrils flared. He chewed his bottom lip.

"I suppose you'll need a uniform," he said at last.

Suzy smiled. "Perfect," she said.

5

ENCOUNTER AT THE TOWER

The train's whistle cut through the night air like a knife. Suzy wondered how far the sound must carry across the empty sands, and who might be out there to hear it.

Wilmot had disappeared into a storage closet at the back of the carriage, so she crossed again to the window and looked out. The desert raced by in a blur. She would have thought they'd be slowing down as they approached their destination, but they actually seemed to be getting faster. That didn't make any sense.

But then, nothing about this train made any sense, she reminded herself.

She heard Wilmot clattering around in the closet, and

she was turning from the window, when she caught sight of something new out in the desert sands. It streaked past too quickly for her to make out, but it didn't look like a tree. It was too small, too gray.

She cupped her hands around her eyes and pressed them to the glass. For a moment, nothing stood out. Then, very close to the train, another gray object flashed past. Then another, farther out into the sands. Then a third, and a fourth. Soon, she was seeing them everywhere.

They were statues, she realized. Hundreds and hundreds of statues of people with arms outstretched and legs raised, as though running. Some were arranged in rows, others seemed to be on horseback, and although the train was moving too quickly for her to be sure, they all seemed to have been carved wearing armor and helmets and carrying swords. And they were all facing the same direction.

She angled her head again, looking ahead along the curve of the train as it followed the tracks snaking in and out among the dunes. What she saw made her gasp.

Rearing up from the desert was a tower so huge, the broad crown of its battlements seemed to prop up the heavens themselves. It was blacker than the night sky surrounding it and reflected nothing of the kaleidoscope of starlight. Instead, the light just seemed to fall into it and be snuffed out. It was like looking at a hole in the world. Suzy shivered. She couldn't help herself.

The statues grew more numerous as the train hurtled closer. They clustered around the base of the tower in great crowds, weapons raised. There were more figures on horseback here, and some riding what appeared to be rhinos.

Rhinos?

Suzy didn't have time to worry about them, though. The base of the tower was rushing closer and closer, wider than a football stadium, and the train showed no sign of slowing. There was no tunnel mouth ahead, just an expanse of black wall.

We're going to crash. The fact popped into her head so matter-of-factly she almost laughed. She just had time to throw herself onto the floor before the whole train bucked beneath her, raining letters down on her from the shelves and sending the lamp flying from Wilmot's desk. She shut her eyes and waited for the splintering of wood.

"Typical. I'll have to pick all this up again now."

She opened her eyes to find Wilmot standing over her, his hands on his hips, surveying the mess with a critical frown. She sat up and looked around. The carriage was still intact, and the rocking motion of the train continued as though nothing had happened.

"They told me they were going to iron out those gravity shifts when it went in for servicing last week," Wilmot went on, flitting back and forth across the carriage, picking up fallen letters as he went. "I haven't got time to re-sort the post every time we go vertical."

"Vertical?" Suzy got uncertainly to her feet and went back to the window. They were still racing along at the same speed, but now the ground beneath the train was jet-black and curved sharply away from them. The same lurid sky was still above them, but something had changed. She looked to her right, the way they had come, and a wave of dizziness hit her so hard she almost fell over. The desert rose like a wall into the sky behind them. She shut her eyes for a moment and looked again. The dizziness passed, and she finally understood what she was seeing. The rails hadn't stopped—they had simply turned at right angles up the side of the tower, and the train was climbing them toward the summit. Far below, she saw the army of statues shrinking into the distance and wondered who had put them all there.

"How is this possible?" she asked, turning to Wilmot. "We're going up. But down is still down. I mean, our feet are still on the floor. The gravity…"

"Is negotiable," he said. "I don't really know how it works, other than it's a mix of troll ingenuity and a bit of borrowed magic. I think it just tricks gravity a bit."

"But gravity's a force. You can't trick a force." Suzy realized she was breathing too quickly and willed herself to slow down. "Can you?"

"Some of them," he said. "And they do say gravity's one of the more gullible ones, don't they."

"No, they don't," she said firmly. "Not where I come from."

"Oh." Wilmot gave an apologetic shrug. "But look what I found in the closet." He produced a battered red cap with a black leather peak and smiled as he reached up to place it on Suzy's head. It was a shade too small, but by tugging it down as far as she could, she persuaded it to stay put. "I couldn't find an entire uniform, but at least you have something official. Oh, and this, of course."

He reached into his pocket and produced a badly tarnished bronze badge. "I checked the regulations, and they say a Postmaster may deputize any suitably qualified person should he have need. And a deputy needs a badge of office." He handed it over. It was a depiction of the same spiral horn embroidered on his jacket, surrounded by a ribbon on which she could just make out the words

UT APOLOGIZE PRO INOPPORTUNITAS

"What does it mean?" she asked.

"It means we must always be thinking of our customers. Do your best to remember that and you won't go far wrong." He drew himself up to his full height, which still only brought him about halfway up Suzy's chest, and raised his right hand. He looked at her expectantly until she did likewise. "Do you solemnly swear to uphold the ideals of the Impossible Postal Express, risking life, limb, and reason in the execution of your duty?"

"Um..." Suzy felt the first doubts creeping into her thoughts. "Is it really that dangerous?"

"Never," said Wilmot. "Almost. Almost never." He gave her a big, encouraging grin.

She wet her lips. If she backed out now, he would have no reason not to call HQ and have her sent back home to have her memory scrambled. But if she agreed, what was she getting herself into? She thought again of the strange sky outside; there was a whole new world out there to be discovered. That itch of curiosity hadn't gone anywhere.

"I do," she said.

"Then I now pronounce you officially deputized, Postal Operative . . . uh, sorry, I don't think I ever caught your name."

"I'm Suzy," she said. "Suzy Smith. And you're Wilmot, right?"

He went red. "Uh, yes, but never while on duty. You should really address me as Postmaster. Please."

"Right," she said. "I mean, right, Postmaster."

He forgot his embarrassment in an instant. "A staff!" Wilmot beamed and jumped up and down on the spot, clapping his hands. "I finally have a staff! Oh, if only old Grandpa Honks could see me now. I've just doubled my productivity!"

The train lurched again as it crested the top of the tower, and the gravity swung back to its normal orientation. Wilmot's enthusiasm died as quickly as his embarrassment had. "We're here," he said. There was a squeal of brakes as the train came to a sudden stop, hurling more letters from the shelves.

Very slowly, and with a trembling hand, he took the

Lady Crepuscula's parcel from the desk and held it out to Suzy. It was only a few inches across on each side, but when she took it, it felt surprisingly heavy.

He darted past her and opened the door. A blast of icy wind pushed its way into the carriage and ruffled the remaining letters on their shelves. Suzy shivered.

"You'd better be quick," said Wilmot. "The later you are, the angrier she'll be. I mean, she's always angry, of course, but she'll be *livid* when she sees you."

"Wonderful," said Suzy, her doubts growing. What was it Wilmot had said? *The most powerful sorceress in the Union?* "Thanks for telling me."

"Oh, you're welcome," he said, apparently immune to sarcasm. "Just remember the plan. Ring, deliver, sign. And no matter what happens, be polite. She puts great store in that sort of thing. Oh, and you'll need this." He plucked a sheet of paper marked PROOF OF DELIVERY from a nearby shelf and thrust it into her hands.

"Wait, what do I do if—" she began, but he planted both hands in the small of her back and propelled her to the door. She stumbled out to avoid tripping on the steps. "Hey, wait! What about—"

The door slammed in her face. "You'll be fine," he called from the other side. He pulled the blind shut.

Suzy took in her surroundings. She was at the very top of the tower, in the center of a large circular courtyard surrounded by high battlements. The floor and walls were the same uniform black stone as the rest of the tower, and a tall archway stood on either side of the courtyard to allow the train access. The Impossible Postal Express bridged the full width from one to the other, idling quietly.

The wind blew stronger, driving a few flecks of ice before it, and she pulled her bathrobe more tightly around her. The air was thin up here, and the stars seemed close enough to touch. So did the familiar shape of the full moon, which was just rising over the battlements.

In front of Suzy was a gatehouse, its large iron doors flanked by torches that burned with sickly green flames. She started toward it, clutching the parcel to her chest with one hand and defending her cap from the wind with the other. She was beginning to understand Wilmot's reluctance to leave the sorting car—the idea of simply dropping the parcel on the doorstep and running was starting to feel like a good one. But she hated being scared, and she wasn't going to act it, even if she felt it.

There were more statues here. They were the same as the ones at the bottom of the tower—knights in armor, with shields and swords at the ready. Perhaps a dozen stood above her on the battlements, pointing down into the courtyard, where a handful more had been placed. They looked human, but now that she was closer to them, she saw that they were larger than life-size—maybe seven or eight feet in height. She passed very close to one and was able to make out what little of its face was visible inside its helmet. It was horrible, twisted in fear or anger, or both. She locked her eyes on the doors ahead of her and tried not to look at any of the other figures, although she couldn't avoid glancing up at the large gargoyle that squatted on top of the gatehouse. It looked like a cross between a bat and a crocodile, its wings folded behind it and its long, tapering snout reaching down almost to the doors themselves.

She tried to ignore the feeling that its black glass eyes were watching her as she stopped underneath it and searched for some way to alert whoever was inside. There was no door knocker, and when she tried knocking with her fist, her knuckles barely made a sound against the thick metal.

She looked back over her shoulder at the train, hoping for some encouragement. The Express sat and steamed, but there was no sign of movement from the crew. She wondered if Stonker and Ursel were as scared of this Lady Crepuscula as Wilmot was.

"And exactly what time do you call this?"

Suzy jumped and spun around. The doors stood wide

open (But how? Surely she would have heard them?), and she narrowed her eyes in confusion at the figure they revealed.

It was a little old lady, who might have been about Suzy's own height but for a slight hunch and the fact that she leaned on a cane for support. She wore a dress of heavy black lace that fell all the way to her feet, with a knitted black shawl pulled tight around the shoulders. Suzy caught the discreet glint of a pearl necklace beneath it. Her hair was silver, and her skin was so pale it almost glowed, like the desert sands far below. She studied Suzy with piercing lilac eyes.

Suzy tried to speak, but only a nervous croak came out. She cleared her throat and tried again.

"I'm looking for the Lady Crepuscula."

"And should I tell you when you've found her, or would you prefer to guess?" the woman said in a voice like cut glass.

Suzy forced a smile, knowing she was being made fun of. "*You're* the Lady Crepuscula."

The woman's own smile was tight and humorless. "You must be new."

"Yes," said Suzy. "It's my first day."

"It shows." The woman looked Suzy over from cap to slippers. "And what manner of troll are you?"

"I'm not," said Suzy. "I mean, I'm a girl. A human being. From Earth."

The smile snapped off in an instant, and Lady Crepuscula leaned forward to examine her more closely. "From

Earth, you say? How curious." She extended a finger and prodded Suzy in the chest, as though checking she was really there. "You're a long way from home, my girl. A very long way indeed."

Suzy, who didn't appreciate being prodded one little bit, did her best to banish the image of her parents that the old woman's words conjured in her mind. "I've got a delivery for you," she said, proffering the parcel.

"I know," said Crepuscula. "But since you've seen fit to make me wait this long for it, I think it's only fair that I take a little of your time in return, hmmm?"

"Um…" Suzy wished she didn't feel so nervous. "I'm very sorry, but I've already apologized for being late, and if I stay any longer I'll be even later for my next delivery."

It was a perfectly reasonable point, but as she watched the Lady Crepuscula's expression sour, she realized it had also been completely the wrong thing to say.

"Then it seems to me, my girl, that you should have been more punctual to begin with." The shadows surrounding Crepuscula seemed to gather and deepen. "And if you will not give it up willingly, perhaps I should just take it from you."

"What do you mean?" said Suzy, but the Lady Crepuscula had already raised her cane and waved it in a circle above Suzy's head.

"There," she said with cold satisfaction. "Half an hour from your life. Now we're even."

Suzy examined the woman's features and tried to discern whether she was being made fun of again. "You can't do that," she said.

"Oh, but I can, my girl. I just have. Half an hour of your time for the half an hour of mine that you wasted." The grim little smile crept back onto her face.

"I don't believe you," said Suzy, who honestly didn't know whether she did or not, but was angry, and still a little scared, and certainly wasn't going to let herself be picked on like this.

"Oh, don't you?" Crepuscula raised her cane again. It was jet-black, with a silver tip that flashed in the lamplight. "I could take more, if that would persuade you. How about a year? Or a decade? I could take a century and turn you to dust where you stand."

Suzy took a deep breath and held up the parcel and delivery slip. "Sign here, please."

Crepuscula's eyes narrowed. For a moment she seemed poised in indecision, but then she reached out with her spare hand and snatched the parcel from Suzy. "I shall open it first," she said. "I won't sign anything until I know you've delivered the right package, and in good condition."

"Fine," Suzy said, and watched as Crepuscula grappled with the parcel. It was small and well wrapped, and her wrinkled fingers had trouble getting underneath the layers of parcel tape. She began hissing with the effort. "Would you like some help?" asked Suzy.

"Certainly not," snapped Crepuscula, but it was another minute before she finally tore through the brown paper to reveal a wooden box, like a jewelry box, but quite plain. Hooking her cane over her arm, she opened the box and withdrew something small and spherical, which glinted in the starlight.

"And there you are, at last," she said, holding the object up to the light. She shook it and gave a grunt of satisfaction.

It was a snow globe: a glass sphere, about the size of a tennis ball, set on a base of ceramic. Inside the sphere was a small, bright green ceramic frog. Multicolored flakes of glitter swirled around it, and Crepuscula held it to her face, so close that her breath fogged the glass.

"You'd better be worth all the trouble I've been to." She tapped a fingernail against the glass. "At least you look rather fetching. If all else fails, I can keep you on my mantelpiece. A nice little souvenir to see me through my twilight years."

She seemed to have forgotten Suzy altogether, and Suzy had to cough, politely, before she looked up again.

"Could you sign for it, please?"

Crepuscula rolled her eyes, but snatched the form from her. "Pen?" she demanded.

Suzy froze. She hadn't even thought about needing a pen. She patted her bathrobe pockets, but it was just for show. "I'm sorry," she said. "Do you have one?"

Crepuscula rocked forward on her toes, bringing her face almost level with Suzy's.

"Standards are slipping," she said. Then, replacing the snow globe in its box, she pivoted on her cane and stamped away into the depths of the gatehouse. "Wait here," she called back. Suzy watched her go, and got her first view of the tower's interior. To her surprise, it wasn't the darkened fortress she had expected. Instead of jet-black stonework, the walls were white and featureless. The floor looked like a chess board, all black and white squares, and a crystal chandelier hung from the ceiling, giving out a clear, cold light.

Crepuscula set the box down on a small wooden table in the center of the room before retreating through an inner doorway and out of sight, muttering under her breath. It might have been a trick of the light, but the shadows in the room seemed to bend toward her as she went.

Suzy waited, hugging herself against the cold. There

was still no sign of movement from the train, but she gave a thumbs-up in the direction of the sorting carriage, in case Wilmot could see her. She doubted it, though—the wind was getting stronger, and the gusts of ice it carried were getting thicker. They hit the floor with a noise like distant wind chimes. The gargoyle still stared down at her from above, its teeth almost close enough to touch.

She shivered and stepped inside the doorway, out of the wind.

"Help me!"

Suzy looked around in surprise. It was a boy's voice, small and faint, and she hurried back to the door, thinking it must have come from the direction of the train. But before she had reached the threshold, it came again.

"Over here! Quick! Please, help me!"

The skin on her arms began to prickle. The voice was coming from somewhere inside the room, but there was nobody in sight. She was quite alone.

"Hello?" she whispered.

"Here! Over here!"

She picked her way inside, letting the voice guide her until she reached the table. "Where are you?"

"Where do you think? I'm in the box."

She looked around again, wary of a trick, but as impossible as it was, the voice certainly *seemed* to be coming from the box. She opened the lid. There was nothing inside except the snow globe, the ceramic frog sitting exactly as she had last seen it. She picked up the globe and gave it an experimental shake.

"Oi! How is that helping?"

The voice certainly seemed to be coming from the snow globe, but the frog remained motionless. Then, as Suzy looked in at it, it blinked.

"You're alive!" she exclaimed.

"Yes, alive and trapped in here." The frog spoke without moving its lips. "Please don't let her take me. She's evil!"

"What do you mean?"

"What do you mean, 'What do you mean?' The Lady Crepuscula put a curse on me! She turned me into this snow globe, and now she wants to take me prisoner!"

"Wait, you mean you're a person?" said Suzy.

"Of course I am. How many snow globes do you know that can talk?"

"Sorry," she said. "I'm new here." She gave a worried glance at the door through which Crepuscula had disappeared. "What should I do?"

"Take me with you," said the frog.

"I don't know...," said Suzy. She could hear the distant sound of Crepuscula's cane against the floor tiles. It was getting closer.

"Please!" whispered the frog. "It's more important than

you know. The fate of all the Impossible Places depends on it."

Suzy's mind raced. This was all happening too quickly. But she remembered Crepuscula's sneer as she waved her cane above her head, the threat to turn her to dust, and she stuffed the snow globe into her pocket, as if by instinct.

"Hurry!" the frog squeaked.

"Shhh!" hissed Suzy. Her mind was still racing, but it had at last chosen a direction. She snapped the lid of the box shut and ran back to the open courtyard doorway, her heart drumming a painful rhythm in her chest. The ice storm was worsening, and she could barely see the train anymore.

She turned back to face the room and leaned against the wall, trying to keep the fear from her face as Crepuscula hobbled back toward them.

"I should deduct another minute from you for making me fetch this," she said, flourishing a quill pen fashioned from what looked to Suzy like an enormous black peacock feather. "But frankly you're barely worth the raising of my wand, and I have more important matters to attend to. Consider yourself lucky." She unfolded the delivery form, stabbed at it with the quill, and thrust it back in Suzy's face. "Now get out of my sight."

Suzy took the form, and ran.

The wind hit her sideways, cutting through her clothes as though they were damp paper. She leaned into it, hurrying onward with her eyes half-shut, clamping her postie's hat to her scalp as ice crystals peppered her face and hands, every one of them a cold, sharp sting. It was like walking into television static, and after just a few yards she realized she had lost sight of the train.

Don't panic, she told herself. *You know it's in front of you. Just keep going and you'll reach it.*

But it was hard not to panic with the guilty secret of the snow globe bumping against her thigh. She was sure the lump in her pocket stood out a mile. She glanced back, expecting to see Crepuscula watching her from the gatehouse, but the doors were already shut. She breathed a sigh of relief and pressed on toward the train.

Then she realized what she had seen and stopped. Very slowly, her body shaking with fear now, rather than cold, she turned back to look at the gatehouse.

The gargoyle was looking at her. Its head had been lowered, its eyes fixed on the spot in front of the doors. Now they were fixed on her. She stumbled backward, not daring to look away, and its head moved with her, keeping her in sight.

Her lungs burned, and she only realized she had been holding her breath when her back collided with something cold and hard, and she let out a scream of surprise.

She whipped around, ready to jump away from whatever danger she had unwittingly walked into. The figure of a knight loomed over her, its mouth open in a silent scream.

She put her head down and ran, not thinking where she was going, just wanting to get away. Away from that thing over the doors, away from these awful statues with their twisted faces, and away from the cruel woman who collected people and years like trinkets.

"When we reach the train, don't tell them about me," said the frog, its voice muffled by her pocket. "If they know you have me, they'll send me back."

"They wouldn't do that," she protested.

"They won't have any choice. It's their job."

She gritted her teeth as she felt everything spiraling out of control. How had it all gone so wrong, so quickly? But there was no time to stop and think, and she ran on until she saw the dark shape of the train ahead of her and, piercing the darkness like a lance, the welcome glow of a lantern.

"Ahoy, down there!" came Stonker's voice. "Hurry up, Postmaster. I want to put this blasted place behind us."

Suzy skidded to a breathless halt. She must have lost her way in her panic, because she was at the wrong end of the train—she was standing in front of the locomotive, not in the back, where the sorting car was. The spotlight of Stonker's lantern found her.

"Good grief! You again."

"Quick!" she called. "We have to get out of here."

"I'm going nowhere with a stowaway on board," said Stonker. "What are you doing here?"

Suzy didn't wait to explain, but ran to the narrow ladder that hung down from the front end of the gangway on which Stonker stood. It was like a fire escape—she had to jump for it, but as she caught the bottom rung, the ladder folded down to touch the ground. She scrambled up it until she was face-to-face with the astonished troll.

"I'm working," she gasped, plucking her deputy's badge from the front of her bathrobe and holding it out like a shield.

Stonker gave it a long, black look. "I think I'll be having words with our young Postmaster," he said.

"Fine!" she said. "But not here."

She picked Stonker up by his collar and, ignoring his protestations, ran with him along the gangway to the cab's open front door, where she bundled him inside. Before she followed him in, she glanced back across the courtyard, and immediately wished she hadn't.

Crepuscula was just visible silhouetted between the open gatehouse doors, the light from her living room casting her shadow across the flagstones. She made no move toward the train, and for a tantalizing second, Suzy thought she might let them go.

Until the old woman raised her hand toward them, and her shadow began to move. It stretched out from her across the courtyard, sliding like a snake between the statues. Suzy watched, horrified, as it began to pull itself hand over hand toward the train.

6

A First-Class Escape

Suzy leaped into the cab and slammed the door behind her, only to find herself face-to-snout with Ursel, who reared up and bared her fangs.

"Young lady!" Stonker said, dusting himself down. "I have never been handled in such a fashion. And on my own locomotive! Why, the indignity of it."

"I'll apologize all you want once we're out of here," Suzy said, wondering whether she should be more scared of Crepuscula's creeping shadow or Ursel's dagger-like claws. "Just, please, hurry!"

"We're not going anywhere until you give a full account of yourself," he said. Ursel growled in agreement.

Suzy leaned past Ursel to argue with him and got her

first view of the inside of the cab. It looked like a neat little sitting room, complete with floral wallpaper, a battered old armchair, and even a small bookcase in one corner. Another door was set into the rear wall, with a window on either side through which she had a clear view of the tender, which was coupled immediately behind the cab. Stonker and Ursel were both facing her, so she was the only one to see the long, skeletal fingers of the shadow creep slowly up the tender's side. She flinched, but clamped her mouth shut. She was determined not to cry out. If the others saw it, they would know something was wrong, and she would have to give up her secret.

But the hand was growing, its fingers as long as tree branches, and within a few seconds it had blotted out everything outside the rear windows. She had to act, before panic overtook her.

"We're still half an hour late," she said, trying to keep the tremor from her voice. "Maybe Wilmot's right."

Stonker narrowed his eyes at her. "Right about what?"

With a tremendous effort of willpower, Suzy leaned against the door and sighed. "Oh, nothing. He just told me the Impossible Postal Express isn't as fast as it used to be, that's all." She saw the flash of anger in Stonker's eyes. She would probably feel guilty about this later, she reflected, but right now she needed that anger. "I'm sure it's not your fault," she went on. "I mean, this train does look pretty old, after all."

"Old." The tips of Stonker's ears had turned red. "*Old!*"

"It's fine," said Suzy. "I'm sure you're doing your best."

She caught her breath as the shadow started to seep in under the back door, spreading like spilled ink.

"Here's my best, young lady."

Stonker threw a large red lever, and the locomotive jumped forward. Suzy was thrown to the floor, but looked up just in time to see the shadow sucked back out of sight beneath the door. She had a glimpse of the courtyard and the distant figure of Crepuscula beyond it through the window, before the whole world tipped on its side, and the train plunged over the edge of the tower. There was another momentary sense of vertigo, which was only made worse as she struggled to her feet and looked out the front window. The rails stretched down the tower to the desert, which raced closer as the train rocketed down, down, down, faster than free fall.

Stonker laughed in triumph and threw himself at the mass of brass pipes, valves, and levers that covered most of the front wall. They twisted around a wrought iron hearth, in which a dazzling blue fire burned. A mantelpiece stood above it, supporting a carriage clock, a telephone like the one on Wilmot's desk, and what looked like an old-fashioned flip-page calendar in a polished wooden frame.

Behind her, meanwhile, Ursel was reaching into an iron hatch she had opened in the rear wall and was pulling out…bananas?

Yes, bunches of bananas, but instead of eating them, she was throwing them onto the fire, where they fizzed and ignited in showers of blue sparks.

"Is this fast enough for you, m'dear?" said Stonker, flashing Suzy a triumphant smile as she clung to the nearest windowsill. She only half heard him—she was more concerned by the wall of desert that was still rushing toward them at incredible speed. She could see the rails ahead of them; they performed a ninety-degree turn at the foot of the tower and stretched off across the sands again. But the train could never hope to make the turn, could it? Their momentum was too great.

Momentum equals mass times velocity, she thought, as a detached part of her mind set about reviewing the details of her impending death. In other words, the heavier you are, and the faster you're going, the longer it takes to change direction. She had no idea what the train's mass was, but it was big. And their velocity? *Fast.* They would crash headfirst into the desert with the speed of a rocket. There would be nothing left of them.

"Ready…" Stonker poised himself at the controls, his fingers hovering over a large dial labeled THIS WAY UP. The fireplace belched more flames, painting the cab an unnatural hue. The sand rushed up to meet them. Suzy sank to the floor and hugged herself.

Stonker turned the dial a second before disaster struck, and Suzy's stomach did a funny little flip. She picked herself up and looked back out the windows. Sure enough, they were racing along the ground at the same terrific speed, the shadow of the tower now receding behind them.

"Voilà!" said Stonker. "That's given us a bit of a kick. An angry dragon couldn't catch us now."

Suzy had no idea how fast an angry dragon could be, but she was tempted to believe him. The whole world was a blur, and the tower was already a tall pencil of shadow on the horizon.

Before she could wonder at their speed any further, the phone rang. Without being asked, Ursel reached out and plucked the receiver from the cradle. "Growlf?" she said, raising it to her ear. She nodded, then extended the receiver to Suzy. "Urf."

"For me?" said Suzy in confusion.

"That'll be the Postmaster," said Stonker. "Do please thank him for his wise counsel. I don't know how we'd cope without him." He busied himself with the controls again.

Suzy put the phone to her ear. "Hello?"

"Postal Operative Suzy!" Wilmot sounded breathless. "Thank goodness! I was afraid we'd left you behind. I don't want to go down in history as the Postmaster who lost his entire staff on their very first delivery."

"You won't," she said, wondering if he would ever know just how close he had come.

"Did you deliver the parcel?" he asked. "Did you get the signature?"

Suzy patted the bulging pocket of her bathrobe and felt a fresh twinge of anxiety. "Well, yes, I did, but—"

"Splendid! In that case, I congratulate you on a successful delivery. I'm sure it will be the first of many."

"I don't know if it was really *successful*," she said, twisting the phone cord around her fingers. She felt trapped and guilty. She had stolen the snow globe and broken her vow on her very first delivery. But the snow globe had asked to be stolen, and if it was being delivered against its will, it was hardly a crime, was it? At the very worst, it was a little crime, to prevent a bigger, much worse one. Probably. All she was sure of was that she couldn't have left the frog with Lady Crepuscula. Nobody deserved that.

"Not successful?" A note of caution crept back into Wilmot's voice.

"Lady Crepuscula was still cross when we left," said Suzy. "Very cross, actually."

There was a pregnant pause on the end of the line. "Do you think she'll file a complaint?"

Suzy pinched the bridge of her nose as she tried to figure out what to say. Surely Wilmot could help her—he was the Postmaster, he must know what to do in this sort of situation. But what if the frog was right? What if Wilmot was duty bound to return the package? Could she take the risk?

"I think she might complain, yes," she said at last.

"Oh dear," he sighed. "I've never had a complaint before. A black mark against our names and reputations." He sighed again. "But I suppose it was inevitable. And you should still be very proud of yourself. You're part of the team now."

"Great," said Suzy, biting her lip against another stab of guilt. "What happens next?"

"Ah yes, our next job. Let me check the itinerary..." She heard the shuffling of papers down the line. "It's a collection, rather than a delivery, and—oh! It's this lot."

"What lot?" she said, gripping the receiver a little tighter.

"Some of our most loyal customers," said Wilmot breezily. "They're perfectly harmless."

"Harmless," she repeated, in a faraway sort of voice, but her thoughts were interrupted by the sound of Stonker clearing his throat.

"Tell the Postmaster we won't get far without a destination on the board," he said, and gave the thing that looked like a calendar a tap. Now that she looked at it properly, Suzy saw it wasn't a calendar at all—it was a miniature destination board. The words OBSIDIAN TOWER were still displayed in the destination box, with TIME DUE listed above and TIME OF ARRIVAL below.

"Don't worry," said Wilmot. "I heard. I'm sending it through now."

As she watched, the destination board began to change, the letters and numbers flipping over one by one, faster and faster, until they clattered by in a cascade of nonsense. Then, in an instant, they stopped, and Stonker's face brightened.

"See?" He grinned, tapping the TIME OF ARRIVAL box. "We've made up ten minutes already. How do you like that?"

But Suzy was more interested in their destination. "The Topaz Narrows?" she said, reading from the board.

"That's right," said Wilmot. "Just pop back to the H. E. C. when we get there, and I'll give you all the details. And tell me, can you swim?"

"Yes," she said cautiously. "Why?"

"Just checking," he said, and hung up. She replaced the receiver and wondered once again what she had signed up for.

Stonker pulled on a short chain hanging from the ceiling, and the whistle let out its mournful howl. "I'm always happy to put this place behind me," he said. "To sunnier climes!"

Suzy craned her neck and looked out the window again. The tower was now lost to sight completely, and even the army of statues was long behind them. There was just empty desert stretching in all directions, broken only by the winding tracks and the arch of another tunnel mouth up ahead.

Her hand strayed to her pocket. She needed time, and some privacy, to figure out what she was going to do about the unexpected guest she was carrying. Who was he, and why did the Lady Crepuscula want him so badly? Something told her that the old woman would do much worse than file a complaint if she ever caught up with them. The thought made her shiver.

Stonker pulled on the whistle again as the train plunged into the tunnel, and with a rush of air the desert was gone.

7

LATE ARRIVAL

Ice crystals ricocheted like bullets off the stones of the Obsidian Tower. They battered the statues, chipping away at the few sharp edges that remained and leaving shallow pockmarks in their once-smooth features. When they came to the Lady Crepuscula, however, they whirled and parted like shoals of fish, slipping around her before carrying on their way. For her part, the Lady Crepuscula didn't even notice them. She might as well have been taking a stroll in a pleasant summer breeze, except for the fact that her expression was one better suited to foul weather.

Crepuscula's forehead wrinkled, and she pursed her lips as she stood on the very edge of the battlements and watched the dwindling lights of the Impossible Postal Express racing away across the desert.

"Foolish girl," she muttered. "You brought this upon yourself." She raised her cane, aiming the silver tip like a rifle at the train.

"Aw, don't tell me I've missed 'em!"

The Lady Crepuscula started, swinging the cane to point at whoever had spoken. The interloper leaped backward from a small pump-operated maintenance trolley that stood on the rails in the center of the courtyard and threw up his hands to shield himself.

"Don't shoot!"

"Why not?" she said. "I don't trust people who creep up behind me. Especially in my own home."

"I'm not creepin'," said the figure, slowly emerging from behind his hands. "I'm just naturally unobtrusive, is all."

"I'll decide if you're obtrusive or not." She looked back over the edge of the tower, just in time to see the train vanish over the horizon. She tutted and lowered her cane. "You're a troll," she said.

"That's right," said the figure. "Name's Fletch."

"I don't care about your name," she said. "I was expecting a visit from a postal troll, but they saw fit to send a human instead. I can't say it was a satisfactory substitution."

Fletch's eyes widened. "She's been 'ere?"

"Evidently. You know the girl?"

"Sort of. Short and fluffy? Light brown skin? Terrible taste in pajamas?"

"One and the same. And in the brief time that she was here, she took something very important to me."

"Yeah, she does that. I'm trying to chase 'er down."

Crepuscula tapped her cane against the flagstones and thought. "We clearly have a common problem."

"Right," said Fletch. He was suddenly aware that he might have said too much, and it made him nervous. "Well, if I've missed 'em 'ere, I'll carry on my merry way. Maybe I could give you a call or somethin', once I've found 'er."

"Oh no you won't," said Crepuscula. "I can't afford to let that girl wander free across the Union. The item she stole is very valuable and very dangerous, and I went to a great deal of effort to acquire it. As you interrupted my attempt to prevent her escape, I think it's only fair that you help me retrieve her now."

"Whoa, wait a minute," said Fletch, backing away. "I'm just passing through. I'm not lookin' for any trouble."

The Lady Crepuscula raised an eyebrow, and Fletch felt a chill that had nothing to do with the wind.

"My poor little creature," she said. "I'm afraid you've already found it."

With a flick of her wrist, she leveled her cane at him,

and he felt his body go rigid. He tried to turn, to run, but couldn't. He was as immobile as the statues.

"I don't know what good you think I'm gonna do you," he gasped. "My job was to build a shortcut from the last delivery in the Western Fenlands to 'ere. They're back on the main rail network now. I've no idea where they're headed."

"Oh, I know perfectly well where they'll end up eventually," she said. "At the only place in the Union with power to match my own."

Fletch gaped at her. "You don't mean ... the *other* tower?"

"Precisely," said Crepuscula. "We both know the price of entry, and it's not the sort of thing that's easy to come by. So tell me, where would your friends go to find it?"

Fletch fought for breath. "No idea."

"I'm afraid I don't believe you."

Very gently, Fletch began to rise into the air. Then he drifted out sideways, beyond the battlements, to hang above the desert. Ice crystals pinged and zipped against his frozen form. He locked eyes with Crepuscula— anything to avoid looking down.

"Let's try again," she said, as though to a reluctant child. "They need a unique piece of knowledge, known only to one person in all the Union. Where would they get it?"

Fletch pressed his lips together and shook his head. Crepuscula sighed. She gave a flick of her cane, and Fletch tilted over until he was facing straight down. Ice crystals battered the back of his head, stinging the delicate skin of his enormous ears before plunging down to the desert below. They took a long time to fall.

"If you're really going to be of no help to me, perhaps we should just part company," she said. "At least the trip down will be easier than the trip up."

Fletch felt the magical bonds holding him start to loosen. He slipped a few inches and cried out in shock. "All right!" he wailed. "I'll tell you, I'll tell you!"

He screwed his eyes shut against the void beneath him, waiting for the thread of magic that held him up to break. Instead, he felt a tug, a short rush of air, and then the impact of cold stone beneath him. He opened his eyes to find himself back in the courtyard, on the spot where he had been standing just a moment earlier.

He breathed a sigh of relief, despite the sight of the Lady Crepuscula standing over him. She was smiling.

"Then why are we wasting time here?" She clapped her hands together. "Come along, boys. We're going on an outing."

Fletch was about to protest being referred to as a boy when he heard a low grinding sound behind him. It sounded like a heavy door swinging open after centuries of disuse. Then he saw that Crepuscula was no longer looking at him, but at something behind him. He turned to look and immediately wished he hadn't.

With slow, awkward movements, every statue in the courtyard was beginning to move.

8

THE HALL OF SPYGLASSES

Captain Neoma was angry. Actually, she was nervous, but she couldn't afford to let anybody know that, especially not here in the Observatory. It was the most secure room in the Union, its existence known only to an elite few, and as Captain of the Guard it was her job to keep it that way, which is exactly what she had done until two days ago, when something went Very Badly Wrong. She still didn't know *why* it had gone wrong, which was why she was nervous, and also why she was hiding those nerves behind a thunderously bad mood.

Word of her temper must have spread, as hardly any of the observers dared glance up from their desks as she stalked past on her patrol, and even the other guards seemed reluctant to make eye contact. That suited her just fine. She was still in charge here, and she wanted everyone to know it.

The Observatory was large, ornate, and circular, with paneled walls of dark wood, and a high-domed ceiling of midnight blue decorated with antiquated star charts. Most of the floor space was taken up with the desks, which stood in three concentric rings, facing outward. Each was occupied by an observer, hunched over their work in silent concentration—five hundred in all, of various species, and most of them children. Kids always saw things adults missed.

That's all her job really was, Captain Neoma reflected. Babysitting. And to think she used to fight monsters for a living...

She ground her teeth and walked on. A few observers were daring enough to sneak a look at her as she passed, but she fixed them with a warning glare and they quickly put their eyes back to their spyglasses.

Even in her good moods, Captain Neoma wasn't a fan of the spyglasses. Frankly, they gave her the creeps. Maybe it was the way they looked so much like normal telescopes—harmless brass tubes mounted on little tripods, one on each desk—but their jet-black lenses always seemed to stare into nothing. The Observatory had no windows, after all. Nevertheless, Captain Neoma could *feel* them watching, their magically charged glass peeling back the layers of reality between the Observatory and the farthest reaches of the Union.

Each spyglass was trained on a different location—Nethertown, Troll Territory, Big Sky Range, and so on—and the observers made careful notes of everything they saw. It was the biggest research project in history. From weather patterns to train timetables, volcanic eruptions to shopping habits, life in the Impossible Places was being painstakingly cataloged, and the air beneath the dome was full of the whispering scratch of pens on paper.

At least the observers didn't take much looking after. The Observatory rules were simple—no talking, no passing notes—and these were smart kids. *Very* smart, in fact, the best and the brightest from throughout the Union. If they performed well, there was a free university place in it for them at the end of it all. None of them were willing to risk that. At least, *almost* none of them...

She spared a resentful glance for the Observatory's only empty desk as she approached it. Its untended spyglass felt like an accusation—a black mark on her otherwise spotless record. These kids weren't allowed to sneeze without her permission, let alone *disappear.* How had this happened? And more to the point, why? Why had this observer chosen to throw away his whole future? Goodness knew, he didn't have much of a past to go back to.

She was still turning the problem over in her mind when she became aware of a whisper running through the room. Heads were turning. A few people pointed. Narrowing her eyes, Captain Neoma followed the commotion to its source, and almost gasped. An observer was away from her post, hurrying between the desks. The other guards saw her, too, but Captain Neoma stayed them with a look. She would be the one to deal with this.

"You there!" she barked, her words amplified by the dome above. "Where do you think you're going?"

The observer—a young girl with blond hair and thick-rimmed glasses—froze in shock.

"I . . . I'm, um . . . ," she stammered as Captain Neoma bore down on her. The girl wore the same dull gray uniform as the other observers, and the name tag pinned to her chest read,

Hi! My name's: MAYA
I'm studying: THE CREPUSCULAN WASTES

"You know the data protection rules," Captain Neoma hissed. "No one's allowed away from their desks without my express permission." She spotted something in the girl's hand. It was a page torn out of a report book, filled with handwriting and folded over. "What's this?" said Neoma.

The girl tried to hide it behind her back. "Please, Captain, I'm not breaking any rules. I'm just following orders. Honest!"

"I didn't give you any orders."

"I know." The girl looked across the room to the door marked CURATOR'S OFFICE. "Lord Meridian did."

Captain Neoma glared intently into the girl's eyes, searching for any hint of a lie. She couldn't find one.

Uncomfortably aware of the attention they were drawing, she took Maya by the hand and led her into the center of the room. There were no desks there, just an open circular space where they couldn't be so easily watched—the other observers all sat with their backs to them. Captain Neoma lowered herself onto one knee and placed a reassuring hand on the girl's shoulder. "Tell me, Maya," she whispered. "What did His Lordship want you to do?"

"He...he told me to keep watch on the Obsidian Tower and to tell him straightaway if I saw anything strange happen. And I did. See something strange, I mean." Maya was breathing hard and, with a trembling hand, brandished the bit of paper. "I wrote it all down, just like he asked."

Captain Neoma made a concerted effort not to tighten her grip on Maya's shoulder. She had no idea why His Lordship would want information on the Obsidian Tower, but she had a feeling it spelled trouble. Anything involving the Lady Crepuscula always did.

"You've done an excellent job, Maya," she said, giving the girl's shoulder a pat. "But I'll take it from here." She held out a hand for the paper.

Maya drew back. "He said nobody else was to read it, Captain. Look." She pointed to the word *Confidential*, which she had handwritten on the outside of the folded paper.

"I promise not to open it," Captain Neoma said. "On my honor." She held Maya's gaze, unblinking, until Maya finally handed the paper over.

"Thank you," said Neoma, standing. "Now get back to your post. There's still work to be done."

Maya grinned with relief. "For knowledge is our treasure!" she said.

"Yes, yes," said Captain Neoma. "And we are its keepers. Now get on back to work."

Maya nodded and hurried away. Captain Neoma watched her until she was back at her desk, then crossed the room to the curator's office, already wishing she hadn't promised not to read the note—what could His Lordship be looking for, and more importantly, why hadn't He told her about this? Perhaps the missing observer had shaken his trust in her. The idea stung more than a little.

She approached the office, sparing a nod for Sergeant Mona standing guard outside it, but was surprised to see the blind was drawn over the window, the words STRICTLY NO ADMITTANCE stenciled on it. She hesitated.

"He's with a client, Captain," Sergeant Mona explained, seeing her confusion. "They've been in there all morning."

Once again, Neoma was forced to hide her surprise. No one was supposed to enter the Observatory without her knowing it, and they certainly weren't supposed to take meetings with His Lordship. "He doesn't have any appointments today," she said. "Are you sure?"

Sergeant Mona, painfully aware of her captain's short temper, wet her lips. "His Lordship brought them in himself, Captain. I thought you knew."

No, I didn't, Neoma thought. *I can add it to the ever-growing list of things I apparently don't know.*

She was raising her hand to knock on the door when it was yanked open from inside and someone swept out, almost knocking her down. "Hey!" she barked, springing clear.

The figure paused and fixed Neoma with a look of simmering fury. It was a woman: tall, raven haired, and richly dressed in a red gown, with a whole wolf skin clasped around her shoulders like a cloak. The creature's head lolled over the woman's shoulder at a drunken angle.

A heavy gold livery collar hung around her neck, and more gold winked at her wrists and fingers as she gathered the wolf skin around her, as though afraid that any contact with Neoma might sully it.

"Excuse me," the woman growled, and swept on in the direction of the exit on the opposite side of the room. The observers all shot her furtive glances, and even Neoma stared after her, mystified, until the armored door of the exit swung closed behind her.

Her thoughts were interrupted by a voice from inside the office.

"Come in, Captain," it said. "I've been expecting you."

The office was cozy, warm, and simple—just a row of bookcases along the back wall, an old wooden desk to one side of the room, and a pair of wingback leather armchairs to the other, where a small figure sat half-hidden in shadow.

"My lord," Neoma said, approaching the chair and snapping to attention. "That woman…"

"Was the chancellor of Wolfhaven." The figure sat forward. He was old and very pale, dressed in a gray suit that matched his thick silver hair. One hand rested on the head of a black silver-tipped walking cane, and he peered at Neoma through half-moon glasses. "She was here on business."

"Wolfhaven!" Neoma had no hope of hiding her surprise this time. "But, my lord, that's one of the richest Impossible Places in the Union. And the chancellor is a state official! I should have been informed."

"The appointment has been in the diary for a while now," said the old man. "Perhaps you overlooked it in all the recent fuss."

Captain Neoma clenched her fists. She was certain she had seen no mention of a visit. "She looked upset, sir."

"Merely overcome with emotion, no doubt," the old man said. "She came here to pledge her support for the research project and was so deeply and personally moved by the extent of our work that she has agreed to extend us some considerable financial assistance. The coffers of Wolfhaven are open to us." He smiled. "Now, I believe you have a report from one of my observers. I was expecting something sooner or later. Which of them is it from?"

So he's given orders to more than one of them, Captain Neoma thought as she handed him the folded paper. "From Maya, sir."

The old man's face fell. "Oh dear. The Obsidian Tower. That's unfortunate." He opened the paper and shifted his glasses up his nose.

Captain Neoma covered her growing uncertainty by standing even further to attention. "Is something wrong, sir?"

"Almost certainly," he murmured, scanning through the notes. "How interesting. A snow globe. The Impossible Postal Express. And a girl, a *human* girl at that. Well, I never." He folded the paper closed again and returned his attention to Captain Neoma. "I'll give you the good news first, Captain. It seems we may finally have caught up with your little mistake."

If she stood any straighter, Captain Neoma thought her head might just pop right off her neck. "At the Obsidian Tower?"

"That's the bad news," the old man said. "It seems the Lady Crepuscula has taken something of an interest in the matter."

Captain Neoma's shock quickly turned to horror. "But why?" she said. "What could she possibly want with an observer?"

"That is a very good question, and I'm willing to bet the answer won't be pleasant. She must have something very specific in mind."

"Let me take a couple of squads out, sir," said Neoma, rising to the balls of her feet in anticipation of a fight. "I'll bring him back myself."

"I'm afraid you're too late. He's aboard the Impossible Postal Express bound for regions unknown. Crepuscula has mobilized her forces in pursuit."

"Then we have to find him first."

"Agreed," said the old man. "But we won't do that by tearing off into the sunset, guns blazing. According to young Maya's report, the Express has already reentered the tunnel system." He pursed his lips in thought. "If memory serves, that particular tunnel leads to seven possible destinations, and we can't take any action until we know which one they're heading for. Luckily for us, neither can Crepuscula."

He settled back into his chair, and Captain Neoma realized he had brought the conversation to a close.

"But we can't just sit here and do nothing!" she exclaimed.

"Of course not," he replied. "We'll do what we do best: watch and learn. One of our own is in danger, Captain. We don't know why he absconded or what Crepuscula stands to gain from him, and when we see an opportunity to act, I promise we will take it. Until then, he is in the care of this human girl. We shall simply have to trust her to stay ahead of Crepuscula until we can reach them."

That didn't sound like a very promising prospect to Captain Neoma, but she knew there was nothing more she could do for now. "I'll have the observers check the destinations of the tunnel, sir," she said. "Will there be anything else?"

"No, thank you, Captain. Notify me the moment you have anything."

Neoma saluted and left the office, positively itching with impatience. She wanted to be out there knocking heads together and getting answers, not stuck in here waiting for news. Crepuscula was on the warpath, and somebody had to be there to stop her. *And I'd really like it to be me*, she thought.

Her mind turned briefly to the chancellor of Wolfhaven. Despite what His Lordship had said, the chancellor hadn't looked like a woman who had just donated to a worthy cause; she had looked angry. Neoma recalled their brief encounter, trying to recapture the look in the woman's eyes. Had there been fear in there as well? It was hard to tell—the chancellor was as much wolf as woman. Skinwalkers could be hard to read.

All she knew for certain was that something strange was going on, and all the answers were aboard the Impossible Postal Express. Its crew had better hope that she caught up with them before Crepuscula did.

9

Sun, Sea, and Explosive Bananas

Sunlight burst into the cab like an explosion as the Impossible Postal Express rocketed out of the tunnel and into fresh, salt-scented air. The chill of the darkness was swept away, and a damp heat replaced it. Blinking away the glare, Suzy hurried to the window.

The eerie starlit desert had been replaced by water—gentle turquoise waves peaked and troughed all around them, broken here and there by tiny islands of sugar-white sand. Gulls sailed alongside them, gliding on the warm breeze, their wings hardly twitching.

"Wow!" said Suzy, turning to Stonker and Ursel in amazement. "It's beautiful."

"The Topaz Narrows," said Stonker, adjusting a few instruments. "A hundred leagues of the richest ocean this side of Landsdown Harbor. Not bad for fishing, when a chap's got the time."

Suzy pulled herself up on the lip of the window and looked down. "But that's impos—" she started. Then she realized it didn't really matter whether it was impossible or not—it was happening. Without waiting for permission from Stonker, she rushed to the door.

Keeping tight hold of the handrail, she leaned as far out as she dared and looked down. There was no land beneath the train. Instead, the rails stretched across the surface of the water, apparently unsupported. The waves slopped over them and withdrew, and the train threw up an arc of spray whenever it cut through one. Tiny droplets were already settling on her face and the fabric of her bathrobe. She stuck out her tongue and tasted the salt and laughed for the sheer joy of it.

"I say there!" Stonker appeared in the open doorway. "You're letting a draft in, young lady."

"Sorry," she called. "I just didn't want to miss this."

The troll's mustache twitched in a reluctant smile. "I suppose I can't blame you. First time out and all that. And you can't beat the view from the *Belle*."

Suzy frowned. "From the what?"

"Why, this old girl, of course," said Stonker, giving the

locomotive's flank an affectionate pat. Suzy hadn't noticed it before, but his hand rested against a bronze nameplate fixed to the boiler. It read BELLE DE LOIN.

"A train can't go anywhere without a locomotive to pull it," said Stonker, beaming. "And the Express wouldn't get much mail delivered without the *Belle* to take her places." He joined Suzy at the railing and looked out across the waters.

"It's a different sky," she said, squinting into the sun. "A different world, a different . . . everything." Her mind was itching with questions, and she turned to Stonker, looking for answers. "We were only in the tunnel for a few minutes. How did it get us so far?"

"Because the Impossible Places aren't all lined up neatly together, except at the Meridian," he said. "Most of them are scattered all over the place."

" 'Threaded all throughout reality,' " she remembered. "What's the Meridian?"

"A long story," he said, waving the question away. "Now, because they're so spread out, there's a lot of empty space between them. Not the sort with stars and planets in it, but negative space where nothing really exists. It's just void: cold, dark, and endless. People used to cross it in ships in the old days, but it's a dangerous journey, and it takes an age. That's why some clever people once put their heads together and invented the tunnels."

"You mean they're wormholes!" she said. "Linking one part of space with another."

"They're shortcuts between the Impossible Places, if that's what you mean," he said. "They skip most of the negative space, and a lot of them intersect with one another, so they connect to lots of different Places at the same time. It's why most people get about by rail nowadays." He pointed out across the water, and she saw the glimmer of several other tracks winding between the distant islands.

"But this is fantastic," she said as the lightning flash of understanding hit her. "It means everything about Einstein's theory of relativity is true! Space isn't flat, it's curved, and you can cut straight from one part of the curve to another! That's . . . wow." The enormity of it left her speechless.

"It's not really curved, so much as lumpy," said Stonker. "But I take your point." He drew himself up short and pushed his chest out. "But we're not here for the view. If you're going to be a member of this crew, you'd better get to the H. E. C. pretty sharpish."

"What's the H. E. C.?"

"That rusty old bucket between the *Belle* and the sorting car. The Postmaster needs you safely inside it before we can make our delivery. So come along. Chop-chop!"

"But how do I get there?"

"Over the tender," he said, ushering her back into the cab with a sweep of his arm.

"What? You can't be serious."

"Fear not, it's hard to slip on the bananas."

"What bananas?"

"You'll see," he said. "Just be sure not to eat any."

Ursel had opened the back door of the cab, giving Suzy a clear view of the tender behind them. A series of shallow handholds was set into the ironwork.

"Why not?" she asked.

"Because you'll explode," said Stonker, giving her a pat on the back. "Now, up you go."

Suzy took a moment to dry her hands on her bathrobe before nervously trying her weight on the first few handholds. She had trouble squeezing her slippers into the spaces but was otherwise able to pull herself up quite easily. After just a few seconds, she had reached the lip of the tender. Sure enough, a hill of bananas rose above her. She had been expecting coal. "Where do I go from here?"

"Straight over the top," said Stonker. "There's another ladder on the other side. Climb down that and cross the footplate to the H. E. C. You'll see a door ahead of you. You can't miss it."

"Right." Suzy took a few steadying breaths. "Wish me luck."

"I don't believe in the stuff," said Stonker. "But I will say, try not to fall off."

"Thanks," Suzy said. "I think." And with one final breath, she hauled herself up and over.

Walking on whole bunches of bananas was a strange sensation, she soon learned. On the one hand, they really did provide good traction, as Stonker had promised. Their thick skins were easy to get a purchase on, and her slippers, though wet, didn't slip at all. On the other hand, the bunches kept shifting beneath her weight, and she was forced to work her way forward in an awkward half crouch, helping herself up the pile with her hands. To her alarm, the bananas fizzed when they made contact with her skin, and crackles of blue energy danced between them and her fingertips. It didn't hurt, but it did set her scalp tingling.

"Trains that run on bananas instead of coal," she said to herself. "How does that work?"

"That's easy," came a small voice from her pocket. "They're fusion bananas."

Suzy looked down in surprise. She had been so focused on the climb that she had almost forgotten about the snow globe. "What are fusion bananas?" she said.

"They're a fuel source," said the frog. "A bit old-fashioned, though. People don't use them much nowadays because they're so unstable."

Suzy froze as more energy crackled around her fingers. "How unstable, exactly?"

The frog seemed to mull this over for a few seconds. "They really only start to go critical once their peels are opened."

The sparks subsided, and Suzy let out a breath. "Stonker sent us up here, so it can't be too dangerous. Right?"

"Right," said the frog. "But you know what troll health and safety rules are like."

"No," she said. "I don't."

"That's because there aren't any," said the frog.

"Thank you so much," she said through gritted teeth. "You know, you still haven't told me who you are."

"Do you really want me to explain right now?"

"Yes, I do." When, after a few seconds, the frog had not replied, she paused her climb and addressed the bulge in her pocket directly. "I'm still waiting."

"All right. Fine. I'm Frederick."

"Frederick who?"

"Prince Frederick," he said with exaggerated patience. "Of the Western Fenlands. Who did you think?"

Suzy snatched the snow globe out of her pocket and stared at the frog in amazement. "You're a prince?"

"Obviously," he said. "And just because I'm not old enough to be king yet doesn't mean you can talk to me like I'm some commoner."

Suzy laughed. "I'm so terribly sorry . . . Your Majesty?"

"It's Your Royal Highness, actually, but it's a start. And what's your name? Or should I just call you postie?"

"I'm Suzy Smith," she said. "From Earth. So why are you a frog? And what does Lady Crepuscula want with you?"

"Do you really want to talk about it here?" he said. Suzy looked around at the pile of bananas and the sea streaking past.

"All right," she said grudgingly. "But as soon as we get the chance, I want the whole story. Okay?"

"Fine," said Frederick, although he didn't sound happy about it.

She slipped him back into her pocket and turned her attention to getting safely over the mound of bananas. When she was ready, she sprang, wanting to get over quickly, but the wind hit her from behind, lifting her bathrobe and filling it like a sail. She tipped forward in an uncontrolled somersault, and rolled down the opposite bank of the pile with a cry of surprise.

"Help!" shouted Frederick, but there was nothing she could do. The world was a pinwheel of blue sky and yellow bananas, swapping ends around her in a dizzying cycle until she landed on her backside, with her hair in her face and her feet braced against the rear edge of the tender.

"Are you all right?" she gasped.

"I think so," said Frederick. "I can't see through all this glitter."

Suzy pulled her hair out of her eyes. The bananas were behind her, the strange metal tube of the H. E. C. was in front of her, and as she watched, a connecting door in its front opened and Wilmot poked his head out.

"Right on time," he said. "Come in."

Suzy scrambled down the ladder to the footplate. It was just a short hop across the gap between the tender and the H. E. C., but Wilmot extended a hand to help her anyway.

"Is everything okay?" he asked, closing the door behind her.

"Fine, I think." She looked around. If the H. E. C. looked a bit like an old tanker from the outside, the inside looked more like the belly of some mechanical whale, braced by wrought-iron ribs. Two large circular hatches were set into the ceiling, with another, larger one in a side wall. The far end of the carriage was taken up with machinery that looked like it might have come from a Victorian mill—flywheels and pistons and dials and springs were all pressed together in a combination that might have been a pump, or maybe some sort of generator. A swivel chair and a complex control panel were mounted in front of it.

The area of the carriage where she and Wilmot stood was full of clothing racks, from which hung what looked like suits of armor. Closer inspection revealed that some of them were just that—dented steel plate, rusty chain mail, and heavy visors, clearly designed with the long ears and nose of a troll in mind.

Other suits were more unusual, however. There was what looked like a space suit, made of padded silver fabric, complete with heavy boots and a reflective domed helmet. Suzy wasn't encouraged to see a number of strips of tape covering what appeared to be burn marks in several places on the suit.

"Welcome to the H. E. C.," said Wilmot. "The Hazardous Environment Carriage. We wouldn't be able to make half our deliveries without it."

The carriage juddered around them, and Suzy had to brace herself against a sudden deceleration. Stonker must finally be applying the brakes.

"You're sending me into a hazardous environment?" she said.

"Normally you'd have to complete your training before we'd let you try something like this," said Wilmot, "but you did such a good job with the Lady Crepuscula I think we'll let you off. What do you say?"

Suzy looked out the nearest porthole as the Express finally came to a wheezing halt. The Narrows looked calm and inviting. She was about to answer, when the whole carriage gave another sharp jolt and she felt the floor drop beneath her. In a panic, she saw the waves rise past the portholes, the churning foam swallowing them inch by inch until the sky was lost to sight.

"We're sinking!" she exclaimed.

"Actually, we're diving," said Wilmot. "It's like sinking, but on purpose." He crossed to the nearest rack and lifted one of the suits down. "You'll be needing this."

"A diving suit?"

He nodded. "It might be a little tight on you, but it's top of the range. At least, it was when they made it."

Suzy took it from him and looked it over. It was similar to the space suit, but instead of silver fabric, it looked like it had been stitched together from old tents. It had thick rubber gloves sewn onto the sleeves and heavy metal boots sewn onto the legs. The helmet was a dented sphere of bronze, with two large glass eyeholes and a long flexible canvas sock on the front for a troll nose. One end of a thick red hose was attached to a nozzle in the top of the helmet.

"I don't think I'm quite as good at this job as you think I am," she said. Outside the portholes, towering clusters of bright pink coral were rising into view, teeming with clouds of tropical fish. It was very beautiful, but she was too nervous to enjoy it. "Couldn't you do it? You seem to be the expert."

"Gosh." Wilmot seemed flustered all of a sudden. "I'm not sure I'd really call myself an *expert*." His shy grin suggested he was very happy that she had called him one, however. "I passed all my theory tests, but there's still so much of the job I haven't done for real yet."

"Why not?" she asked. "How long have you been doing it?"

"Just over a year now. Ever since I dropped out of school."

"You were in school?" This surprised her. "How old are you?"

"A hundred and fifty."

"How old?"

"I know," he said, blushing. "I'm the youngest troll ever to hold the job. Normally, I'd have spent a few decades in the Postal Academy, started as a junior postie, and then worked my way up, but the Impossible Postal Express has been understaffed for years, and when Dad died I was the only one who could take his place." He blushed even harder. "The Impossible Postal Express has been a hobby of mine since I was in diapers, you see. I'd studied all the postal routes, the delivery prices, the rules and regulations. It's a great privilege to be here."

110

This confession only served to renew the sense of guilt gnawing at Suzy's insides.

"I'm sorry about your dad," she said. "I had no idea."

Wilmot smiled, though there was sadness in his eyes. "He died with his boots on," he said. "That's all any troll can ask."

Suzy wasn't quite sure what this meant, but she was preoccupied with another question. "So how long do trolls live? Most humans are lucky to live to a hundred."

"Really?" Wilmot looked horrified. "How do you get the time to do anything?"

"We keep busy," she said.

"No wonder," said Wilmot. "Most trolls can expect to live to at least a thousand, although I know lots who are older."

"Like Fletch," she said. "He told me he was a thousand and ten."

"And still two centuries from retirement," Wilmot sighed. "As he keeps reminding everyone."

Suzy shut her eyes and made some rough calculations in her head. "I think," she said, opening one eye again, "that one human year must be about the same as twelve troll years. Roughly."

"How old does that make you in troll terms, then?" said Wilmot.

Another quick calculation. "One hundred and

thirty-two," she said, and laughed. "It was my birthday last month. My cake should have had more candles."

"And how young am I in human years?"

"Twelve and a half," she said.

They both laughed and, for a moment, Suzy's fear of the Lady Crepuscula felt very small and far away.

"I might not have all the experience I need yet," said Wilmot, "but this pickup is a part of the job I *have* done before. So trust me when I tell you you'll be fine. Besides, I'll be here to help."

He skipped to the strange machine at the opposite end of the carriage and flipped a few switches on the control panel. The machine wheezed to life, its flywheel turning, spewing a cloud of dust into the air. "This will keep you breathing," he said between bouts of coughing.

"Are you sure it's safe?"

"Absolutely. This is troll engineering. Guaranteed to last a century, or your money back."

"And how long have you been using it?" To Suzy's alarm, bits of the machine seemed to have been repaired with the same tape as the space suit.

"Don't worry about that now," he said, a little too quickly for her liking. "You'd better get dressed. The quicker you get out there, the quicker you'll be back. We're still behind schedule, remember." He took a seat at the controls and began fiddling with the machine.

Suzy looked at the suit again. There were no obvious tears, although she wasn't sure just how waterproof the stitching between the various sections of fabric would be. Still, it wouldn't matter as long as the air pressure inside the suit was strong enough to keep the water out.

Pressure is measured in units called atmospheres, she told herself. *Pressure at the surface is one atmosphere. Every ten meters of depth increases the pressure by one more atmosphere.* A glance out the nearest porthole suggested they were about twenty meters down. *So, two extra atmospheres. Three atmospheres in total.* She still had no idea whether the suit would hold the water out, but the calculation had made her a little calmer, at least.

She shrugged off her bathrobe and climbed into the suit. The boots were so heavy she had trouble lifting her feet, but she suspected that would be less of a problem once she was in the water. The suit was tight, as Wilmot had predicted, but the arms and legs had sections of concertina'd fabric sewn into them, so they stretched to fit.

"Don't just leave me here!" Frederick's voice was muffled by the fabric of her bathrobe, but it was loud enough to prompt Wilmot to look around.

"What was that?" he said.

"It was me," said Suzy in a voice that she was sure was too loud, and too false. "I was just... talking to myself."

"My mom always says that's the first sign of going mad," he replied. "Of course, the last sign is painting yourself orange and sticking carrots up your nose." He looked worried. "You're not about to do that, are you?"

"Don't worry," she said, trying to smile. "We've only got bananas on board."

The H. E. C. gave a final shudder as it came to rest on the sea floor.

"Right." He grinned. "Are you ready?"

"Almost." She turned her back on him and knelt down, pretending to fiddle with the helmet. She slipped a hand into the pocket of her bathrobe and drew out the snow globe. "Be quiet," she whispered, raising it to her lips. Then she reached into the helmet and pushed the snow globe into the nose sock, which dangled down in front of her like an elephant's trunk once she had pulled the helmet into place.

"Let me do you up," said Wilmot. It was dark and echoey inside, and the sound of him fastening the clasps that sealed the helmet was deafening. Suzy had never suffered from claustrophobia before, but as the seconds dragged on, she started to sweat with nerves. How would she cope outside, under the water, if she couldn't even handle this?

This thought was interrupted when Wilmot gave the

helmet a tap and, holding his hand up in front of the eye-holes, gave her a thumbs-up. "This way."

He guided her to the large hatch in the wall, spinning the big brass wheel that unlocked it and pulling it open to reveal an air lock—a space the size of a cupboard, with an identical hatch on the opposite side. Suzy hesitated, suddenly hating the idea of being sealed inside that tiny space.

"You'll have to attach your air hose once you're outside," Wilmot shouted, bringing his mouth up as close to the helmet as he could. "It's the bright red valve to your right."

Suzy forced herself to focus on his instructions. If she had a clear objective, it might help keep her rising fear at bay. "Okay," she called back, and winced as her voice bounced around inside the helmet. "Where do I go after that?"

"It'll be straight in front of you," he shouted. "Oh, and you'll need to deliver this." He reached into his pocket and pulled out a green glass bottle.

"I thought I was picking something up, not delivering," she called, taking the bottle and holding it up to the eye-holes. An old-fashioned label on the front bore a picture of the moon and the title SEA OF TRANQUILITY—FINEST DARK RUM. The neck was sealed with black wax, although the bottle seemed to be empty. She gave it an experimental shake, and something light and feathery rattled around inside it. She did her best to see what it was, but the glass of the bottle was too thick and dark to see through properly. She fumbled it into a large leather pocket attached to the front of the suit.

"You are, technically," said Wilmot. "But there won't actually be anything for you to pick up. Well, there will be, but you won't be able to pick it up, if you see what I mean."

"No," said Suzy, "I don't."

"Don't worry," he said. "It'll all make sense once you meet the captain. Are you ready?"

"I think so. Who's the captain?"

"He's a nice man, really," said the Postmaster. "Once you get past all the, y'know." And here he pulled a face, sticking his tongue out, rolling his eyes, and waving his hands around his face. "Best of luck!"

Before she could protest, he swung the air-lock door shut with a crash.

❧

"What was he talking about?" Frederick asked from the depths of the nose sock.

"I have no idea," she said. "I suppose there's only one way to find out."

A moment later, the air lock began to flood with water. It came gushing in through a grate in the floor, rising rapidly, and was around Suzy's knees in just a few seconds.

"What's that noise?" Frederick cried. "I can't see anything in here. Why didn't you put me somewhere I can see?"

"Because I had to hide you," she said.

"That sounds like water. Are we going to drown? We're going to drown, aren't we!"

"Sshhh," said Suzy. "Calm down. This is an air lock. It has to fill with water before we can open the outside door. Otherwise the sea would rush in all at once and squash us."

"Oh," he said. "If you say so."

"I do say so," said Suzy, although she had to stop herself from holding her breath as the water reached the helmet's goggles. "It's all about equalizing the pressure, so it's the same in here as out there. It's physics."

"Physics." He tested the word. "Is that a bit like fuzzics?"

"No," she said, gritting her teeth in annoyance. "Physics always makes sense."

The water reached the ceiling of the chamber, and she unlocked the outer hatch.

Her boots sent up puffs of fine white sand as she stepped outside. Towers of neon coral rose all around her, and clouds of fish glimmered and darted between them. The surface rolled like a broken mirror far above them, letting through fractured spears of sunlight.

"It's wonderful," she breathed.

"I'll have to take your word for it," grumbled Frederick. "Aren't you supposed to do something with that pipe on your head?"

"Oh yes!" Suzy had forgotten all about Wilmot's instructions to attach her air hose. Without it, she only had the air already in the suit to keep her breathing, and she doubted that would last more than a minute or two.

She looked around and saw the bright red circular nozzle protruding from the side of the carriage next to the air lock. She reached up and, a little clumsily, took hold of the trailing hose and fed it through her hands until she found the brass screw fitting at the end. Her thick gloves made it difficult to attach the one to the other, and she was short of breath before the hose finally clicked into place and she was able to screw it tight to the nozzle. A thin whistle of air filled the helmet, and she felt its cool touch on her face and neck. She heaved a deep sigh of relief.

"That was close," said Frederick. "You're looking after royalty now, remember. You should be more careful."

"Thanks, Your Highness," said Suzy. "I'll take extra care not to drown."

"Good idea."

Suzy paused to wonder whether sarcasm simply didn't exist in the Impossible Places, before remembering she had a job to do and that, as beautiful as this place was, she would feel much safer once she was looking at it from inside the carriage again. She looked around until she saw a large, jagged shape sticking up from among the coral a short distance away.

"That looks like a shipwreck," she said. "Do you think that's where we're supposed to go?"

"I've no idea," said Frederick. "You're the postie."

Suzy chewed a stray length of hair that had fallen across her face. "I can't see anything else around here," she said. "Maybe we're going to meet a mermaid." She gave a weak laugh and started toward the wreck, being careful not to tread on any of the coral. "Could we actually meet a mermaid?" she asked. "I mean, do they exist here?"

"Maybe," he replied. "Mermaids, mermen, merbeasts, weresharks, weresquid, flying squid, land squid, giant eels, electric eels, nuclear eels... They all exist somewhere in the Union."

Suzy shivered, and wished she hadn't asked. Some of those creatures sounded decidedly unpleasant, and although the reef looked tranquil, she tried to keep an eye on the darker crevices within the coral.

"So, Your Highness," she said, looking for a distraction, "how does a prince end up stuck inside a snow globe? And how does the snow globe end up getting mailed to an evil witch?"

"It's a long story," said Frederick.

"So I guessed," she said. "I'm all ears."

He sighed again. "I won't bore you with the details, but I'm next in line for the throne. That means I'm going to be king one day, and that's kind of a big deal."

"It sounds like it," said Suzy.

"And not to boast or anything, but the people of the Western Fenlands can't wait until I'm in charge. I'm just really, really popular there."

"Naturally," said Suzy flatly. "So what happened?"

"I was in the wrong place at the wrong time, and I overheard something I wasn't supposed to," said Frederick. "A plot to overthrow the kingdom."

"Wow," said Suzy, genuinely shocked. "That's pretty serious."

"I know," he said, sounding morose. "When I tried to raise the alarm, a remote spell came out of nowhere and I found myself stuck in this stupid ornament."

"Crepuscula's curse!" gasped Suzy. "So she's behind the plot?"

"D'you know what the worst thing is?" said Frederick. "As soon as I'd been cursed, my bodyguards—the two people I trusted most in all the Union—packaged me up and put me in the mail to the Obsidian Tower. They'd been working with Crepuscula all along." His voice wavered, and Suzy felt a rush of sadness for the boy.

"I'm sorry," she said. "That's terrible."

"It is," he agreed. "I mean, a novelty frog! She didn't even turn me into something classy, like a candlestick or a clock."

Suzy plodded on toward the wreck. It was certainly a troubling story, and it had raised the specter of Crepuscula again in her mind. If Frederick knew the old woman was behind the plot, surely she would do anything to silence him? The shadows beneath the coral seemed a shade darker than they had a moment ago, and she tried not to look at them too closely.

But there was something else as well. She could feel that little itch in her brain again; something didn't quite add up.

"Hang on," she said, coming to a sudden stop. "When you asked me to rescue you, you said the fate of all the Impossible Places depended on it."

"Did I?" Frederick's tone of surprise didn't quite ring true. "Are you sure I didn't say the fate of *an* Impossible Place depended on it?"

"I'm positive," she said. "It's one of the reasons I helped you."

"You were under a lot of stress," he said. "Perhaps your memory's just playing tricks on you."

My memory's perfect, Suzy thought. *Which means you were either lying then, or you're lying now.* She almost gave voice to the thought, but instinct told her to keep it to herself for a while longer. Maybe Frederick had just been exaggerating his importance to make sure she saved him from the tower. But now that she had, why not just admit to it? The itch refused to fade—she had a puzzle to solve. She didn't have all the pieces yet, but she knew Frederick would clam up if she pushed him too hard. She'd have to wait, and hope he gave something away accidentally.

"Perhaps you're right," she said with studied patience. "Come on. I want to see what's in that wreck."

10

A Watery Grave

I wonder when I'll get a nice, straightforward job," said Suzy. "Like sticking a letter through a mail slot." They had reached the wreck, and now stood outside a ragged hole in the side of its barnacle-encrusted hull. It must have been a magnificent ship once—a large, oceangoing vessel with three huge masts, now all broken. The nameplate on the prow was still just barely discernible—LA ROUQUINE.

The hole in the hull was big enough for a man to walk through without bending over, but only darkness was visible inside. Suzy lingered on the threshold, wishing she had a flashlight.

"What are you waiting for?" said Frederick. "They're expecting us, aren't they?"

"If only we knew what *we* should be expecting," she said. "Oh well, here goes." She cleared her throat and shouted as loud as she could. "Hello? Is anyone there? I'm here to pick up the mail."

"Ouch," winced Frederick. "I think I've gone deaf in one ear."

"You don't have ears, Your Highness," she said. "Now, shush."

They both listened, but no reply came from inside the wreck.

"What now?" he asked.

"Only one thing to do, I suppose," she said, and swallowing her fear, she stepped through the hole into the shadows.

"Are you sure this is a good idea?" he whispered.

"No," she said. And now that she was there, peering through the small lenses of the helmet into total darkness, she really wasn't sure at all. There could be anything in there with her. Sharks, eels, nuclear squid. She waited for her eyes to adjust to the darkness, but this wasn't the sort of darkness your eyes could get used to. This was proper, total blackness, with not a wink of light to see by.

Until a faint blue-white glow faded into being somewhere in the depths of the ship's ruined interior. It was very slight, and she wasn't even sure she was seeing it at first, but it gradually grew in size and strength until it illuminated the vague shapes of old barrels and chests, an overturned table, a rusted cannon...and a few white objects scattered about in the sand that covered the floor.

"Bones," Suzy whispered. There were lots of them, strewn here and there. They could have been from any sort of creature at all, if it weren't for the skulls that protruded from the sand. She counted five altogether.

She took a step back toward the tear in the hull, but then she saw the source of the light and stopped. It looked like a cloud—formless, and rippling through the water toward her, casting out light as it went.

"What's happening?" said Frederick. "I can't see."

"It's...it's algae," she said. "Yes. Bioluminescent algae. I saw a nature documentary about it once. That's all it is."

"Then why do you sound so scared?" he asked.

She planted her boots more squarely in the sand. "I'm not."

Yessssss, yoooouuuu aaaaaarrrre...

The voice seemed to come from everywhere at once, making her jump. She was alone, but a second glowing cloud was seeping from the ground behind her, blocking her escape. She backed away from it and saw a third cloud materializing above one of the spilled chests. Two more descended through the solid wood of the deck above. Within seconds, she was surrounded.

Doooon't ruuuuun..., said the voice. It came as a

whisper from the heart of the light. *Weeeeeee haaaaave beeeeeen waaaaaiiiting…*

"Who are you?" she said, not bothering to shout this time.

Loooook agaaaaaain…

The clouds drew in on themselves, becoming denser and brighter, their edges receding and their cores twisting and folding in on themselves, forming elaborate patterns. They had edges now, and textures, and when the cloud right in front of her raised an arm she realized with astonishment what she was looking at—they were people.

Five men, in fact, most of them bearded, wearing some sort of old-fashioned hat, frilled shirts, and long coats that fell to their... well, not to their feet, because they still didn't have any; their legs just sort of petered out into wispy glowing strands, each trailing down into one of the empty skulls. Suzy watched as one figure, with its hand outstretched, revealed a small stack of sealed envelopes, as blue and transparent as the rest of it.

Taaaaaake theeeeeeeem...

She reached out to take the letters, but a voice of caution in the back of her mind made her pause.

"What are they?" she said.

Our laaaaaast missives hoooooooooome . . ., said the figure, who was a head taller than the others and wore a larger, more impressive hat. *Pleeeeease . . . Taaaaaake word to our faaaaaaamilies . . .*

"Why are you talking like that, Cap'n?" said one of the other figures. "You got a fish in your throat?"

Taaaaaaake theeeeeeem . . ., the taller man said, a little more pointedly. He waggled the letters in Suzy's direction. *It is my dying wiiiiiiish . . .*

"Your dying wish was that the boat would stop sinking," said a third figure. "I remember it. You got quite sweary."

"I wished to be rescued by a beautiful mermaid," said another, who was round and broad shouldered. "And seriously, Captain, are you feeling all right? You sound a bit hoarse."

I'm fiiiiiine . . ., said the captain, scowling. *I'm fiii—* "Oh, never mind. You've all ruined it now." He let the arm drop to his side. "Honestly, you lot. Our first new guest in years. I just thought she deserved a little spectacle, that's all."

"New guest?" The pirate—Suzy was sure by now that they were ghostly pirates—who had wished for a mermaid narrowed his eyes at Suzy and floated closer to her, the strand connecting his body to the skull stretching and

128

bending like the string of a balloon as he did so. "Y'mean this isn't wossisname? Li'l Wilmot?"

"Of course not, Gavin," said the captain. "Haven't you been paying attention? The voice is all wrong. This is a young lady."

"Oooh!" The stooped and elderly figure of the fifth pirate grinned. "The Postmaster's finally got himself a staff."

"Oh, terrific!" the captain beamed. "Congratulations. Wilmot's always dreamed of having a postie or two to call his own. Oh, good for him." He clapped his hands together in delight, which shouldn't have been possible underwater, but Suzy supposed that ghosts could do whatever they liked.

She shook herself. She should probably have been scared, she thought, or at least astonished to find herself face-to-face with a group of ghosts, but for some reason her anxiety was actually fading. Maybe it was because they seemed to think *she* was the oddity. "My name's Suzy," she said. "I'm here to collect something." She pointed at the letters in the captain's hand. "Is that it?"

To her confusion, the pirates all started laughing.

"What?" she said, annoyed. "What is it?"

"Wilmot didn't tell you, did he?" said the captain.

"Tell me what?" said Suzy.

"Oh, nothing to worry about. It's just a bit of a tradition we have here. Isn't that right, lads?"

"Aye," they all chorused, and gathered round. Whatever the captain was about to say, they were eager not to miss it.

"You see, Miss Suzy, it's a lonely existence, sleeping with the fishes, and we've been down here a long time. Sailing the Eight Oceans, we were, in search of treasure."

"So you *are* pirates," said Suzy. "I knew it." But to her surprise, the crew's expressions all darkened.

"Pirates?" spluttered the captain. "Young lady, do we look like common ruffians to you?"

"Oh, no," she said hurriedly. "It's just, I thought, you know, with the hats? And the coats?"

"These are uniforms," the captain said, striking a noble pose. "For we are the Society of Adventure and Discovery." The others all snapped to attention alongside him and put their hands on where their hearts would have been, if they'd still had them. "'If no one's ever been there, we'll go there,'" they chorused. "'And if someone's already there, we'll have discovered them, too.'"

"I'm very sorry," said Suzy. "I didn't know."

"Consider yourself forgiven," the captain said. "We all learn from our mistakes."

"Like you learned not to steer a ship through a coral reef in the dark," said one of the crew.

"Quiet, Neville." The captain flicked an imaginary speck of dust from the sleeve of his coat. "As I was saying, we ventured west in search of treasure, and by golly we found it—the lost city of Condóro, where everything from the roof tiles to the gutters is made from solid gold."

Suzy bit her lip. She had heard stories similar to this in her history lessons. "Did you steal it?" she asked.

"Good heavens no," said the captain. "We all took jobs on a building site, hauling golden rubble away. The Condórons were happy for us to take it."

"Oh." Suzy blushed, ashamed that she had assumed the worst of them.

"We set sail with our hold full to bursting," said the captain, and the crew all smiled with him. "We were so impatient to get back to port we decided to take a shortcut through the Narrows."

The others all made quite a performance of clearing their throats.

"All right, *I* decided," said the captain. "And it would have worked if it hadn't been impossible. No moon to navigate by that night, y'see."

Suzy looked down, past the floating wisps of blue

ectoplasm to the lonely skulls lying in the sand, and felt a rush of pity for them all. "So you sank," she said. "That's awful."

The captain shrugged. "You get used to it after a while. My only regret is that we never had the chance to report our success. The lost city of Condóro remains lost. We had the only map."

Suzy looked again at the papers in his hand. "Is that what you want me to deliver?"

He didn't laugh this time, but he did smile. "Take them and try," he said, offering them to her. She reached out but, as she had already half suspected, her hand passed right through them.

"The original dissolved years ago, along with our letters home. There's nothing left to deliver, and no recipients left to deliver them to."

"Then I don't understand," she said. "Why am I here?"

"It's just a little game we play. As the ship was sinking, I had time to scribble our coordinates on a scrap of parchment, along with a plea to come and salvage the map before it was too late. I sealed them in an old rum bottle, then cast the bottle into the sea, hoping that a fair current would carry it ashore. Rescue was hopeless, of course, but I couldn't die knowing that our expedition was unfinished." It was hard to tell, because they were underwater and he was translucent, but Suzy thought the

132

captain's eyes were shining with repressed tears. "Alas, nobody came. One of the disadvantages of being corporeally challenged is that we're tied to our final resting place, you see, and we spent many years alone in here, waiting. Until, one day, a strange little figure appeared, wearing that very diving suit you're in now. None of us knew what to make of it, until it held up the bottle I'd thrown into the sea all those years before and said, 'Someone's got a map to pick up?'"

"Wilmot!" she said.

"No," said the captain with a smile. "His grandfather. He was just a young troll then, a postie, like yourself. And like you, he almost jumped out of his suit when he first set eyes on us." He laughed. "Poor old Honks. We were so starved of company we talked him half to death. We thought it would be our last ever chance to socialize, you see. Once he realized there was no post to collect, he'd leave us there forever."

"But he didn't, did he?" said Suzy. "Otherwise I wouldn't be here now."

"Quite right. Once he'd figured out what was going on, I think he felt sorry for us. In any case, he returned the bottle and let us know that if it were ever to wash up on shore again, the Impossible Postal Service would be obliged to call on us. And that's the way it's been ever since. Every year or so, the bottle makes its way back to us and we get to catch up on what's been happening in the Union. You're the latest in a proud line."

With a shock, Suzy realized that all the ghostly faces were now turned toward her, smiling in expectation. "Oh," she said. "What do you want to know, exactly?"

The outburst of questions was instantaneous and loud.

"What's the price of fish in Landsdown Harbor these days?"

"Read any good books lately?"

"Did the Western Fenlands win the Impossible Places Song Contest again this year?"

"Do you know any mermaids?"

Suzy raised her hands, appealing for quiet. "I'm sorry," she said. "I don't know how to answer any of those questions. Except the mermaid one—I've never met a mermaid."

"Me neither," said Gavin, hanging his head.

"Wait a minute," said Suzy as her brain caught up with her. "Did one of you ask about the Western Fenlands?"

"Aye," said Neville. "I reckoned we were in with a chance of winning this year, as long as Dalemark don't beat us again." The others all nodded in agreement.

"Sssshhh!" Frederick hissed at Suzy, as quietly as he could manage. "What are you doing?"

"Is that where you're from?" she asked Neville.

"Yes," he said proudly. "We're Fenlanders through and through."

"Tell me about it," she said, brightening.

"Why, it's the greatest seafaring nation in the Union," said the captain. "Lots of trade, lots of wealth, lots of history."

"Lots of cows," said Neville.

"What?" The captain floundered. "Well, yes, I suppose so, but—"

"An inordinate number of cows, when you think about it."

"I'll grant you, Neville, we do have a lot of cows, but that's not what I—"

"As a nation, we're positively pecorous."

Every head turned to Neville in bewilderment.

"Pecorous," he said. "It means 'full of cows.' No?" He looked around for a sympathetic face, but found none. "It's a terribly useful word, in the right circumstances," he muttered.

"But this is wonderful," cut in Suzy. "You're exactly the people I need!"

"No!" Frederick hissed. "Stop it!"

"Who said that?" said the captain. "Are there two of you in there?"

"Yes," she said. "You won't have heard yet, but your

kingdom's in danger. A witch called the Lady Crepuscula is plotting to steal the throne, and I'm here with Prince Frederick, the real heir. He's on the run."

"What have you done?" wailed Frederick.

"It's fine," she said. "Don't you see? They can't leave the ship, so they can't tell anyone about you. And they might be able to help us." But when she looked at the circle of faces, she saw only pinched expressions. "What's wrong?" she said.

The captain cleared his throat, a little embarrassed. "I'm afraid you're mistaken, m'dear. The Western Fenlands hasn't had a king since the great revolution. We elect a premier now. It's been that way for centuries."

"What?" she said. "But that's impossible. He told me..." Realization dawned. Furious, she took hold of the nose sock, shaking it until the snow globe rolled out into the helmet. It lay against her cheek, and by straining her eyes and looking straight down, she could just make eye contact with Frederick inside it.

"I can explain everything," he said.

11

THE GREAT SPYGLASS

Neoma snapped off a salute as she entered the curator's office. "My lord, we've found the Express. It's in the Topaz Narrows."

The old man looked up from a report he had been reading. "Good work, Captain. Is the girl still with them?"

"We think so, sir, but part of the train has dived below the surface, and the spyglasses aren't powerful enough to penetrate that deep. We need the Great Spyglass."

"Splendid," said the old man, springing to his feet. "I've been looking for an excuse to dust it off."

Captain Neoma followed him out into the Observatory and the open space in the center of the floor where she had spoken to Maya earlier. The old man rapped the tip of his cane three times against the tiles. The noise echoed off the domed ceiling like a trio of gunshots, but the sounds had not died away before they were joined by a deep rumbling from somewhere beneath the floor. The rumbling grew steadily stronger, and they both retreated to the safety of the desks in anticipation of what came next.

The tiles began to shift and fold themselves away, revealing empty darkness below. The opening continued to grow, widening like an iris until it claimed the whole space in the middle of the room. Then, with the soft whir of well-oiled gears, something rose up out of the darkness.

It was a telescope, easily twenty times the size of its counterparts on the desks, but identical in every other respect; it stared blindly at the ceiling through a lens of black glass that was as tall as Neoma herself. It was mounted on a circular base that neatly filled the gap left by the tiles, and the old man hurried across it, easing himself into a reclining chair beneath the telescope's eyepiece. Captain Neoma took up a position at his shoulder.

"Sir, if I may make a suggestion," she whispered, "we know exactly where the Express is, but we've not seen the Lady Crepuscula and her forces since they entered the tunnel system. We need to ascertain their whereabouts before we can take any action."

"Very true, Captain, very true." The old man adjusted the eyepiece and peered through it. "There's certainly no sign of her in the Topaz Narrows," he said after a moment's study. "If she knew where the Express was heading, she'd be there already."

"Excellent," said Neoma, happy to get a little good news at last. "I'll take a squad out there now and retrieve Frederick."

"Don't be so hasty." The old man tweaked the eyepiece again. "The Impossible Postal Express never stops for long. They'll have moved on before you can reach them."

139

"But we have to do something before the Lady Crepuscula finds them, sir."

"I agree. But I'm not convinced she's following them."

"What do you mean?"

The old man sighed. "I'd never say it to her face, but Crepuscula is too clever to get lost. If she hasn't followed the Express to the Topaz Narrows, then she has something else in mind, and that troubles me. Until we know what she's up to, we need to be careful." He pursed his lips in thought. "Put the guards on full alert, please, Captain. I want them ready for action at a moment's notice."

"Yes, sir!" A thrill of anticipation ran through Neoma. *At last*, she thought. *A little bit of action*. But that feeling of unease was still whispering to her from the dark recesses of her mind, and she lingered a moment longer. "Sir," she said, approaching the subject as carefully as she knew how. "We still don't know what Crepuscula wants with Frederick, or why he's under a curse, or even why he ran away in the first place."

"Those are very important questions," said the old man. "Perhaps he can give us some answers once he's safely back under our wing." He smiled, and returned his attention to the spyglass.

"All three things have to be related somehow," Neoma continued, thinking aloud. "But how? He's just an observer, the same as all the others. What could he possibly have that Crepuscula wants?" Her brow creased in thought. "Unless he saw something through his spyglass."

"It's an observer's job to see things, Captain," the old man said absently.

"I mean something important," she replied. "Something...different." She looked over at the empty desk again and steeled herself for her next question. "I know it's classified information, sir, but what was he researching before he disappeared?"

The old man took his eye from the spyglass and looked very hard at her for a moment. She stared right back.

"That information is classified for good reason, Captain," he said very quietly. "Our data protection rules are sacrosanct."

"Yes, sir. And I wouldn't normally ask, but something is clearly very wrong here, and I can't be expected to fix it if I don't have all the facts." She could feel her frustration starting to boil up, like a furnace deep inside her, filling her with a hot, sputtering energy. She had to open her mouth to let it escape, and it came out as words. "We are in the business of collecting information, after all."

The old man's eyebrows came together in a scowl. "Collecting it, yes. Giving it out willy-nilly to anyone who asks for it, no." He gestured toward the vault.

"Information is a treasure, Captain—more precious than gold and more dangerous than magic. It can reshape whole worlds, in the right hands."

"Or the wrong ones," said Neoma. "Which is why we need to keep it out of Crepuscula's reach, whatever it might be."

The old man folded his hands over the head of his cane and studied her for a moment longer. Then he closed his eyes. "He was studying the farming practices of the Western Fenlands," he said at last. "Lots of fields, cows, and milking sheds. I don't know what else you think he's likely to have seen." He chuckled at the idea, and Captain Neoma knew that, very gently but definitely, he was putting an end to her questions. She still didn't have everything she needed but knew she was unlikely to get anything more from him right away.

"Thank you, sir," she said, snapping off an especially crisp salute. "There's just one more thing."

He raised an eyebrow and took a theatrically deep breath. "Yes?"

"The chancellor of Wolfhaven. I checked the official diary, and there's no record of her visit at all, sir. No appointment, no security arrangements. Nothing." She let the last word hang there between them, watching for his reaction.

He simply blinked, smiled amiably up at her, and said,

"How careless of me. I must have forgotten to write it down. My apologies, Captain."

Captain Neoma smiled back. "No need to apologize, sir. We all make mistakes."

Except you, she thought as she marched away, her mind more alive than ever with questions. *You never forget* anything. *There's something you're not telling me, and I'm going to find out what it is.*

12

A TALE OF TWO TOWERS

Anger boiled in Suzy's chest like acid. "You lied to me!" she said. "You told me you were a prince."

"It wasn't a lie," protested Frederick. "It was a cover story. That's different."

"How much of it was true?" she demanded.

"Some of it." Frederick's embarrassment was audible. "Crepuscula really did put this curse on me. And you were right, I did say the fate of the Impossible Places might be at stake. I wasn't lying about that."

The captain cleared his spectral throat and tried to bat away a passing fish, which swam straight through his hand, unperturbed. "The lads and I are a little confused," he said, looking decidedly uncomfortable. "If your friend here isn't a prince, who exactly is he?"

"He isn't my friend," she said. "And I've no idea who he is. He claims his name's Frederick."

"It is," said Frederick. "That bit's true as well."

"Then why did you lie about everything else?" said Suzy.

"Because some things are dangerous to know," he said in a plaintive voice. "And the less you know about them, the safer you'll be."

Suzy glared at him. "I'm already in danger, thanks to you," she said. "I saved you, and you're going to tell me what's going on."

"You haven't really saved me yet, though, have you?" said Frederick. "I'm still stuck in this ridiculous snow globe. And as if that wasn't bad enough, I'm also stuck in this diving suit, with you breathing on me."

"I'm sorry, would you like me to hold my breath?"

"You're fogging my glass! Plus, I can see right up your nose."

"Perhaps you'd prefer the view from Crepuscula's mantelpiece," Suzy said, and immediately regretted it. She would never dream of handing anyone over to somebody like Crepuscula, but her anger had made her mean. She was about to tell Frederick as much, but he spoke first.

"You're right," he said in a humble little whisper. "I'm sorry. I'll tell you everything."

"Good," she said, although she didn't feel good about it at all.

The ghosts huddled closer, not wanting to miss a word.

"I'm not a prince," said Frederick. "But I really am a Fenlander. And I'll be a hero, too, if I can ever break this curse and get back to my proper form. You see, there really is a plot and I'm the only one who can stop it."

"Why you?" said Suzy.

"Because I'm the only one who knows about it, of course," he replied. "Why do you think Crepuscula wants to get her hands on me so badly?"

"Hang on," said Suzy, narrowing her eyes at him. "How can there be a plot to steal the throne when there isn't even a throne to steal?"

"Because it's not a plot to rule the Western Fenlands," he said. "It's a plot to rule the Impossible Places. Every single one of them."

Nobody spoke for a moment, and the words weighed heavy on Suzy. Could she believe them? She didn't want to, but the memory of Crepuscula's shadow crawling toward her like a living thing reared up in her mind, and she pictured it sweeping out from the tower like an oil slick, enveloping everything in its path. The idea seemed horribly plausible.

146

Worse, it made her feel very small and vulnerable, like a mouse that feels the shadow of a circling hawk sweep across it. Crepuscula was out there somewhere right now, hunting for them. Suzy didn't want to think what would happen if she caught them.

"So Crepuscula wants to conquer the Union," said Suzy, trying to wriggle out from under the feeling. "All right, I can believe that. But how did you find out about it?"

Frederick hesitated. "Because I'm a genius," he said.

The ghosts all made appreciative noises, but Suzy snorted. "Is that a fact?"

"Hey," he protested. "Just because I grew up on a farm doesn't mean I can't be clever. You don't know what it was like, stuck out there in the middle of the marshlands. No brothers or sisters, no neighbors, no friends, no school, no money, no prospects. And my parents, who thought I was just taking up space."

"Poor lad," said the captain. The rest of the crew nodded sadly, and the wreck grew darker as their ghostly luminescence dimmed a little in sympathy.

"Oh." Suzy hadn't been expecting such a frank confession, and it made her feel awkward. "I'm sorry. It sounds awful."

"Life was . . ." He sighed. "Pecorous. But it meant that if I wanted something, I had to do it for myself. I taught myself to read before I was five years old, and I'd mapped every star in the night sky by age six. Not to boast, but I'm a bit of a prodigy."

"And how old are you now?" said Suzy.

"Ten," he said. "Almost eleven."

"But how can a ten-year-old uncover a secret plot by the most dangerous woman in the Union?" said Suzy. "I'm eleven, and I still can't find a matching pair of socks most mornings."

"I just talked to the right people," said Frederick. "I put all the evidence together, but before I could use it, Crepuscula's curse got me. And here I am." His voice trailed off.

"But you can still talk," said Suzy, hoping to brighten his mood a little. "That means you can still report what you've found, doesn't it?"

"But it'll be my word against hers, and that's not enough," he said. "I've got loads of evidence, but I was holding it when the curse hit me, so it's stuck in here with me. It's part of the snow globe now."

"Then we need to break the curse somehow," she said. "Change you and the evidence back to normal."

"Yes, but how?"

Suzy shrugged. "The trolls can do magic. Maybe they can help."

To her annoyance, Frederick laughed. "Troll magic? It's fine for machines, but not people."

"Then what do you suggest?" she said, feeling the edges of her patience beginning to fray.

"May I take a look?" said the captain. She nodded, and he leaned forward, putting his face through the skin of the helmet. She couldn't help recoiling as his glowing blue features appeared inside the helmet, barely an inch from her own face.

"Sorry," he whispered with an apologetic smile. "This will only take a second." He scrutinized Frederick's snow globe, and his brow furrowed. After a minute, he withdrew his face and floated back to rejoin the others. "I'm afraid the boy's right," he said. "That's some quality spell craft at work there. Very powerful stuff."

"Told you so," muttered Frederick.

"So how do we undo it?" said Suzy.

"With an equally powerful counter-spell, of course," said the captain. "And there's only one place I know of that can match the magic of the Obsidian Tower."

"Oh no," said Frederick. "Don't say it."

"Say what?" asked Suzy.

The captain drew himself up. "The Ivory Tower," he said in a somber tone.

"I knew it," wailed Frederick. "Isn't there anywhere else you can think of?"

"Wait a minute," said Suzy, who could feel the conversation running away from her. "What's the Ivory Tower?"

The ghosts all looked at her in astonishment. "Perhaps Gavin here can enlighten you," said the captain. "He's the ship's historian, and he spins a good yarn."

"It'd be a pleasure, sir," said Gavin, clearly thrilled to be called upon. He drifted up above the others and waited until he was sure he had their full attention. "It's a tale as old as any I've heard told," he said in a half whisper. "Countless ages ago, when the Impossible Places first agreed to live together in union, two mighty towers were built. They were to be symbols of hope, to which all could turn in times of need—one tower of strength, and another of knowledge.

"For centuries, the magic of the Obsidian Tower offered protection to the helpless, justice to the wronged, and courage to the weak. Its strength shone like a beacon for all who needed it. But strength is power, and power corrupts. As the years passed, the lords and ladies appointed to rule the tower began to wonder why the strong should serve the weak at all. Thus, it became a symbol of fear, from which the mighty could reach down and punish those who displeased them."

Suzy gave an involuntary shudder inside the suit. If there was one thing she was certain of, it was that she had displeased Crepuscula. She tried to put the feeling to one side as Gavin continued.

"The Ivory Tower, meanwhile, was a storehouse of wisdom, fostering understanding between the newly joined peoples. Its library gathered texts from across the Union, and brought enlightenment to many. But knowledge is power, too, and the keepers of the tower grew arrogant and aloof, setting themselves apart from those they served. Never cruel, never dangerous, but cold. Now the tower guards its knowledge closely, granting access to a select few, and then only in exchange for its most valued currency—new information. That is the price of knowledge now: a truth for a truth."

His tale concluded, Gavin drifted back down with a nod of satisfaction. There was a smattering of applause from the rest of the crew.

"Well done, Gavin," said the captain. "Couldn't have put it better myself."

"So we need to get to this Ivory Tower," said Suzy, glad of a clear objective at last. "Where is it?"

"Getting to it is easy," said Frederick, sounding morose. "Getting in and out again is almost impossible."

Suzy picked over the things that Gavin had said. "You said we need new information to get in. 'A truth for a truth.'"

"Aye," said Gavin. "That's the one inviolable rule of the tower."

"But what does it mean?" she said.

"It means a secret," said Frederick. "Something that only one person in all the Impossible Places knows."

"I see." Suzy chewed her lip and thought. Then it struck her. "But we've already got one!" she said. "Your evidence against Crepuscula. You're the only one who knows it, right?"

"Wrong," he said. "I gathered it from other people, remember?"

Suzy slumped in disappointment. The crew were all bowed in concentration as well, stroking their spectral beards and muttering to themselves. Looking at them, Suzy had another idea. "What about the location of Condóro?" she said. "You're the only ones who know it, now that the map's dissolved."

"But the whole crew knows it," said the captain. "That makes five of us already."

"But don't any of you have *any* secrets?" she said. "Anything at all?"

The captain laughed. "Not after all these years together. Besides, even if we did, the moment we shared them with you, they'd cease to be secret." He gave a shrug of defeat. "I'm sorry. We're not much help to anyone these days."

This softened her. "You've been a great help," she said. "I didn't even believe in ghosts yesterday, but I'm very glad you exist."

The crew all seemed to glow a little brighter at this. "It's very nice of you to say so," said the captain. "And may

152

I say, it's been a pleasure to make your acquaintance. We're already looking forward to your next visit."

Next visit? The words hit Suzy like a shock of cold water, and for the first time she was forced to confront the question she had been keeping at arm's length since jumping onto the train—just how long could she keep this whole thing up? She hadn't even thought about how much time it might take her to get back home; she had just been in a hurry not to let this chance escape. But now that she had taken it, was she stuck with it? The trolls couldn't make her stay, surely? But how could she possibly find her way back home without them? And what would be waiting for her if she did? Had her parents woken up and found her missing? Was Fletch still out there somewhere, ready to scramble her memories? And what about poor Wilmot, toiling all alone in the sorting van? She hated the idea of abandoning him, but what else could she do? She couldn't stay with the Impossible Postal Express forever. Now that she had faced them, she finally began to appreciate the scale of her problems, and they reared up like mountains, surrounding her on all sides. She began to sweat a little.

"Where do you want me to leave this?" she said, fumbling the rum bottle out of the pocket of the diving suit.

"Just pop it out of that porthole over there, and we'll see where the sea takes it." The captain pointed to a circular hole in the hull, its edges softened by a growth of coral.

She did as he asked, being careful not to stand on any stray bones as she clumped her way across the ship's interior and stuck the bottle out through the opening. She let it go, and it rocketed away like a cork, swirling upward out of sight.

"Thank you," said the captain.

"You're welcome," she said, feeling terrible at the idea she would never see them again. "Are you sure you're going to be all right in here all by yourselves?"

"We've grown quite accomplished at passing the time," said the captain. "The months just fly by. Although I do think we've exhausted all the possibilities of Eye Spy by now."

"I spy with my little eye," piped up Neville, "something beginning with *sea*." The others all groaned.

"Now, go and find that secret," said the captain. "Get this boy to the Ivory Tower, get him back to normal, and save the Union. And then come back and tell us all about it."

"I'll try," Suzy said, not wanting to make any more promises she couldn't keep. The ghosts each raised a hand in farewell and began dissolving back into amorphous clouds. Only the captain retained his form, and as she stepped outside the wreck and looked back, he was still there, watching her, a sad but hopeful look in his eyes.

13

SUBTERFUGE

"We need to get a move on," said Frederick as Suzy picked her way back through the reef toward the H. E. C. "We've got a lot to do, and I don't want to spend any longer in this bubble than I need to."

Suzy didn't reply. Her encounter with the ghosts had left her sad and troubled, and she wanted a moment's peace to put her thoughts in order. "You said the Ivory Tower is easy to get to," she said at last. "Can the Express get us there?"

"Of course," said Frederick. "Every rail line in the Union leads to the tower eventually. But what good will that do us if we can't get inside?"

"It'll be a start," she said. She watched the fish dart

out of her way as she plodded on and started thinking aloud. "The Impossible Postal Express delivers to the Obsidian Tower, so it must deliver to the Ivory Tower as well. Right?"

"Yes," said Frederick, starting to sound impatient. "It delivers everywhere."

"Which means the posties must have a way of getting in," she said.

"Maybe. But deliveries to the tower are very rare. The Express might not get one for months. I can't afford to wait that long."

She was too busy putting a new idea together to respond, and they were almost at the outer hatch of the H. E. C.'s air lock when she stopped abruptly.

"What's wrong?" said Frederick. "We need to get inside."

"And we will," she said, "once you've made me a promise."

"Fine. Anything. Just hurry up!"

"No more lies, is that clear? If I'm going to help you, I have to know you're being honest with me. Otherwise you're on your own."

"I *am* being honest," he said. "I've told you everything now."

"You haven't told me who gave you the information

about Crepuscula's plot," she said. "Or why you knew to ask them about it in the first place."

"Why bother?" he said. "It's not as if you'd know any of them. But I happen to have friends in high places."

This answer did absolutely nothing to help Suzy's mood. "How?" she said. "I thought you lived on a farm in the middle of nowhere."

"No, I said I grew up there. But I'm a genius, remember? I've gone up in the world."

Suzy balled her fists in frustration. "Then why don't we just go to these friends of yours and ask them to help us?" she said. The question must have struck a nerve, because Frederick's voice became clipped and terse.

"Maybe *friends* wasn't quite the right word to use," he said. "They're more like acquaintances."

"Friendly acquaintances?"

Frederick paused. "Not really," he said quietly. "I don't really get along with many people."

"There's a surprise," said Suzy.

"I can't help it if people find my intellect intimidating," Frederick said. "Anyway, you don't have to worry about them. You just have to trust me. Right now, you and I are the only ones who can save the Union, and we're running out of time. If Crepuscula catches up with us, it's all over—there'll be no one to stop her."

The thought sent a cold tingle of worry down Suzy's back. "I think I can get us to the Ivory Tower," she said, "but I want something from you in return."

"What's that?"

"I need you to help me find a way home."

"Can't the Express do it?" he said.

She opened her mouth, but the words suddenly became very difficult to say. "If my plan works, I don't think they'll want to," she said. Because she had already broken her promise to Wilmot, and she was about to do something even worse. And if they reached the Ivory Tower, she wouldn't be able to hide it from him anymore.

"I can do that," said Frederick. "The Ivory Tower has information on everything. I'm sure I can help you find what you need to know once we get there."

"Great." She would have breathed a sigh of relief, except she wasn't relieved at all—she was well and truly in league with Frederick now. She still wasn't sure just how much she could trust him, but what choice did she have? He was annoying, but he was also alone and helpless. The fate of the Union depended on him, and he was depending on her. She hoped she was making the right choice.

"How did it go? Were they surprised to see you? What did the captain say?" Wilmot started asking questions the second he had hauled the inner hatch open, and he didn't wait for Suzy to reply as he helped her unscrew the bolts holding the helmet in place. She gave a silent prayer of thanks that she had already tipped Frederick's snow globe back into the nose sock, where it wouldn't be seen.

"I hope they didn't bore you," Wilmot went on. "They're terribly nice, really, and they've got some fantastic stories to share. Although they do tend to go on a bit." He heaved the helmet clear of Suzy's head and set it down on the floor. "So?"

"It was fine," she replied, enjoying the touch of fresher air against her face. "I liked them."

"You did? Oh, I am glad. I like what you've done with your hair, by the way."

"With my what?" She pulled a strand of it down in front of her face and gasped. "It's gone blond!"

"Only a little," he said.

Suzy inspected her reflection in the polished visor of the nearby space helmet. The tips of her hair had turned bright yellow. She stared at them in fascination. "How did this happen?" she asked.

"It's a side effect of contact with the fusion bananas," said Wilmot.

"So that's why Ursel is yellow?"

"That's right," he said. "The effects wear off after a day or two."

Good, she thought as she wriggled her way out of the suit, casting an eye around the chamber in search of Wilmot's delivery schedule. She soon spotted it, balanced precariously on top of the air pump. Now all she had to do was get to it. "Does everyone in the Impossible Places become a ghost when they die?" she said, pulling her bathrobe on.

"Goodness no. You wouldn't be able to put a pin between them if they did. It's usually just those with unfinished business who hang around like that." He shook a few drops of water from his hands. "Did you deliver the bottle?"

"Yes," she said. "Although I think the suit has sprung a leak." She handed him the suit and prayed that her guilt wouldn't make her blush too badly. She hated the idea of tricking Wilmot, but it was the only thing that would work.

"Oh dear," he said, holding it up and prodding at it with a finger. "Is it a bad leak?"

"Uh, yes," she said. "Quite bad. Somewhere on the front, I think."

He put his head in through the neck of the suit, groping around the outside with both hands. "I can't see anything," he said.

"Keep looking," she said, stealing across the chamber to the pump. "It's definitely there."

160

She picked up the delivery schedule and looked it over. It was an orderly table of destinations, recipients, and items, filled out in pencil in neat, blocky handwriting. As she had expected, there was no sign of the Ivory Tower on it anywhere; their next delivery consisted of a package number (the package itself, she assumed, was sitting on a shelf in the sorting car), the name Calvus Rayleigh, and a destination: Cloud Forge.

She glanced back at Wilmot, who now appeared to be in a certain amount of distress—he wore the suit upside down over the top half of his body, and she wasn't sure he was able to get out again. He seemed to be trying to brazen it out, though, by making very knowledgeable noises and occasionally muttering things like "I see" and "Very interesting."

She was running out of time. She took up the stubby pencil that was attached to the clipboard by a length of string. It had a bright yellow eraser on the end, and she used it to scrub out the entry for Cloud Forge, before hastily writing in a new one: the Ivory Tower. She matched Wilmot's handwriting as best she could, but there was little she could do about the faint smudge of pencil lead left behind by her rubbing-out. And she had to trust that Wilmot hadn't had the chance to consult the chart while she'd been out on the seabed. As plans went, it was far from ideal, but it was all she had time for. She was barely able to replace the clipboard on the pump and dart back to Wilmot's side before he finally wrestled the suit off his head.

"I can't see anything wrong with it," he gasped, red-faced. "And it seems dry in there."

Suzy pressed her lips together and blushed, not knowing what to say.

"There's no time to worry about it now, though," he went on, slipping the suit back onto its hanger. "We've got work to do." He grinned at her and dashed to a small control panel against one wall. He threw a lever, and the H. E. C. lurched around them, before slowly rising off the sea floor. Suzy took the opportunity to return the diving helmet to the rack, making sure to retrieve Frederick from the depths of the nose sock as she did so.

"What's going on?" he whispered.

"Ssssh!" she hissed, and slipped him into her bathrobe pocket.

"That's two successful deliveries under your belt already," said Wilmot, turning back from the controls. "Let's make it three, shall we?"

"Sounds great," she said through a smile that felt too false and tight. "Where are we going?"

"Good question," he said, and made for the clipboard. Suzy's momentary flutter of relief—*he hadn't already checked the chart!*—was immediately overcome by fresh anxiety as she watched his eyes work their way down the table and then widen in shock.

"That can't be right," he said in a choked little voice. "That can't be right at all."

Suzy looked on, wishing she could be anywhere else, but unable to look away as the color slowly drained from Wilmot's face. She clenched her fists so hard that her fingernails bit into her palms, but it didn't lessen her discomfort. She was lying to someone who trusted her, just as Frederick had lied to her, which made her every bit as bad.

But what other way was there?

"What's wrong?" she said, feeling like a fraud for asking the question. He turned a look of vacant panic on her.

"How can I have missed it? I thought I'd checked." His finger stabbed at the clipboard. "This is serious."

As he said it, the H. E. C. broke the surface and reconnected to the rest of the train with a metallic *clunk*. No sooner had the sound died away than a phone on the instrument panel began to ring. Wilmot blinked at it, as though he'd never seen it before. "Oh dear," he said, and picked it up.

Steeling herself, Suzy moved to stand beside him as he stammered into the receiver. "Yes, Mr. Stonker, I was just about to do it, but I've been busy with the pump and . . ." A moment's silence. "Well, I'm afraid there's been a bit of an oversight. You see . . . Yes, yes, I will. Right away."

Taking the phone from his ear, he picked up the stub of pencil attached to the clipboard and tapped the tip three times against the entry for the Ivory Tower. Suzy watched, fascinated, as the handwritten letters glowed a brilliant gold. Then they shifted, tumbling over themselves in a blur. She had seen this before, on the tiny destination board in the cab, and knew instinctively that this was how the board was updated; it was linked to Wilmot's clipboard with magic.

After just a few seconds, the letters settled down into their former order and their glow faded. The phone emitted Stonker's bark of shock as loudly as if he had been standing in the H. E. C. with them.

"I'm so sorry," said Wilmot into the mouthpiece. "I must have been so preoccupied with our delivery to the Obsidian Tower that I completely overlooked this one."

Suzy couldn't quite make out what Stonker was saying in reply, but it didn't sound happy.

"No, I know that's not an excuse," said Wilmot, who was sounding increasingly miserable. "I take full responsibility. Yes, I know how much time it's going to add to our route. No, you're right, it's not acceptable."

Suzy was horrified to see the early sign of tears in Wilmot's eyes, and placed a supportive hand on his shoulder. He must have forgotten she was there, because he flinched. But he didn't protest when she took the phone from him and replaced it in its cradle.

"Are you all right?" she asked.

"No," he said. "I've made a huge mistake, and now we're going to be even further behind schedule."

The words dug into Suzy's heart like hot needles. "I'm sure it isn't your fault," she said.

"But it is!" His agitation wouldn't let him keep still, and he pulled free of her touch and started pacing in frantic circles around the center of the chamber. "The Ivory Tower! Of all places! Do you know how often the Express visits it?"

"How often?" she said.

"Never! At least, almost never. My dad had to make a delivery there once, years ago. And now it's my turn, and I didn't even notice. Oh, my mom's right, this job's too much for one troll alone to handle. I'm letting things slip."

"Don't say that," she pleaded. "You're a great Postmaster, you really are." The train bucked into motion. "Are we going there now?"

He shook his head, still pacing. "No, we can't just turn up. Lord Meridian never lets anyone in for free."

"Who's Lord Meridian?"

"The keeper of the tower. The curator of all its knowledge. That's his job, you see—gathering information. So if you want to learn something from him, you have to be able to offer him something he doesn't already know. That *nobody* else knows."

"And you can do that?" Suzy asked hopefully.

"Not without making a detour first." He hurried to the nearest porthole. Suzy joined him. The afternoon had drawn on, and the sun was growing fat as it dipped toward the horizon, staining the tips of the waves gold and crimson.

"Where are we going?" she said, wishing she could feel better in the face of such a view.

"Home," he said.

Then the darkness of the tunnel swallowed the train with one snap of its jaws, and the Topaz Narrows was gone.

14

A Bird's-Eye View

Captain Neoma paused in front of Frederick's empty desk. She had passed it three times on her latest patrol of the Observatory floor, her nagging sense of disquiet urging her to stop each time she approached it, but she had always lost her nerve at the last second and hurried past it on another lap of the room.

Now her disquiet was too great to ignore, even as she cast a nervous glance toward the center of the room, where Lord Meridian was still engrossed in whatever the Great Spyglass was showing him. She wet her lips—her mouth had gone dry—and leaned down to address the observer at the neighboring desk.

"Has anyone touched this spyglass since the boy disappeared?" she whispered.

The observer—a young boy with the face and fur of a dog, whose name, according to his badge, was Jim-Jim—flinched in surprise. "No, Captain," he said, his voice tight with worry. "We're not allowed to touch each other's desks. It's the rules."

"And none of the guards have touched it?" she asked, before dropping her voice to an even lower whisper. "Not even... His Lordship?"

Jim-Jim flattened his ears and gave an almost-imperceptible shake of his head. "No one," he said.

"Thank you," said Neoma, who briefly considered adding "Good boy" before deciding against it. Jim-Jim turned hurriedly back to his work and made a very obvious effort to pretend she wasn't there. She shot another quick look in Lord Meridian's direction, then eased Frederick's chair out from the desk and sat down in it.

She hated sneaking around like this. It felt dishonest. But she hated her feeling of uncertainty more, and she knew the only way to banish it was to get to the bottom of whatever had gone on here. Something had made Frederick leave the Observatory—something so dangerous that he had almost ended up in Lady Crepuscula's clutches as a result. That wasn't the sort of thing that happened when you sat around watching farms all day. He *had* to have been watching something else. And if nobody had touched his spyglass, then it would still be trained on the last thing he had seen with it...

Repressing a reflexive shiver of revulsion at the thing, Captain Neoma leaned forward and pressed her eye to the spyglass, gazing out across the reaches of reality for the very first time.

She saw a cow.

In fact, she saw several cows milling around in a small, muddy yard between a sagging barn and a tiny, ramshackle old shed of a house. She was looking down on the scene from above, and as she adjusted the eyepiece her view zoomed out, revealing a patchwork of dull green fields, all of them full of cows. Their chorus of snorting and lowing reached her as if from underwater.

"Looking for something, Captain?"

Neoma leaped to her feet so quickly her knees struck the underside of the desk with a bang that echoed around the whole room. She winced at the sudden pain, but snapped off a salute. Lord Meridian was standing beside the desk. He raised one eyebrow in polite inquiry. "Well?"

"My lord!" she stammered. "I was just...just..."

"Just checking up on me?" He grimaced. "I'm a little hurt by your lack of trust, Captain, although I suppose I should commend you for it. No one should be above suspicion. Not even me." His grimace melted into a smile. "What have you discovered?"

Captain Neoma fought to keep her own grimace in check. "Nothing, sir. Just farmland, exactly as you said. Whatever made him leave, it wasn't this." Her cheeks burned with embarrassment, but Lord Meridian just gave a nod of satisfaction.

"I'm glad that's settled. If you had only waited, I could have explained his motives to you myself."

"You know something, sir?"

"I do now," he said, and beckoned her to follow him back to the Great Spyglass. Out of earshot of the observers, he spoke again. "I tracked him and the human girl, Suzy, to the sea floor, where he imparted a few worrying truths. It seems that Crepuscula's ambitions are greater than I ever suspected." His expression hardened. "I believe she plans to seize control of this observatory, Captain. That's why she needs Frederick—he knows where to find it, how to get in, and how it all works."

Anger and dread began mixing in the pit of Neoma's stomach. "You mean he's sold us out?"

"That's my current theory, yes." Lord Meridian gave a sad smile. "It's hard to stomach, after all we've done for him. He must have had second thoughts and tried to escape from her, though, which explains the curse she put on him. Poetic justice, wouldn't you say?"

"You have to let me take a squad out, sir," Neoma said, flexing her hands. She imagined Frederick's neck between them and felt a little better. "I'll make that curse look like a joke when I catch up with him."

"There'll be no need for that, Captain," said Lord Meridian. "You'll have plenty of opportunity to show the boy the error of his ways once he arrives."

It took Captain Neoma a few seconds to realize what he meant. "You mean he's coming back?" she exclaimed. "He only just left!"

"It seems that having Crepuscula on his tail has prompted a change of heart," said Lord Meridian. Then, to Neoma's surprise, he reached out and caught her forearm. His grip was surprisingly strong. "This is vital, Captain," he hissed. "Frederick is the key to all this, and my guess is that Crepuscula will come here to intercept him. We can't afford to let that happen. Double the perimeter guard. Triple it."

Slowly but deliberately, Captain Neoma pulled her arm free of his grip. "Sir, are you sure about this? The Obsidian Tower has never moved against the Ivory Tower, not in all the history of the Union."

"History is one thing, Captain," he said. "The future is another. And if we're not prepared for it, the Union of Impossible Places itself is at risk."

His eyes blazed with a cold fire. Neoma was about to

answer him, when the radio clipped to her belt suddenly squawked to life.

"Secure the Observatory!" came a panicked voice from the speaker. "Hostile approaching. Hostile approaching!" Before Captain Neoma could respond, she felt the floor tremble as something huge and heavy approached the outer door at a run. The observers all leaped to their feet, and the guards scrambled to take up defensive positions.

"She's already here!" she cried. "Secure the door!"

Too late. The door crashed open, and a huge figure burst into the room, pursued by a squad of guards.

Neoma had been expecting one of Crepuscula's statues, but it was a man, twice her height and as wide as a tractor. He was clad in leather armor, his face was purple with tattoos, and he snarled as he thundered across the room toward her, revealing teeth that had been filed to jagged points. He upended desks and swatted aside every guard who tried to stop him.

Captain Neoma dropped into a fighting crouch and took aim with her rifle. "A Berserker!" she cried. "Take shelter in the office, sir! I'll hold him as long as I can." *How did he get here?* she thought. She was about to pull the trigger, when the old man stepped in front of her.

"Berserker Chief, so nice of you to accept my invitation. I wasn't sure you'd come."

Neoma stared in amazement as Lord Meridian spread his arms to greet the Berserker like an old friend. The Berserker thudded to a halt and glowered down at him. "You want to talk," he said in a voice so low that Captain Neoma felt it in her bones. "So talk."

"Certainly," said Lord Meridian. "Shall we step into my office?" The Berserker Chief just growled in response, while the pursuing guards stumbled to a breathless halt behind him. Their armor was dented, their uniforms torn, and most of them sported fresh cuts and bruises. They all looked to Captain Neoma for guidance.

"He had the price of admission, Captain," one of them said. "But he wouldn't stop for the security check."

"My lord!" Neoma's heart was still, and her finger was still curled around the trigger of her rifle. "What's going on?"

"Preparation for the future, Captain. As leader of his Impossible Place, the Berserker Chief learned about our project and is keen to be an active part of it." He stepped aside and ushered the Berserker Chief toward the office with a sweep of his arm. The creature was so big that he had to get down on all fours to squeeze himself through the doorway.

"But, sir!" Captain Neoma caught the old man's arm as he turned to follow his guest. "Berserkers bite people's fingers off for sport. They eat raw dragon flesh." She dropped her voice to a whisper. "What could we possibly have that they'd want?"

The old man patted her hand and smiled. "I'll be fine, Captain. Trust me." He surveyed the path of overturned desks, scattered papers, and open-mouthed observers that the Berserker Chief had left behind. "You'd better get back to work. We have a lot to do." With a parting smile, he shut the office door behind him and pulled down the blind.

"Understood," Neoma grumbled, but it was a lie. Berserkers! Of all the hundreds of species that populated the Impossible Places, they were the last ones she would ever have expected to see here. They were warriors, not scholars. They could only count to ten on their fingers. Sometimes to twenty, if they used the fingers they'd bitten off other people.

She gave the office door one last dark look before turning back to the waiting guards. "Don't just stand there," she barked. "You heard His Lordship. Let's get this place cleaned up."

15

HOMECOMING

The Impossible Postal Express was only in the tunnel for a few minutes, but it was long enough for a change to come over Wilmot. His despondency gave way to a nervous energy, and he flitted restlessly around the H. E. C., checking his pocket watch every few seconds and peering out the portholes with an almost-hopeful expression.

"It'll all be fine," said Suzy, trying to reassure herself as much as him.

"Almost there," he said, looking at his watch again.

A few moments later, the train burst from the tunnel with a whoosh of air and a corona of dissipating magic and immediately began to slow.

"We're here!" he said, and leaped to the nearest port-hole. He waved her over, and she hurried to join him.

Flat beige light washed into the cabin from a flat beige sky, punctuated here and there with columns of black smoke rising from formidable brick chimneys. A hodge-podge of industrial buildings rose beyond the tracks—warehouses, factories, mills—all built from the same dirty yellow bricks, with coal-black roof slates. Far beyond them, Suzy could just make out the peaks of distant moun-tains, brown and lumpy and half-hidden in the haze.

The Express was weaving through a broad ribbon of multiple rail lines, all of them intersecting and overlap-ping in a confusion of points and junctions.

A few other trains hurried this way and that. Some of them were big and regal, pulling lines of carriages that seemed to stretch on without end, while others looked al-most handmade, like garden sheds on wheels.

She glanced at Wilmot, not sure whether he was ex-pecting her to be impressed, but he was watching it all with a slight smile.

"Where are we?" she prompted.

"We're home," he said. "This is Trollville."

The *Belle de Loin* slowed to a crawl as it cut across the other lines, finally drawing the Express into a clutch of

178

sidings—lengths of dead-end track to one side of the main lines—on which a collection of freight trains were being serviced and unloaded. Wilmot had his hands on the release handle for the H. E. C. door before they had even come to a complete stop.

"We've got to hurry," he said, leaping out. Suzy followed him down onto a narrow platform between the Express and a row of freight cars loaded with goods on the neighboring track, barely wide enough for two people to pass each other. It was choked with dozens of trolls in work overalls loading and unloading crates, all jostling and shouting for space. Suzy hugged herself and pressed in close to Wilmot to avoid being swept away.

"There you are!" Stonker came striding along the platform toward them, the yellow bulk of Ursel close behind him. Suzy sensed Wilmot go rigid beside her.

"I don't know how it happened, Mr. Stonker," he began, but the older troll silenced him with a look.

"It doesn't matter how it happened. All that matters is how we deal with it. Can it be done quickly?"

"Yes," said Wilmot. "I mean, I think so. I've never had to—"

"Then why are you both still standing here?" Stonker's mustache bristled. "I want to be under way again in an hour."

"Right!" said Wilmot, who spun on his heels and grasped Suzy by the elbow. "Let's go!"

Before she could speak, he had struck out along the platform, dragging her with him.

"Where are we going?" she said, jogging beside Wilmot as they emerged from the siding into a small yard between warehouses. More trolls, most of them in hard hats and safety jackets, shuttled back and forth, stacking crates and pushing wheelbarrows loaded with equipment. They stopped to stare at Suzy as she passed, and she couldn't help blushing, painfully self-conscious at the attention. There was no way to hide from it; she was at least a foot taller than every troll they passed.

"We're going to HQ," said Wilmot.

She dug her heels in, bringing him to a halt. "HQ?" she said, aghast. "They're the ones who wanted to scramble my memory."

He gave her a pained smile. "Technically, yes. But that was before I'd deputized you. You're part of the staff now."

"But they don't know that."

He see-sawed from one foot to the other, not wanting to linger. "It's probably fine," he said. "Besides, you're with me. You can't get into any trouble."

She pressed her lips together. As far as she could tell, she had got into nothing but trouble with Wilmot, but she stayed silent and followed him as he set off at a run again.

"How is this helping us get to the Ivory Tower?" whispered Frederick from inside her pocket, but she pressed it shut until he took the hint and fell silent.

Wilmot led her out of the courtyard into a narrow street lined with more warehouses. Half of them seemed to be empty, and Suzy guessed that the area had seen better days, but the farther they got from the freight yard, the cleaner and more orderly everything appeared and the wider the streets became.

Suzy also started to notice bundles of glowing cables strung back and forth like washing lines between the upper floors of many of the buildings they passed. They looked a bit like telephone wires, except they were a luminous white and pulsed with occasional flashes of light. She tried to ask Wilmot about them, but he was deaf to her questions, leading her from one street to the next until they finally stepped out onto a broad boulevard lined with big, regal buildings that looked like banks or department stores. Trolleys jostled for space with motorized tricycles, and there were even things that looked a bit like cars, albeit cars assembled from random bits of scrap. One hurried past that looked like two antique bicycles welded to an old sofa, with a washing machine for an engine.

Horns blared, drivers shouted, pedestrians shouted back. But despite the noise, Suzy could tell almost immediately that everything was under control. It sounded like chaos—it even looked like chaos—but every vehicle was traveling at the same steady speed, changing lanes in calm and fluid motions. No brakes squealed. And when she really listened, she noticed that none of the shouting was angry. It seemed almost . . .

"Excited?" She didn't realize she had spoken aloud until Wilmot replied.

"Yes, it's always like this at rush hour," he said. "Everyone loves showing off what they've been working on."

She looked at the throng of vehicles again with a new sense of respect. "You mean they made these themselves?"

"Mostly."

She couldn't suppress a grin. "They're incredible!"

He led her along the crowded pavement toward a large, open square at the end. "We're trolls. We build things. It's what we do."

She tried to ignore the heads that turned in her direction as she passed. "What about you? What do you build?"

He paused for just a second, then redoubled his speed, but he had given her enough time to see him blushing. "I'm, uh, not much of an engineer, I'm afraid. I've just never had the knack." He pressed on, not looking back, although the tips of his ears were still bright red with embarrassment. "I mean, engineering's very important, but it's not the only thing in life, is it."

"I never said it was."

He looked back at her then, with something like surprise. "Good," he said. "That's not a view many trolls take."

They had reached the square, one whole side of which was dominated by a building the size of a cathedral. Suzy stared at it in wonder as they approached—it was built from blocks of stone as big as cars, and a row of soaring columns ran along its front, supporting a huge triangular lintel. The lintel was alive with elaborate carvings of trumpets and trains, rockets and trolls in postal uniforms, all radiating out from a crescent moon in the center. Beneath this were carved the words TROLLVILLE CENTRAL POST OFFICE.

"This is it," he said, spreading his arms wide. "The place where it all started. The nerve center. The hub."

"It's a post office," she said.

"It's *the* post office. The first and greatest. The heart of the Impossible Postal network."

She was too wary to be impressed. "Are you absolutely sure they won't mess with my brain?"

"Almost positive," he said. "Let's go."

Far from reassured, Suzy followed him up a broad flight of stone steps between the columns, through the entrance, and into a vast and echoing foyer of pink marble and gold fittings. Despite the enormous space, they were the only people present, with the exception of a small gray troll with a perm, who sat alone behind a wooden reception desk against one wall. She peered at them over her spectacles as they approached.

"What do you want?"

Wilmot cleared his throat and straightened his lapels. "I am Postmaster Wilmot Grunt of the Impossible Postal Service, and this is Postal Operative Suzy Smith. We have a delivery to make to the Ivory Tower, and we're here to collect one of the Facts of Entry." He followed this with a big showman's grin, which was met with a blank stare.

"Have you made an appointment?"

"No," said Wilmot. "Was I supposed to?"

"Yes. You do it online."

His smile tightened into a grimace. "Can't I just make one here?"

The receptionist rolled her eyes and started tapping away at her keyboard. It was attached to a riveted steel box, which Suzy realized must be the troll equivalent of a computer. It connected to a bundle of the glowing wires she had seen out in the street.

"I didn't know you had the internet here," she whispered to Wilmot. "Is that what those wires are? Are they fiber optics?"

"The Ether Web," he said with a disapproving hiss. "Instant communication. It's changed everything."

"Isn't that good?" she said, suspecting she already knew the answer.

"Not if you work in the postal service." He waved a hand at the empty hall. "When Grandpa Honks was a junior postie, there were almost two hundred Impossible Postal Express trains riding the rails. Just imagine! And that's not counting the airships, the mail missiles, the deep-drill couriers, and the guaranteed-delivery eagles. Almost every message in the Union passed through this building—more than a million a day—and it was an army of ordinary people like you and me who took care of them. And now look at it."

Suzy looked again at the grand marble hall and saw, for the first time, the hairline cracks running through the slabs, the dirty carpets, the tarnished and dented fittings.

"We're lucky to get a thousand messages a day now, and there are barely a hundred staff left to manage them."

"I'm sorry," she said. "I had no idea."

"It's the end of an era," said Wilmot, his shoulders slumping. "Why send a letter when the Web is quicker? We're just left handling the odd package that can't go any other way."

"How many Postal Express trains are left?" she asked.

His brow furrowed. "Why, one, of course. We're the last."

Suzy was too shocked by this news to think of anything helpful to say. All she could feel was sadness.

"I'm not just the youngest-ever Postmaster," he said. "I'm probably the last as well. At least it guarantees my place in the history books." He hoisted his face into a lop-sided smile, but there was no real happiness in it. Suzy reached out and squeezed his hand.

The receptionist cleared her throat. "No," she said.

"No, what?" said Wilmot.

"No, you can't withdraw any of the Facts of Entry," said the receptionist. "You're not authorized."

"But I'm a Postmaster!"

The receptionist's stare didn't waver. "The Facts of Entry are strictly confidential," she said. "Only the trolls who deposited them are allowed to take them out again."

"But no one's deposited a Fact of Entry for years," he said. "All the trolls who left them here must be dead or . . ."

"Or what?" said Suzy.

"I'll be back," he said to the receptionist, before seizing Suzy by the hand again. He was about to take off back across the hall when something made him stop. "Just one more question," he said, sounding a bit sheepish all of a sudden. "I don't suppose we've received any complaints today, have we? From a Lady Crepuscula, perhaps?"

The receptionist stabbed at her keyboard again before lifting her bored eyes to his. "Computer says no."

Suzy could practically see the weight lifting from his shoulders. "Jolly good," he said. "Thank you very much."

He practically skipped across the hall and took the steps at a run. "Perhaps we're in luck," he said over his shoulder. "She must have decided not to complain after all."

The image of Crepuscula's shadow picking its way among the statues toward the train flashed back into Suzy's memory. "Good," she said, although the word felt false and brittle in her mouth. *We're almost there*, she told herself. *If we can stay ahead of Crepuscula just a little farther, we'll be at the Ivory Tower. We'll be safe.*

As they left the post office behind them, neither of them noticed the angular gray shape perched atop the lintel. Had either of them glanced back, they might have realized it hadn't been there on their way in. And Suzy would certainly have recognized it—it was a gargoyle, with wings like a bat and a snout like a crocodile. And it watched them closely with its lifeless glass eyes as they hurried away across the square.

16

THE UNDERSIDE

I've got an idea," said Wilmot, leading Suzy away from the post office and back across the bustling square, dodging traffic as they went. They arrived at a narrow building clad in white and green tile, with a large red neon sign above the entrance that read UNDERSIDE. Beneath this were two doorways, one labeled DOWN, the other UP. Trolls streamed into the first and out the second, and Wilmot only slowed his pace as they joined the small throng pushing its way toward the DOWN door.

"Where are we going?" she said.

"To find one of the posties who deposited a Fact of Entry," he said. "They'll be able to withdraw it for us so we can get into the Ivory Tower."

"What sort of facts are they?"

"They could be anything. Any piece of information known only to the person who deposited it. It's the price required by the Ivory Tower in exchange for its own information. They won't even let us in without one. They're pretty rare, so whenever posties found themselves with one, they'd seal it in the post office vault."

"So they could withdraw it again if they ever needed to make a delivery to the Ivory Tower," she said. "Clever."

"All we need is the right postie," he said. "And I know just the place to look. Next stop, the Underside!"

Suzy tried to make herself as small as possible as they stepped in through the DOWN doorway and onto a narrow spiral staircase of wrought iron that had obviously been designed with only trolls in mind—she had to stoop to avoid grazing her scalp on the low ceiling. Hundreds of work boots rang out on the stairs, and a chaos of troll voices echoed off the walls. The crowd swept on, forcing her farther down, down, down the tight curve.

"What's the Underside?" she shouted.

"Yes, it is!" Wilmot shouted back, cupping a hand to his mouth. "Very noisy!"

Suzy grimaced and covered her ears as the crowd carried them down below ground level. She was beginning to feel uncomfortable echoes of the claustrophobia she had experienced in the diving suit, until all of a sudden the walls surrounding them were gone and the staircase was descending through an echoing space the size of a large aircraft hangar. Suzy gawked in astonishment. It was some sort of factory, but its machines were still and silent, and the whole space was cloaked in shadows and dust. In the vague distance, she could dimly see other staircases like theirs spiraling down through the darkness. The sound of thousands of footsteps rang like a great, dull bell in the huge space.

Suzy tapped Wilmot on the shoulder. "Is this where we're going?" she shouted into his ear.

"No," he called back. "This is the old manufacturing level. It's where we used to make technology for the whole Union." He gestured to the broken machines. "But these past few years it's all fallen apart. Not the machines," he added hurriedly, "although that does sometimes happen. I mean ... everything else. Nobody wants troll tech anymore. Nobody wants the postal service. Everything we do is starting to, well ... stop."

This elicited a chorus of resigned sighs from the trolls around them, and more than a few resentful looks.

Trying to fend off her mounting unease, Suzy reached into her pocket and, after making sure that Wilmot wasn't looking, pulled out the snow globe and held it up to her mouth. "Frederick," she whispered. "If we make it to the

Ivory Tower, what happens then? How are you going to break the curse?" She moved the snow globe to her ear and was just able to make out Frederick's reply over the din.

"I've already told you," he said. "With magic."

"But you're trapped in the snow globe. You haven't even got any hands."

"That's easy," he retorted. "You're going to do it for me."

"Me?" She almost raised her voice in surprise. "But I don't know any magic."

"Really? Then why are you carrying around that wand?"

"What wand?"

"The one in the pocket you keep shoving me into, of course."

The wheels of Suzy's mind spun fruitlessly for a few seconds. What on earth could he be talking about? The only thing in her bathrobe pocket was . . .

"That metal thing I took from Fletch?" she said. "I thought it was just some sort of tool."

"A troll wand *is* a tool," he said. "And a very basic one—not much more than a blunt instrument, really—but it might still be useful. Anyone can perform magic if they have the will, the knowledge, and the wand. We've got two out of three already, and if we ever make it out of here, we might just get the third. There's a book at the Ivory Tower that can help us: *Harmful Spells and How to Break Them*. It'll tell you everything you need to know."

Suzy returned Frederick to her pocket, where she felt the cold length of the wand against her fingers. It didn't feel very magical, but Frederick's words had sparked a new worry—if she didn't make it home in time, not only would her mom and dad wake up to find her missing, they'd find themselves in a house that was bigger on the inside, with two open tunnel mouths in the hallway. Because what was it Fletch had said before she'd jumped onto the train? *Can't do the job without it...* She had taken his wand. How was he supposed to put the house back to normal if he couldn't use magic?

She remained preoccupied with the question as the stairs carried them down through the factory floor, and the walls closed in again.

"Almost there!" shouted Wilmot.

"Thank goodness," said Suzy. "I'm not used to being this deep underground."

He gave her a curious look. "We're not underground," he said.

She was about to tell him how absolutely ridiculous that was—of *course* they were underground, where else *could* they be?—when the stairs took them down into the open again and into ... daylight? Yes, dull and half-hearted perhaps, but definitely daylight.

Suzy looked around in confusion, but before she could process what she was seeing, the stairs ended and she stumbled off them onto a metal walkway, bumping into half a dozen trolls as she did so.

"Are you all right?" Wilmot said, turning to her with concern. She didn't answer. She couldn't take her eyes off what she was seeing. Nor could she believe it.

She wasn't underground anymore; she was above it. A very, very long way above it. The walkway was suspended over a canyon so deep she couldn't see the bottom, and so wide its rocky walls were hazy with distance. She staggered to the nearest handrail and clung to it, fighting the sudden onset of vertigo that threatened to make her legs go all weak. "Where are we?" she gasped. "Are we in a new Impossible Place?"

"Of course not," said Wilmot in obvious confusion. "We're just on the Underside, that's all."

A gust of wind pulled at Suzy's bathrobe. "But we're so high up," she said. "Where's Trollville?"

Wilmot gave a chuckle of polite embarrassment. "It's exactly where we left it," he said, and raised his eyes to the sky. Except there was no sky, she realized as she followed his gaze.

Instead, a vast expanse of stone, brick, and iron arched

above their heads, stretching from one canyon wall to the other, and at least a mile from side to side. It was like an immense, dirty rainbow and, even more impossibly, Suzy could see houses clinging to the underside of the arch. Lots of houses. An entire town, in fact—shops and spires and blocks of apartment buildings, all hanging by their tops from the arch like stalactites from a cave roof. Lights burned in windows, washing hung from lines, drainpipes disgorged water into the bottomless chasm below.

"Suzy? Are you sure you're all right?" Wilmot put a hand on her arm. She shut her mouth, which had been hanging open, and blinked away her disbelief. "I'm seeing it," she said, "but I'm still not understanding it."

"It's quite simple, really," said Wilmot, holding his hand out flat in front of him, the palm facing down. "We were here, on the Overside." He tapped the back of his hand with a finger. "That's where all the civic buildings like the post office are. Y'know, the stuff we show the tourists." He grinned. "Then we came down through the superstructure"—he drew his finger down the side of his hand toward the palm—"and now we're here, on the Underside." He tapped the finger against his palm. "It's the residential district."

She took a moment to reevaluate her surroundings. "The Underside," she said, testing the name. Understanding was beginning to creep into the edges of her mind, but she wasn't sure she believed it. "Wilmot, are we ... are we underneath a *bridge?*"

Wilmot laughed. "Well, where else is a troll supposed to live?" When she didn't laugh back, he blinked at her in astonishment. "You mean you really didn't know?"

She shook her head.

"Oh." It took a moment for him to take this fact on board. "I'm sorry. I just sort of assumed you did. I mean, everyone knows."

"That your entire city is a bridge?"

"The greatest troll bridge ever built," he said, puffing with pride. "The Fourth Bridge."

The name made her start. "My world's got a Forth Bridge as well. It's in Scotland."

The tips of his ears twitched. "Oh yes? How did you lose your first three?"

"I'm sorry?"

"Our First Bridge fell down," he said. "The Second Bridge fell up. The Third Bridge ... well, nobody's sure quite what happened to that one, although bits of it still phase in and out of reality sometimes. But this one's stood strong for centuries."

"How?" she said. "A bridge this size shouldn't be able to exist. It should collapse under its own weight." He opened his mouth to answer, but she cut him off. "And *don't* tell me it uses magic, because that's cheating."

He stood there with his mouth open for a few seconds before finally speaking. "Let's just call it a testament to troll determination, shall we?"

Suzy smiled, but redoubled her grip on the railing. "That's great," she said. "Now, where are we actually going?"

17

THE OLD GUARD

It didn't take Suzy long to realize that the iron walkways were like sidewalks in the sky. They all interconnected and finally led them in among the suspended buildings at the lower curve of the bridge's huge arch.

Wilmot halted in front of a large, square house called the Valley View Rest Home, according to the plaque by the front door, and, instead of knocking, he produced a key from his pocket and let them in.

Suzy looked around, glad to have something solid beneath her feet again. It looked like a perfectly normal building on the inside, albeit one built at a scale more suitable for trolls than humans. They had stepped into a spacious entry hall, whose wood-paneled walls were decorated with large paintings of various troll locomotives. One depicted the *Belle de Loin*, its funnel spewing sparks and steam, its wheels a blur. The air smelled of mint and lavender, and the whole place had an air of patient quiet about it, despite the team of trolls in gray nurses' smocks who shuttled constantly back and forth, bearing trays and stacks of linen and pushing carts. Like the traffic on the Overside, they gave the impression of a well-choreographed routine, but with none of the fanfare. Suzy immediately felt safer, just watching them.

"Oh, hello." One of the nurses—older and rounder than the others, with honey-colored skin—spotted them and diverted her course, giving Suzy a quick appraising glance as she approached, but saving most of her attention for Wilmot. "Is that our Wilmot?"

"Hello, Aunty Dorothy." Wilmot beamed and inclined his head to accept the loud wet kiss she planted on his nose. "Sorry to drop by unannounced, but we need some help. Is Mom around?"

"I'll just check," said Dorothy, and filled her lungs. "GERTRUDE? GERTRUDE, YOUR BOY'S HERE!" Suzy and Wilmot both winced at the noise, which echoed around the hall for several seconds. As one, the other nurses all paused and took up the cry, and Suzy heard it carried away to distant and unseen corners of the building.

Then, the message delivered, the nurses all carried on as though nothing had happened.

"She'll let us know where she is in a sec," said Dorothy, smiling. "So I see you've brought a girl home?" Her eyes flicked to Suzy again. "Not much of a nose on her, but she's good 'n' tall, I'll give her that."

"What?" Wilmot's ears went such a shade of red that Suzy thought they might combust. "Oh no, Aunty, it's not like that, it's—"

"I've been waiting for the day," said Dorothy, ignoring his embarrassment and addressing Suzy directly. "His mom keeps telling me to mind my own business, that he'll find someone when he's old enough, but I keep thinking, how's he going to manage that? I mean, there's no opportunity for a young troll to step out with anyone when they're holed up by themselves in a sorting carriage day and night, is there? But here you are." She stepped back, the better to take Suzy in. "I don't mind admitting you're not quite what I expected, but I'm sure I'll get used to it. Welcome to the family!"

"Aunty!" Wilmot was wringing his cap between his hands and chewing his lip as though he were trying to eat himself. "I'm only a hundred and fifty! I don't want a girlfriend!"

"It's never too early to start planning for your future,

dear," said Dorothy, before turning back to Suzy. "He always was a bit sensitive. You'll have to get used to that."

Suzy, who had been deriving a slightly guilty pleasure from Wilmot's discomfort, laughed. "I'm sorry," she said. "But I'm not his girlfriend."

"Oh." Dorothy's face fell a little. "Are you sure? 'Cause he's available. And he's very clean."

"Show her your badge," said Wilmot, straining the words through his teeth. Suzy nodded, and flipped over the lapel of her bathrobe. Dorothy leaned in, squinting at the badge. Then her eyes widened, her mouth popped open, and she jumped straight up in the air. When her feet hit the floor again, she was staring at Wilmot.

"It's not true!"

"It is," he said, unable to stop the smile creeping across his face. "I finally have a staff."

"Oh, just wait until your mother hears about this!" said Dorothy, sweeping them both up into a ferocious hug. "She'll be over the moon!"

A new call echoed in another part of the house. It was repeated, closer, taken up by one nurse after another until it reached the hall. "I'M IN THE RESIDENTS' LOUNGE."

"There, see?" said Dorothy, releasing them. "I told you she'd get back to us."

The residents' lounge was a long, high-ceilinged room, with tall arched windows along the back wall. Suzy could see a broad balcony outside them and, beyond that, nothing but the void beneath the town. The lounge was littered with armchairs and sofas, which in turn were littered with elderly trolls wrapped in tartan blankets and woolen shawls. Some of them chatted together quietly, some snoozed, some just sat and stared into nothing. One of them, she noted, was bright orange and had a pair of carrots up his nose.

"This is the Old Guard," Wilmot whispered in Suzy's ear as Dorothy hustled them in through the door. "Veteran posties, all of them. There's nowhere they haven't been, nothing they haven't delivered. They're heroes."

A matron glided from one old troll to another, tucking in blankets, pausing to rest a comforting hand on a shoulder, refilling water glasses with the jug she carried. She was taller and thinner than Dorothy, but the family resemblance was unmistakable. She turned an imperious look first on Wilmot, and then on Suzy.

"Look who's stopped by, Gert," said Dorothy, giving Wilmot a little shove in the back.

"So I heard," said Gertrude with a slight knotting of

her brow. "Wilmot? What brings you here outside visiting hours?"

"Sorry, Mom," he said in a small voice. "I know you're busy, but I'm in a bit of a fix, and I think the Old Guard might be able to help."

There was a creak of old bones as some of the elderly trolls turned to watch the conversation. Then Suzy saw a funny thing happen: A ripple of delighted recognition ran out to the far edges of the lounge, and within a few seconds every troll in the room was looking at them. No, not at them, but at Wilmot. Smiles broke out, hands were raised in greeting, and a buzz of excited conversation rose all around them.

Gertrude noted this with a sideways glance. "Can it wait? I've just settled them all down."

"Not really," he said, his eyes darting around the room in nervous acknowledgment of the attention he was receiving. "I need someone who can withdraw a Fact of Entry from the post office vault." He swallowed. "Suzy, my new postal operative here, is making a delivery to the Ivory Tower." His smile wavered as he watched his mother's face for her reaction.

At first, there wasn't one. She simply looked Suzy over again, from her (by now filthy) slippers to the crazed bird's nest of her hair. The assessment complete, Gertrude directed her gaze back to Wilmot, and arched one pencil-thin eyebrow. Then the other eyebrow rose to meet it, and her own smile blossomed, big and bold and sincere.

"Oh, my boy, I knew you could do it!" She dropped the water jug, rushed forward, and scooped him up in her arms, planting a barrage of kisses on his nose. Then she danced with him, spinning him around in a circle so quickly his feet didn't touch the floor. They both laughed, and the room erupted in applause. "Postmaster to your own postie," she said, finally setting him back on his feet, and fanning herself with her hand. "Just like your dad. He'd be so proud." She reached up and wiped away a single tear.

"So you'll help?" he said.

"Oh, darling, of course I will."

She looked around at the elderly trolls, smoothing down her apron and bringing her smile under control. But she couldn't keep the happiness from her voice. "Ladies and gentlemen? The Impossible Postal Service needs your help. If any of you has a Fact of Entry in the post office vault, please make yourself known to the Postmaster and his new staff."

The words had barely left her mouth before Suzy and Wilmot were surrounded. The elderly trolls all sprang from their chairs and closed in on them with surprising agility, gummy lips smiling, withered hands stretching out to shake theirs, clap them on the back, and finger Suzy's deputy's badge.

"Welcome to the club!" they said.

"Never thought I'd live to see another delivery to the Ivory Tower."

"Always good to see new blood."

"Are you taking dinner orders? I'll have the jelly rolls."

Suzy smiled and shook as many hands as she could, as the crowd shuffled ever closer. Wilmot, to her surprise, seemed to have put the matter of the Ivory Tower to one side for the moment and was lapping up the attention, greeting the trolls like old friends.

"Mrs. Horne! So good to see you. How's the leg?" and "Mr. Litch! Are those teeth still giving you trouble?" and "Yes, yes, I'm thrilled, Mr. Rumpo. She's already got two successful deliveries under her belt."

We'll never get anywhere if he keeps on like this, she thought, and was just about to say so when a strong hand seized hers and pulled her clear of the throng. Dazed, she found herself eye to eye with Gertrude.

"You'll have to excuse them," she said, releasing Suzy's hand. "They don't often get visitors, and between you and me, I don't think Wilmot meets enough people, either." She gave Suzy an appraising stare. "Although I might be underestimating him."

"We sort of bumped into each other," said Suzy. "I'm just helping out for a bit."

"Well, I'm very glad you are," said Gertrude. "The Impossible Postal Service is like a family, and it's been shrinking for far too long. It's good to have you with us, Suzy." Gertrude's smile returned, wise and reassuring, and Suzy found it easy to smile back.

The commotion of the crowd died away suddenly, and they both turned to see the knot of old trolls opening up, leaving one individual in the center. His skin was ruddy and liver-spotted, and his nose was as sharp as a pickax blade. He held aloft a fine gold chain, from which dangled a small key.

Wilmot's eyes lit up. "Mr. Trellis? Can you help us?"

"Aye," the old troll said. "I've got one. I've got a Fact of Entry in the vault."

"Marvelous," said Gertrude. "The Postmaster and his staff are very short of time, so the rest of you, please make your good-byes." She beamed at Wilmot and Suzy for a second. "While I fetch the bus."

The "bus" was a large cable car, which rose from beneath the rest home with much creaking and grinding of gears. It looked to Suzy's eyes like a converted railway carriage, its peeling burgundy paint revealing old wood beneath, and its few surviving windows all rattling as it hauled itself level with the balcony outside the lounge.

Suzy, Wilmot, and Mr. Trellis were standing on the balcony, hugging themselves against the cool wind picking at their clothes. Behind them, Dorothy and the remainder of the Old Guard had their faces pressed against the windows, watching them.

"Are you sure it's safe?" Suzy whispered to Wilmot as Gertrude waved from the driver's cabin.

"Oh yes," he said, waving back. "Grandpa Honks built it. It was one of his proudest achievements."

"And how long ago was that?" she asked.

"D'you know, I'm not sure," he said, reaching out to open the bus door. The handle came off in his hand. "It just needs a bit of spit and polish," he said with a smile that didn't look as confident as he probably wanted it to.

The door swung open, and Mr. Trellis sprang aboard. The bus groaned and dipped under his weight. Suzy made a conscious effort not to look down as she stepped over the narrow gap from the balcony—she didn't want to be reminded of the fathomless depths of the canyon beneath her—and looked up instead. The cable to which the bus was attached was an outlying branch of a thick web, pulled in an ugly cat's cradle between the largest buildings under the bridge. There seemed to be some complex system of joints connecting them, and she even saw what looked like traffic lights at some of the larger intersections. What few vehicles she could see looked like antique roller-coaster trains slung beneath the cables, rattling past at some speed.

She took a seat beside Wilmot and prayed that the bus wouldn't be traveling that fast.

"All aboard?" called Gertrude.

"All present and correct," Wilmot said. He pulled the door shut after him, and Suzy noticed that he fastened it with a length of string around a nail.

With another screech of cold metal the bus swung into motion, rising in fits and starts up the cable. Suzy watched the rest home drop out of sight below them, the Old Guard clustered at the windows, waving them off.

"I'm so glad you got to meet them," said Wilmot. "They're a great bunch. A lot of them were friends with my dad and grandpa."

"Yes, they were very nice," she said, glad of the opportunity to take her mind off their climb. Mr. Trellis gave her a gummy smile from the seat opposite.

"Working as a postie was the greatest adventure of my life," he said. "The places I saw! The people I met! You're going to love it, lass."

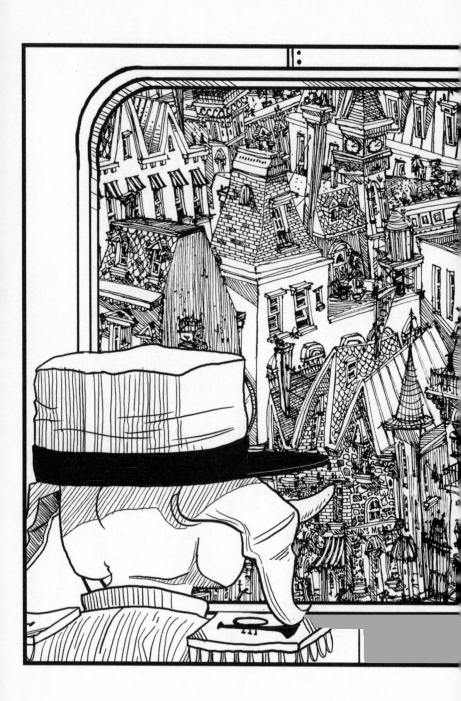

"Uh, thank you," Suzy said, trying not to stare at her reflection, horribly distorted, in the steel plate screwed to the old troll's scalp.

"Spotted this, eh?" He grinned and rapped his knuckles against it. "I got this delivering a birthday card to the princess of Upelstäht."

The bus rode over a set of pulleys with a jarring shake that rattled the windows again.

"A birthday card?" said Suzy. "It doesn't sound that dangerous."

"It wasn't supposed to be," he said, "but she'd been kidnapped by her uncle, the archduke, who was holding her at the summit of the palace clock tower. You know how these royals are. Anyway, it was quite a climb, and when he saw me coming, he panicked and came at me with his sword."

"That's terrible," said Suzy, horrified. "How could he do that to you for delivering a card?"

"Oh, he didn't. The silly oaf tripped over his own feet and plunged to his death. But once the princess opened the card and realized there wasn't any birthday money in it, she threw a tantrum and pushed me off the tower."

Suzy was speechless.

"Luckily, the archduke broke my fall."

"That's horrible," she said.

"I can't hold it against her. She was only three." The

troll cackled. "Of course, then there's the time I lost my leg to a giant clam in the swamps of Grununda." He tugged at his trouser leg, revealing yet more shining steel beneath.

"I don't like to cut you short, Mr. Trellis," Gertrude said, "but we're nearly there."

Suzy looked out the window and saw Gertrude was right. They were close under the curve of the bridge, the jumble of the Underside spread out around them.

A few seconds later, the bus rose into an opening in the stone. Iron girders and patches of old brickwork slid past the windows as they climbed back up through the super-structure. Suzy caught glimpses of more abandoned spaces, of dormant machinery and half-hidden passages, before they finally emerged into daylight. Muted and grubby though it was, it was positively blinding after the twilight of the Underside.

The bus ground to a noisy halt, and Gertrude applied the hand brake. "The Overside," she called. "Everybody off."

18

THE VAULT OF SECRETS

W ilmot led their small procession into the post office. The mean-faced receptionist was still behind her desk and glared at them disapprovingly as they approached. Suzy glared back, hoping the fussy little creature wouldn't cause them any more delays.

"Can I help you?" the receptionist said, as though she didn't already know.

Wilmot gave her his best smile and nudged Mr. Trellis.

"What?" the old troll said, startled. "Oh yes. Hello!" He stepped forward and slapped a hand down on the desk. The receptionist shrank back from it a little. "Bertrum Trellis, former postie. I've got a little something in the vault."

The receptionist sniffed. "Do you have your key?"

Mr. Trellis reached into his shirt and pulled out the length of chain with the key on the end of it. "Will this do?"

The receptionist looked from the key to Mr. Trellis to the rest of the group. "Do you know the way?"

"Perfectly well, thank you," said Gertrude, holding her head high and sweeping past the desk. Suzy couldn't help taking a small amount of satisfaction in the receptionist's obvious annoyance, before setting off in pursuit.

"That receptionist must be new," Wilmot said, grinning as he trotted alongside Suzy. "Otherwise she'd have been nicer to Mom."

"Why?" said Suzy.

"Because I used to work here," said Gertrude. "People knew me."

"She's being modest," said Wilmot. "She didn't just work here. She was in charge."

"What?" said Suzy. "Of the post office?"

"Of everything," said Wilmot, beaming with pride. "She was Postmistress General. When most of her best posties retired, she founded the rest home to look after them. Everyone here called her Her Majesty. But only behind her back, of course."

"As if I couldn't hear them," said Gertrude with a knowing smile.

They reached a tall pair of polished bronze doors. An elderly troll in a postal uniform was slumped on a stool in front of them, snoring gently.

"Who's that?" Suzy whispered.

"The Post Provost Marshal," Wilmot whispered back. "Very prestigious. Very well respected."

Mr. Trellis walked forward and kicked the old troll's stool away, sending him crashing to the floor on his backside. "Wake up, Derrick, you great wazzock," he said.

"Intruders! Villains! Pirates!" The Post Provost Marshal hobbled to his feet and pulled a small truncheon from his belt, but didn't seem entirely sure in which direction he should be facing. "You won't sneak past me!"

"A herd of woolly mammoths could sneak past you," said Mr. Trellis. "Now, let us in."

Derrick blinked heavily and peered at Mr. Trellis through rheumy eyes. "Is that you, Bertrum? What are you doing topside?"

Mr. Trellis removed the chain from around his neck and held up the key.

Derrick lowered the truncheon. "You mean, you've finally come for it?"

"I have," said Mr. Trellis. "The Postmaster here's on urgent business."

"Well, why didn't you say so?" Derrick was suddenly businesslike. Suzy had expected him to have to unlock the huge bronze doors, but they swung open easily when he gave them a shove. "We lost the key a while back," he said, by way of explanation, as he led them inside. "But it's been so long since anyone wanted anything from in here, we figured no one's going to try to break in. And I'm always on guard."

Mr. Trellis cackled. "Making money in your sleep, more like." He paused and looked around the vault. "They've redecorated. I like the statues."

Suzy followed his gaze. The vault was tall, its ceiling half-hidden in shadow. Rows of small, square iron lockers filled the walls, and twin rows of columns formed a central aisle down the length of the room. The spaces between them were filled with ancient-looking statues, all standing at attention, broadswords raised in front of their faces. Suzy couldn't help but be reminded of the stone figures at the Obsidian Tower and tried not to look too closely at these as Derrick led them down the aisle to a locker near the back of the room.

"Box number 82517, if memory serves," he announced.

"Sounds about right," said Mr. Trellis, inserting the key in the lock. It turned with a satisfying click.

Suzy and the others leaned forward to watch as he opened the box, reached in, and withdrew a small glass sphere about the same size as Frederick's snow globe.

"What's that?" asked Suzy.

"A NeuroGlobe," said Wilmot. "It holds memories, and lets you share them with others." Suzy leaned in for a closer look and saw that the NeuroGlobe was full of tiny brass cogs and wheels, slowly ticking around like the workings of an old watch. They passed a fine thread of crackling red energy between them—it looked like a neon caterpillar burrowing in and out of the clockwork.

"Is that the memory?" she asked, pointing at the thread.

"It is," said Mr. Trellis, holding the globe up to the light. "D'you know which memory?"

"Don't tell us!" cried Suzy. Mr. Trellis laughed.

"A long time ago, I was standing alone on top of the Mountains of Madness, when the wind whispered in my ear and offered me something extraordinary in exchange for my sanity." He tapped the sphere. "This is my record of what it offered me, and I don't mind telling you, I was tempted. But it's yours now." He handed it to Wilmot, who took it reverently in both hands. "Make good use of it."

"Thank you," said Wilmot. "We will."

But before he could secure it in his pocket, a great commotion reached them from the corridor outside, and they turned as a noisy tide of people swept into the room.

"Intruders!" yelled Derrick, drawing his truncheon again.

"Don't mind us," said Wilmot's Aunt Dorothy, bustling past him. What looked like most of the remaining

216

members of the Old Guard jostled and poked and nosed about behind her.

"They've not kept this place up," one of them said.

"I hear they've installed that Ether Web and everything."

"Is this where they keep the jelly rolls?"

"Dorothy?" Gertrude raised one questioning eyebrow. "What are you doing here? And why are the residents with you?"

"Sorry, Gert," she said with a big grin that looked anything but sorry. "I couldn't make 'em stay put. They want to see Suzy lick the queen's backside."

Suzy went rigid with shock. "They what?" she said.

The Old Guard sniggered, including Mr. Trellis, but she heard Wilmot gasp.

"Of course," he said. "I've been so busy I completely forgot."

"Forgot what?" said Suzy. The question sounded like an accusation, which she supposed it was.

"It's sort of a tradition," he said. "They say you're not a true postie until you've done it."

"We've all done it, haven't we, lads?" shouted Mr. Trellis. The others cheered and waved their canes.

"They just didn't want you to miss out," said Dorothy, although she was looking at her sister, who let her mask of disapproval slip for a moment.

"Very well," said Gertrude. "As long as it doesn't take too long."

"I knew you'd say yes," said Dorothy. "That's why we took a little detour to the stamp room on our way here and got her out of her case."

She turned and nodded to the Old Guard, whose fussing and chattering came to an abrupt halt as something was passed hand to hand from the back of the group to the front. It was a small velvet cushion with something gold resting on it.

"You do the honors, Wilmot," said Dorothy, passing him the cushion with a proud smile. Blushing with pride, Wilmot pressed the NeuroGlobe into Suzy's hands and took the cushion.

"I never thought I'd get to do this," he said, looking around the sea of eager faces. "Thank you, everyone."

"Don't keep her waiting, lad," said Mr. Trellis, clearly as excited as the others. "This is her big day."

All eyes turned to Suzy, who squirmed. She had no idea what was happening, but she didn't like being at the center of it.

"Of course. Sorry." Wilmot cleared his throat and addressed the crowd. "Ladies and gentlemen, I, Postmaster Wilmot Grunt, am proud to present the newest member of our Impossible Postal family." He nudged Suzy in the ribs.

"What? Oh. Uh, it's me. Suzy Smith. Postal operative. Hello."

"Suzy Smith," intoned Wilmot. "You swore to uphold the ideals of the Impossible Postal Service, risking life, limb, and reason in the execution of your duty, and have been found equal to the task."

Suzy tried to smile, but Frederick's snow globe was starting to feel very heavy in her pocket. "Listen," she whispered to Wilmot. "Maybe this isn't such a good idea."

"Sssssshhhhhhh!" To her horror, every troll in the room put a finger to their lips and shushed her. She blushed a furious red and kept quiet.

"Now step forward and behold Her Majesty, Queen Borax the First," said Wilmot.

She looked to Gertrude, wanting to plead with her to stop this before it went too far, but Gertrude just gave an encouraging nod in return. Swallowing her awkwardness, Suzy did as she was instructed.

Wilmot held the cushion out to her, and she finally saw what the flicker of gold was—it was a postage stamp. It seemed to be fashioned from actual gold leaf and glowed with a warm brilliance that was both beautiful and captivating. But the most remarkable thing about it was its shape. It was the height of a normal stamp, but incredibly wide: almost six inches from one side to the other, and the entire width was taken up with the profile of Queen Borax. A troll queen, of course, with a nose mightier than any Suzy had seen thus far, stretching to the far edge of the stamp.

"The original *Queen's Gold*," said Wilmot. "The very first troll stamp ever printed. In recognition of your part in its legacy, I now invite you to lick its reverse."

With great reverence, he turned the stamp over, and Suzy almost laughed with relief as she realized what the others had been talking about. Sure enough, there were a few suppressed giggles from the crowd behind her.

But her relief was short-lived, as Wilmot gave her an expectant smile and she realized that everyone in the room was waiting for her to act. Her mouth went dry.

"Go ahead, Suzy," Wilmot whispered.

Why not? she thought. *Just get it over with, and you can get out of here. What's stopping you?*

She didn't know, but something definitely was. The respectful silence of the room was filling up with nervous mutterings. Wilmot proffered the cushion again. He was starting to look nervous.

Not knowing what else to do, she stuffed the Neuro-Globe into the pocket of her bathrobe not taken up by Frederick and the wand, bent forward over the cushion, and tried to stick her tongue out, only to find it was glued to the roof of her mouth. She peeled it free and rolled it around inside her cheeks, trying to wet it, while Wilmot, Gertrude, and everyone else looked on.

"Is everything all right?" said Wilmot.

A simple question, but it was suddenly all she needed. "No," she exclaimed, the word echoing round the room like a gunshot. She looked him in the eyes. "I'm sorry," she said. "I can't do it."

There were gasps of shock from all sides, but Wilmot remained silent. Somehow, that felt worse. "But why?" he said quietly. "You've been doing so well."

"I haven't," she said. "I know you think I have, but I haven't, and I don't want to go on lying to you." She reached into her pocket and grasped Frederick's snow globe.

"What are you doing?" she heard him hiss. She ignored him.

"I broke my promise, Wilmot. I told you I'd uphold the values of the Impossible Postal Service, and I meant it, I really did, but something happened, and I couldn't. I'm sorry."

Wilmot looked dismayed. "What are you talking about?"

This was it. The moment of truth. She could feel her chest tightening as the secrets she had been hoarding strained to get out. She pulled Frederick from her pocket and held him aloft.

Everyone stared in confusion.

"A snow globe?" said Wilmot.

"It's not mine," she said. "It's the Lady Crepuscula's. I stole it."

The silence was broken by a collective gasp of shock, and Wilmot's eyes opened wide. For the merest fraction of a second, she thought it was because of what she'd said, but then she saw the movement reflected in his pupils and just had time to throw herself forward, catching him around the waist and hurling them both to the floor.

CRACK! The spot where they had been standing erupted in splinters of granite.

Suzy rolled off Wilmot and onto her back as a statue withdrew the tip of its sword from the fissure it had cleaved in the floor. She looked up in horror at its twisted face, as it raised the blade above its head, ready to strike again.

19

SURROUNDED

R un!" Suzy shouted.

She jumped to her feet, dragging Wilmot with her, but there was movement all around them now, as every statue in the room stepped forward, sword drawn, and Suzy cursed herself for not recognizing them sooner. They had been hiding their faces, but she should have realized these were the same statues she had seen at the Obsidian Tower.

"What's happening?" said Wilmot, then let out a squeal of fear as the second sword blow whistled a few inches over his head. Suzy ducked and felt the stone blade brush the tips of her hair. While the statue was still twisted around, she sprinted past, pulling Wilmot with her behind the nearest pillar.

"We need to get out of here," she said. "Is there another door?"

"There's a secret exit." It was Gertrude's voice, and they turned to see her behind the adjacent pillar. She had Derrick and Mr. Trellis with her. "At the back of the room, behind two of the lockers."

"Get everyone out through there," Suzy ordered. "I'll try to lead the statues away."

Stone hands reached around the pillars and grabbed at them, forcing them to break from cover. Two more statues swung their swords at Suzy as she raced across the aisle, but they hadn't had time to prepare and their blows both fell short. She made it to the cover of the opposite pillar, pursued by flying shards of granite. Wilmot joined her a second later, pale and breathless.

"How will you do that?" he panted.

"I've got what they're after," she said. "They're bound to follow me. You help get the others to safety."

Before he had a chance to argue, she slipped into the middle of the aisle, straight into the midst of four of the large figures. Fear made her catch her breath before she found her voice.

"I'm here!" she shouted, holding Frederick aloft for all to see. "If you want him, come and get him."

"You're going to get us killed!" Frederick cried. But the ploy had worked. All four statues lunged for the snow globe, momentarily forgetting their swords. And each other.

They crashed together with a noise like a cannon firing, as Suzy threw herself down on the ground and crawled on her belly between the nearest statue's legs. The blow seemed to disorient them, giving Suzy just enough time to regain her feet and start a desperate sprint down the aisle away from them and toward the main doors.

"Everybody out!" she shouted at the Old Guard, who had taken shelter behind the other pillars. "Follow Gertrude! Through the back."

The statue nearest to her raised its sword, and Suzy saw, too late, that its aim was sound. She skidded to a halt but slipped, landing on her back and staring helplessly up as the blade swung down in a vicious arc toward her head. She didn't even have time to close her eyes.

That's why she saw the tip of Mr. Trellis's stick appear and strike a glancing blow on the statue's arm. The stick shattered into matchwood, but it was enough to deflect the statue's swing by a few inches, and the sword buried itself in the marble beside Suzy's head. The noise it made was deafening and ran through her like a bolt of electricity, making her scream, but when she rolled clear and put a hand to her ringing ear, it was still attached to the rest of her. She scrambled to her feet, dizzy and in shock.

"Upstart furniture!" Mr. Trellis shouted. "Overblown shopwindow dummies!" He gesticulated with the shattered nub of his stick, until Dorothy appeared and seized him by both arms. She dragged him away toward the back of the room, where Gertrude had succeeded in opening the hidden door.

Suzy turned and fled. The distraction had saved her, but it was over too quickly, and as one, all six statues marched on her. There was nothing between her and the doors now, but she felt no sense of triumph as she reached them, just a finely tuned panic.

I can fix this, she told herself. *I've got the NeuroGlobe. If I can get to the Express, I can get to the Ivory Tower, turn Frederick back to normal, and fix this. I can fix everything.*

She crashed through the doors but, instead of finding the corridor, ran face-first into a smothering darkness. It was as black as night, as cold as frost, and had hard, pinching claws that held her fast. She fought against them, but was carried, helpless, back into the vault.

With a crash, the statues stopped their pursuit and stood to attention.

The shadow set her down on her feet and flowed around her, pouring itself into the room like a tidal wave of ink.

"What have you done?" wailed Frederick. Suzy barely heard him—she was too intent on the hunched figure now emerging from the seething darkness. Her one consolation was that the trolls had had time to escape.

"There you are, my girl," said Crepuscula, drawing to a halt in front of her. "Aren't you tired of running yet?"

20

A Good Deal Goes Bad

Y ou've kept up quite a pace," said Crepuscula, folding her hands over the head of her cane. "I might choose to be impressed if the experience hadn't been so utterly frustrating."

Suzy looked around for a way out, but she was surrounded. Crepuscula and the shadow blocked the main doors, while the statues stood in a tight semicircle behind her. So she was a little surprised to discover that her earlier panic was receding. She had spent so long worrying about Crepuscula catching her that it was almost a relief to have it actually happen. It gave her mind a little room to think.

"How did you know we'd be here?" Suzy asked. Then

she noticed the tiny figure slinking into the room behind Crepuscula, as though trying not to be noticed. "Fletch," she said.

The engineer flinched. "None of this was my idea," he muttered. "I'm just here for what's mine."

"As are we all," said Crepuscula, extending a hand toward Suzy.

"Don't do it!" Frederick cried. "Don't let her take me!"

Suzy clutched the snow globe to her chest. "You're not having him."

Crepuscula sighed. "I'm a reasonable woman. Return Frederick to me, and I might be persuaded to let you walk away."

"Why should I trust you?"

"That's a little rich coming from a thief, my dear." She flexed the fingers of the outstretched hand. "Come on. My patience isn't infinite."

"Run, Suzy," said Frederick. "Or fight her. But don't just stand here. Do something!"

Crepuscula's face twisted into a grim smile. "You know, Frederick, it occurs to me to wonder precisely what you told this young lady to convince her to run off with you like this. I bet it wasn't the truth."

"I've told her everything," Frederick protested.

Crepuscula turned a questioning look on Suzy, who wanted to squirm. She knew Frederick hadn't given her the full story, but she wasn't about to give Crepuscula the satisfaction of knowing that. "It doesn't matter what he told me," she said, hardening her resolve. "I wouldn't leave him with someone like you."

"Then you're even more foolish than I feared," said Crepuscula. "But since you're so clearly open to persuasion, and you've nowhere left to run to, perhaps you would accept an exchange. Something of yours, for something of mine."

"Don't listen to her!" said Frederick.

"I'm not making any deals," said Suzy.

"Wait until you hear my offer." Crepuscula reached into her jacket and drew out an empty glass jam jar, sealed with a lid. Suzy gave it a look of suspicion.

"What's that?"

"The thirty minutes of your life that I took from you," she said, holding the jar up to the light. "Yours in return for Frederick. Oh, and for this pitiful creature's wand, which I understand is also in your possession." She indicated Fletch, who looked as though he was waiting for the ground to open up and swallow him. "I think that's more than fair, don't you?"

"You must think I'm stupid," said Suzy. "It's just an empty jar."

Crepuscula scowled. "And what, exactly, did you

expect time to look like? Would you prefer me to fill it with tinsel?"

Suzy didn't know what to say in response to this, so said nothing. She was still trying to think of a way out.

"This is a measure of the most precious resource in existence," Crepuscula continued. "Every living soul wants more of it. And it's yours, if you just give Freddie back to me."

"Suzy..." Frederick sounded scared. She was certain he couldn't be trembling inside his globe, but it felt like he was. Or was it her own hands shaking? "Suzy, please don't."

She planted her feet more firmly on the floor and looked Crepuscula in the eye. "No deal," she said. "It's only thirty minutes. It's not worth a person's life."

Crepuscula's expression was quick to darken. "Are you sure about that? I trimmed the end of your mortal span. Your life ends thirty minutes sooner than it should. Imagine what you could do with that time back."

"Not much." Suzy was trying to sound like she didn't care, but the awful truth was, Crepuscula's words were sowing doubt in her mind. What *could* she do with that time?

"They're the most important minutes of your life," said Crepuscula, her voice low and urgent now. "Your chance to make your last decisions, to bid a final farewell to family and friends, to tell a secret love of your true feelings, to finally set right what once went wrong."

Cold sweat glued Suzy's pajamas to her skin. "The end of my life," she said. "Have you seen it?"

Crepuscula's smile was like a shark's. "Would you like to know when it's due?"

"No," said Suzy, with absolute certainty. "And I don't care what you tell me. I'm not giving you Frederick."

Crepuscula stared hard at her for a moment, then sighed. "In which case, we shall have to resort to unpleasantness."

Suzy backed away quickly as Crepuscula stalked toward her.

"Stop!"

Suzy froze in surprise, and even Crepuscula paused, a look of impatient confusion on her face. Suzy turned toward the source of the voice. "Oh no," she breathed.

Wilmot stood in the hidden doorway, his baggy uniform pooling around his ankles and his cap at a drunken angle on his head.

"Wilmot, don't—" she started, but he silenced her with a look of fire. She had never seen him like this before. He was furious.

"Lady Crepuscula," he said, striding down the length of the room toward them. The statues parted to let him pass. "I must ask you to unhand my employee."

"And who might you be?" said Crepuscula.

"I am Postmaster Wilmot Grunt of the Impossible Postal Service," he said, drawing to a halt beside Suzy. "This postal operative is my responsibility, and, as such, I believe I owe you an apology."

Crepuscula raised an eyebrow. "I don't care for apologies, boy. I simply require restoration."

"I understand," said Wilmot, ignoring the slight against his age. "Nevertheless, let me apologize, fully and sincerely, on behalf of the Impossible Postal Service. Our operative stole from you, and we take such breaches of our ethical guidelines very seriously indeed."

Suzy put herself between Wilmot and Crepuscula. "What are you doing?" she whispered.

He calmly brushed her aside, but as he did so, replied out of the corner of his mouth, "Trust me." He straightened his cap and addressed Crepuscula again. "Consequently, the Impossible Postal Service will be happy to return your item and to compensate you for the inconvenience caused. The disciplinary proceedings for Postal Operative Suzy Smith, however, must remain an internal matter."

Before Crepuscula could reply, the sound of rapid footsteps made everyone turn again, and Gertrude emerged from the hidden exit at a run. She skidded to a stop in the middle of the hall, the statues blocking her path.

"Wilmot!" she cried, trying to fight her way past them. "Wilmot, darling, get away from here!"

Suzy chewed her lip, but Wilmot turned back. "Don't worry, Mom," he said. "I'm just doing my job."

Crepuscula sniffed and turned her attention back to him. "You want me to leave your little pet alone? After everything she's done?"

"She is not my pet," said Wilmot, "but yes. And you of course have the right to file a formal complaint, if you so wish. I have the necessary form here." He reached inside his jacket and pulled out a small rectangle of paper, which he held out to Crepuscula.

For a moment, the hall was silent. Then Crepuscula began to laugh, softly at first, but growing louder and louder, until her shoulders shook. Suzy took an involuntary step back, but Wilmot stood his ground, the complaint form not so much as wavering. Crepuscula pointed at him, and the shadow rushed forward.

"No!" Suzy lunged for him, but it was already too late. The shadow swallowed him whole. His dwindling cry reached her as though from a great distance, and when the shadow receded, nothing remained but his cap, lying crumpled and forlorn on the flagstones.

Suzy stood, immobilized with shock. She could hear Gertrude screaming.

"I've had enough of these distractions," said Crepuscula, bearing down on Suzy. "If you won't hand Freddie over, I'll take him myself."

Panic struck, and Suzy's mind went blank. All she could think about was Wilmot, vanishing into darkness. It was all her fault.

"Suzy, please!" Frederick's voice cut through the fog in her brain, and she saw that Crepuscula was almost on her. She couldn't bargain. She couldn't run. All she could do was fight. And so, in a final act of desperation, she reached into her pocket, pulled out the only solid thing she could lay hands on, apart from Frederick, and threw it at Crepuscula, hard.

It was Fletch's wand. Crepuscula saw it coming and brought a hand up to shield herself. It was the hand holding the jam jar.

The rod struck the jar, which exploded in a nimbus of glass. Suzy shut her eyes.

And that's when everything stopped.

21

A GLITCH IN TIME

Suzy opened one eye a sliver, expecting some sort of horror to strike her. Instead, there was just silence, and an unnatural stillness.

Very cautiously, she opened both eyes and looked around. Crepuscula stood before her, her outstretched hand just a couple of inches away. But she didn't move. She didn't speak.

And the jam jar, which Suzy had just had time to see shatter before she shut her eyes, was exactly as it had been—a burst of glass shards frozen in mid-air, winking in the light of the chandeliers.

Very tentatively indeed, Suzy reached out and touched one. It didn't fall, but it did move under a little pressure from her fingertip. It also cut her, and she snatched her finger back and stuck it in her mouth as she took in the rest of the room.

Everything was frozen. Fletch had been caught reaching for his wand, which had bounced away from the breaking jar and now sat in the air just beyond Crepuscula's elbow. Behind Suzy, Gertrude still reached for the spot where Wilmot had stood, her face a mask of sadness and pain, the tears as solid and immobile as glass on her cheeks. Suzy looked away from her quickly, feeling her own tears start.

"What happened?"

Frederick's voice was so unexpected that she nearly dropped him. "I don't know," she sobbed. "Everything just... stopped."

"Except us," said Frederick. "What did you do? Was it a spell?"

"No, I..." Her voice felt thick and sluggish with tears. "I don't know what I did."

"Well, whatever it was, it worked," said Frederick. "This is our chance. Let's go!"

"No," she said. "What about Wilmot?"

"What about him?" said Frederick. "You saw what happened. He's gone. Finished."

"No!" She ran to the shadow, banked like a static thundercloud behind Crepuscula, and passed into it as easily

237

as if it were smoke. The room looked dark from inside it, the light from the chandeliers stained a sickly purple. She cupped her free hand around her mouth and shouted. "Wilmot! Wilmot, are you in here?"

"He won't answer," said Frederick, and she very nearly hurled him across the room. This was all *his* fault. His... and hers.

"Wilmot?" She raced from one side of the vault to the other, groping through the darkness for any sign of life. But when she stumbled back into the light behind Crepuscula, she knew Frederick was right. Wilmot was gone.

"Please, Suzy," Frederick pleaded. "I don't know what's happened here, but we have to get away before it all unsticks. The fate of all the Impossible Places—"

"I know!" she snapped, pawing the tears from her eyes. "Just give me a minute, will you?"

He was right of course—that was the worst part. Whatever was happening, it was their only chance at escape. They couldn't afford not to take it. She blinked the salt sting from her vision and looked around. "We still need the wand," she said.

It didn't give as easily as the glass had, but it twisted a little, and by leaning back and applying her whole weight against it, she was able to drag it slowly free of its spot in the air.

"Now we can go," said Frederick as she stuffed it back into her pocket.

"Not quite," she said. She patted her other pocket to make sure the NeuroGlobe was still safe, then crossed to the point where Wilmot had stood and picked up his fallen cap. She straightened it, dusted it off. Then she threw her own cap aside and pulled Wilmot's down over her hair. It was tight, but it just fitted. "*Now* we can go," she said.

"None of this would have happened if you hadn't told them about me," he went on. "You promised to keep me secret."

"I also promised to do my best as a postie," she said, squeezing between two of the statues. "I couldn't keep doing both. Besides, things had changed. I thought they would be able to help us. And anyway, the statues were already here. They were *waiting* for us."

She paused in front of Gertrude and finally looked her in the eyes. The life was still in them, but Gertrude was as unresponsive as a photograph. Suzy placed a hand on the troll's shoulder. "I'm sorry."

She paused at the secret exit and took a final look at the room. Then she turned and ran.

She had expected to step out of the post office into the noise and bustle of a living city, but the silence outside was absolute as well. The Old Guard stood frozen in various attitudes of flight in the alleyway behind the building. Dorothy had taken the lead, pulling Mr. Trellis along by the arm. Suzy waved her hand in front of Dorothy's face and called her name, but knew it was fruitless. Turning sadly away, she hurried around the building and into the square.

It was a snapshot of chaos. Statues blocked every street, while the cars, bikes, and various unclassifiable vehicles were trapped in the midst of evasive maneuvers, their drivers shaking their fists or jumping clear of impending disaster.

"She must have brought every single statue," she said, awed. "A whole army."

"At least they're stuck, too," said Frederick. "What d'you suppose happened? It's everywhere."

"It must be something to do with the jar," she said, fighting her way through the stalled traffic toward the opposite side of the square. "Or the wand? I don't even know how it's supposed to work."

"I think you point it at something and just sort of *feel* what you want to happen," said Frederick. "But I don't see how that could cause a whole city to stop."

She bit her lip with worry. "Can we call someone?"

"What do you mean?"

"I mean, is there any way of contacting someone in

charge? The Union must have a prime minister or a president or something. Someone to send help."

"No," he said, starting to sound uncomfortable. "At least, not officially. There are things we all share, like the postal service and the Ether Web, but each Impossible Place is supposed to govern itself. The trolls have their council of elders, the Clockwork Kingdom has its chief automaton, and nobody even knows how the Wicker Women of High Heath do things, because nobody who's asked them has ever been seen again. Everywhere's different."

"It sounds like chaos," she said.

"That's not the point," he said. "Each Impossible Place makes its own rules. No one's supposed to be in charge of the whole thing."

They slipped past the blockade of statues onto the main boulevard. Suzy watched carefully, trying to remember exactly which side street she and Wilmot had emerged from on their way to the post office earlier.

"Where are we going?" he said.

"Back to the train. We need to get out of town."

"But how are we going to get it to move if everything's frozen?"

"I don't know yet," she said, feeling the threat of tears prickling behind her eyes again. "I don't know anything, but we can't stay here."

She paused at the entrance to one of the streets. It looked like it could be the right one, but the same was true of the last two they had passed. And as if that weren't bad enough, there was at least one statue standing guard in every one of them. Even though they were immobile, Suzy didn't quite have the courage to look at their pitted, twisted faces. She put her head down and ran on. "Is this Crepuscula's plan?" she said. "Invade the Union with statues?"

"No, this is just to recapture me," said Frederick. "Her real plan would be much worse."

The thought spurred Suzy on. She felt exposed and vulnerable out in the streets like this. She wanted the warmth of the Express. "Let's try down here," she said, trusting to luck and leading them into a side street. Even if it wasn't the one she had taken earlier, it shouldn't take them too far away from the freight yard. As she wove through the crowd, her mind raced.

"I can move things," she said. "Like the glass shard, and the wand. If I try hard enough, I can ... unstick them."

"Do you think you can unstick the train?"

"Maybe. The glass was easy. The wand was harder. Maybe it's something to do with size."

"In which case, the train will be impossible," he said.

"Yes, thanks for that."

A minute later, they reached a small junction, and at

last she saw a shop she recognized. "It's that way!" she exclaimed, setting off in the new direction with a greater sense of purpose. They passed two more statues in the next street, which she did her best to ignore.

"Do you think that's why I'm not frozen?" asked Frederick. "Because you were holding me when all this started?"

"Maybe," she said. "If I can unfreeze other things by touching them, I suppose it makes sense."

Frederick ruminated on this for a moment. "Then don't let go of me," he said.

"I won't," she said. "I promise."

They took two wrong turns and a convoluted detour before they finally arrived back in the freight yard. Suzy's elation at seeing it was quickly tempered by the sight of another statue standing guard at the near end of the platform. Its sword was drawn, and it seemed to have been scanning the faces of the fleeing crowd when everyone was frozen.

Her hand strayed instinctively to Fletch's wand, although she wasn't sure how she could use it to defend herself, should she need to. She still had no idea how magic worked, or what it could do. Had the wand malfunctioned when it hit…

"...the jar!" She stopped in her tracks as her imagination spat out a big, fat, tantalizing idea.

"What about it?"

"There was time inside it. But it was *my* time."

"What do you mean?"

"Crepuscula said she'd taken the time from the end of my life. It was time only *I* was supposed to have."

"So?"

"So, what if I'm having that time *now*? Instead of putting it back where it came from, breaking the jar gave it back to me here and now. But it's only mine, so the rest of the world doesn't get to live it with me."

"You mean, you're getting half an hour of life back while the rest of the world is on pause?" said Frederick.

"Yes. I think. I mean, maybe." She shook her head to clear it. "Does any of that make sense?"

"I've no idea," he said. "I'm not a temporal fuzzicist. I suppose we'll find out when the thirty minutes are up."

A shock ran through her. "Oh no! How long have we got left?"

"I don't know. They don't make watches in my size."

"We can't have long." She redoubled her grip on Frederick and broke into a run, forcing her way between the frozen trolls blocking the platform between her and the Express. "Maybe only minutes!"

It was less, as she discovered when the world snapped

back into motion around her, and a troll worker, fleeing the invader in the freight yard, crashed into her, sending her flying. She just had the presence of mind to land on her back, clutching Frederick's globe to her chest as she landed.

"Watch it!" the troll barked as he leaped over her and ran on.

Panic surrounded Suzy on all sides as the trolls stampeded up the platform, threatening to crush her underfoot. She struggled upright, only to lock eyes with the statue in the yard. For an awful second, the trolls' panic infected her, and she found she couldn't move, even as the statue turned and lumbered toward her. Only Frederick brought her back to her senses.

"Run!" he screamed.

Jostled and buffeted, Suzy turned and joined the stampede.

22

RED ALERT

With mounting alarm, Captain Neoma read the hastily scrawled report the Troll Territory observer had just handed her.

"And this is happening right now?" she said.

The observer, a young troll called Scrunge, according to his name badge, nodded frantically. "The human girl was there in the vault one second, and the next she was gone. Vanished!"

Neoma folded the paper. "Find her," she said. "Check the Express."

Scrunge nodded and dashed back to his desk, while Neoma made straight for Lord Meridian's office. Sergeant Mona had the good sense not to stop her as she marched straight up to the door and threw it open, ignoring the STRICTLY NO ADMITTANCE sign—meeting or no meeting, this wouldn't wait.

"My lord," she started, before trailing into silence at the remarkable scene that met her eyes.

Lord Meridian sat in one of the leather armchairs, calmly reading a book, while on the floor at his feet lay the Berserker Chief. The huge man was curled into a ball, hugging himself and rocking slowly from side to side, whimpering. He started to his feet when he saw Neoma and bared his jagged teeth at her, but then his bottom lip trembled, and to Neoma's amazement, a tear glimmered in his eye. He must have seen her surprise because he tried to hide his face, and shoved her effortlessly aside as he squeezed out through the doorway. The observers all ducked beneath their desks when they saw him coming, but he ignored them and loped hurriedly away toward the exit, his face downcast.

"What happened in here?" said Neoma, getting to her feet.

"Enlightenment, Captain." Lord Meridian put down his book. "The Berserker Chief came here to expand his horizons. It can be an emotional experience."

If that answer was intended to put her mind to rest, Neoma thought, it had failed—she had had no idea until now that Berserkers were even capable of crying, let alone being reduced to quivering wrecks. But there was no time to worry about that now. She handed him the folded paper.

"Crepuscula's closed in on Frederick and the girl in Trollville, sir. I'm taking a squad out to extract them, and I'm not taking no for an answer."

Lord Meridian had scanned through the note and risen from his chair before she had even finished speaking. "Blast! I should have anticipated this." He shooed her toward the door. "Put your team together and take my personal train. It's the quickest we have."

"Thank you, sir."

But as she hurried to gather her troops together, she found she was unable to banish the memory of the Berserker Chief's eyes welling up in the second before he had turned and fled. Yes, *fled*, because she was sure now that he had been running from something. And Berserkers never ran—it just wasn't in their nature. The chancellor of Wolfhaven had stormed out of her meeting as well. What was going on in that office?

She pushed the thought to one side—all her unanswered questions would have to wait. It was time to fight, at long last. She had a Union to save.

23

BACK UP TO SPEED

A tinkling of glass.

The fragments of the jar scattered across the floor and were promptly ground underfoot by Crepuscula, who snatched at the empty air where, from her perspective, Suzy had been standing less than a second earlier. Fletch finished his flying leap for the wand and landed empty-handed. By the time he regained his feet, looking around in confusion, Crepuscula was sifting through the shards of glass with the tip of her cane, her back to him.

He crept silently toward the edge of the room, hoping to make a discreet exit before anyone thought to notice him again. The statues seemed distracted by the girl's vanishing act, and the shadow . . . well, it was hard to tell. But he'd take his chances.

"She's a lucky one," Crepuscula said, picking a shard of glass from the tip of one finger and teasing a drop of blood free. It was dark blue. "She got her time back and used it to make off with my prize. I'd say that's very lucky indeed. Wouldn't you agree?"

Fletch tried to move as silently as possible, lifting each foot carefully and placing it down flat. He had only taken two steps when, without looking round, she clicked her fingers and pointed straight at him.

"Where do you think you're going?"

He started, then felt angry with himself for being so easily unsettled. "I'm going to find someone who can sort out this mess," he said. "And by 'mess,' I mean you."

"Charming," she said flatly. "But I've not finished with you yet."

"Well, I've finished with you." He shook his fist at her. Now that he was speaking his mind, he found his anger came tumbling out, driving him onward. It felt like freedom. "I might not have liked that slip of a Postmaster much, but I respected him. All he wanted was to follow his dad, and he busted a gut, day in and day out. He didn't deserve what you did to him."

Crepuscula, who had maintained a look of polite patience throughout Fletch's diatribe, simply nodded and said, "Where has the girl gone?"

"How should I know?" he spat. "She just vanished, along with my wand. And as long as she's out of your reach, good luck to her!"

"Let me rephrase the question," said Crepuscula. "She came here on that infernal train of yours. Where is it stationed?"

Fletch folded his arms. "Not telling."

Crepuscula sucked her breath in through her teeth. "Why must people always make this so difficult?" She pointed the tip of her cane at the kneeling figure of Gertrude, who went rigid and promptly shot ten feet into the air, where she hung, rotating slowly, her eyes wide with fear and anger. "Tell me where the Impossible Postal Express is," said Crepuscula, "or this dear nurse will suffer some deeply unpleasant experiences."

"You wouldn't!" Fletch cried, although he knew already that Crepuscula would. He could see it in her face.

"Don't tell her a thing, Fletch!" cried Gertrude. "She killed Wilmot! And I'd sooner die than help her."

"You just might," said Crepuscula, giving her cane a

flick and putting Gertrude into a swift triple somersault. "Now be quiet, please. I want to hear what your friend has to tell me."

She turned her flinty gaze on Fletch, who swallowed and cursed himself. He already knew he had lost.

24

LAWS OF MOTION

*A*hoy, down there!"

Suzy looked up into the face and mustache of Stonker and realized they had arrived. The *Belle de Loin* stood over her, steaming and ready for action. A noise behind her made her turn, and over the heads of the stampeding trolls, she saw the statue advancing up the platform toward them.

"Remember to keep me hidden!" Frederick hissed as she scrambled up the ladder. "For my sake and theirs."

Suzy didn't need to be told twice and buried Frederick deep in her pocket. She wasn't about to let anyone else suffer the consequences of what she'd done.

"What took you so long?" said Stonker as she reached

the gangway. "Where's the Postmaster? And can someone please tell me what the blazes is going on out there?"

"It's an attack," she said. "We have to get out of here."

Stonker started at the sight of the approaching statue and bundled her into the cab, where he slammed the door shut. Ursel had stuck her head out one of the side windows and was watching the unfolding drama with obvious alarm.

"Unk!"

Ursel backed into the middle of the cab, but her warning came too late, as the terrible face of the statue rose into view, blotting out the light. The *Belle de Loin* creaked and leaned to one side as the stone figure smashed the window into fragments with one blow of its fist.

Suzy threw herself to the ground to avoid the flying glass, but there was nowhere to hide. The statue let out a bellow of triumph, as loud as a foghorn. Its lips didn't move, it had no throat or lungs to draw breath, but the cry kept coming, until Suzy thought it would drive her mad. The thing had found its prey. It was calling its fellows.

Something moved over her, very close to her head, and she looked up, expecting to see a stone hand reaching for her. Instead, she saw Ursel. The bear reached into the firebox and plucked out a burning banana. There was a sizzling sound, like bacon frying, and the flames licked hungrily at the fur of her paw. Then, with one leap, she threw herself at the window and shoved the banana straight into the statue's face.

There was an eruption of blue sparks, and the statue fell away. A second later, they all heard the heavy crunch as it hit the platform. They raced to the window to see.

The statue lay below them, its head wreathed in blue fire. Its cry died away as the flames blazed brighter.

"Get down!" barked Stonker. Suzy was about to ask him why, when the statue's head exploded. She threw herself flat as fragments of stone pinged and whistled off the body of the locomotive.

She blinked away the purple blob that the explosion had left on her vision and raced back to the window. There was very little left of the statue—just a pair of stone legs, lying at the fringe of a smoldering crater.

"That was horrible!" she exclaimed.

"That was lucky," said Stonker, springing to Ursel's side. "Of all the dashed silly things..."

Suzy joined him, and together they helped Ursel into a sitting position against the wall of the cab. The bear let out a low growl and clutched at her paw—the fur had burned away up to the elbow, leaving angry red blisters.

"I've seen some irresponsible maneuvers in my time, but that one tops them all," said Stonker. "You could have blown yourself sky high."

"Growlf," said Ursel.

Stonker smiled. "Yes, I'll admit, it was rather wonderful. Thank you."

Suzy threw her arms around Ursel's neck in a hug. Ursel grunted and extended her uninjured paw in what looked suspiciously like a thumbs-up.

They all turned at the sound of another foghorn cry. It came from some distance away, but was still too close for comfort. Another cry went up, and another, until the city seemed to throb with them.

"The other statues," said Suzy. "They're coming."

"We'll make a move as soon as the Postmaster's aboard," said Stonker. "Why isn't he with you?"

The weight of Suzy's grief came crashing down again, squeezing the breath from her. She tried to speak, but her voice broke in her throat, and she had to choke back a fresh rush of tears. "He's gone."

"What d'you mean, 'gone'?" said Stonker. "Gone where?"

She took off Wilmot's battered Postmaster cap and showed it to him. "It was Crepuscula," she said thickly. "He tried to stop her from hurting me. He got in the way, and she ..." Her voice trailed off into silence.

"Crepuscula?" Stonker's voice dropped to a whisper. "Is that old witch behind all this?"

"It's my fault," she said. "I stole the package I was supposed to deliver to her."

"Then for pity's sake give it back," said Stonker. "Before anyone else gets hurt."

"I can't!" she cried. "It wasn't hers in the first place, and now I have to get it to the Ivory Tower."

Stonker's mustache twitched as he digested this. "You mean we were handling stolen goods? That's a pretty steep charge." He exchanged a look with Ursel. "So what is it? Treasure? Cursed artifact? Forbidden codex?"

"It's . . . secret," she said, and cringed a little at the sharp looks they both turned on her. "I'm sorry, but it's better if you don't know. I told Wilmot because I thought he could help me, and instead it just got him . . ." The word felt so big and heavy, she had to force it out. ". . . killed." Saying it made it real, and for the first time since stepping aboard the Express, she wished she had stayed at home and let Fletch scramble her memories. Because she didn't want to remember this moment at all.

"If we get this package to the Ivory Tower," said Stonker, "Crepuscula will stop chasing us?"

"Yes."

Stonker regarded her for a moment, weighing what she had told him. Finally, he accepted it with an almost-imperceptible nod. "Then we'd better make ourselves scarce," he said. There was no sign of his usual exuberance as he turned to the controls, but a steely resolve. He released the brake lever and began backing the Express out of its siding.

Suzy looked out the porthole at the Trollville skyline sliding past. More statues were coming. She could see them climbing over the stationary freight cars in their sidings and marching along the platforms toward them. She counted five. No, six. Seven already. Something circled in the air overhead, and she knew without looking that it was Crepuscula's gargoyle.

"They're almost here," she said, biting her lip.

"And we're almost there," said Stonker. "Let's give them a run for their money, shall we? For Wilmot."

Ursel growled in agreement, and their determination lent Suzy a little more courage.

"For Wilmot," she said. "Let's do it."

They had backed out of the siding onto the main lines, and Stonker threw the locomotive into forward gear.

"Where are the tunnels?" she said.

"The far end of the bridge," said Stonker. "A couple of minutes away."

They gathered speed quickly, but the leading statues vaulted the last of the rail cars in the freight yard and cut across the tracks toward them.

"Faster!" gasped Suzy.

The nearest statue closed the gap between them. Casting its sword aside, it leaped for the train, hands grasping, but fell just short, sprawling across the neighboring tracks.

Suzy laughed with relief, but the next statue was right behind it, running hard. The Express was still accelerating, but not quickly enough, and when the statue leaped, it struck the H. E. C. By leaning out the window, Suzy could just see it pulling itself hand over hand onto the roof.

"It's on board!" she shouted.

"Blast it all," said Stonker, his hands flying over the instruments. "Do me a favor and throw a few more bananas on the fire. We need to balance out the extra weight."

"Hurmph." With obvious pain, Ursel levered herself onto her hind legs.

"Not you," said Stonker without looking round. "You're in no state to do anything. Suzy, shake a leg."

But Suzy was too preoccupied to shake anything, as Stonker's words had triggered an avalanche of thought. "Weight," she murmured to herself. "Weight and speed." Then, without warning, she threw open the back door of the cab and leaped across to the tender.

"Oi!" Stonker shouted after her, but she was already scrambling up the ladder to the pile of bananas. It was the same route she had taken in the Topaz Narrows, but there hadn't been a killer statue waiting for her then.

"What's happening?" cried Frederick from her pocket.

"I know what to do!" she said, wincing as energy escaped from the bananas, sparking and snapping against her bare hands. "My homework!"

"Homework!" he cried. "At a time like this?"

"I mean Newton's laws of motion," she said. "I know how to fix this!"

She was already over the bananas and slithered quickly down the ladder to the footplate at the rear of the tender. A length of thick chain coupled it to the H. E. C., locked in place by a stout metal pin.

"Newton's second law of motion," she said, wrapping her hands around the head of the pin. "Apply force to a mass—in this case a train—to make it accelerate. If you keep the force the same but reduce the mass, you increase the acceleration. So if I can pull this free..."

She strained with every ounce of strength she had, until it felt like tongues of fire were crawling up her arms. She arched her back with effort, looking straight up into the sky. And that's when she saw the dreadful face of the statue looking down at her from the roof of the H. E. C.

It lunged for her, and she leaped back in terror. Her back collided with the rear of the tender, and, in a moment of cold horror, she realized she had nowhere to go. Fractured stone fingers reached for her...

...and closed on empty air, just inches in front of her

face. Suzy blinked in astonishment, then looked down at the object she hadn't realized she was still holding—the coupling pin.

The statue howled in frustration, but it was too late. As the *Belle de Loin* got faster, the H. E. C. started to slow down. It happened so gradually that Suzy wasn't sure it was even happening, until the statue tried to grab the tender and got a handful of empty air instead. It roared in frustration, but it was too late—the gap was widening by the second, and when it made a last-ditch leap for the tender, it crashed to the tracks, just a few feet short.

A giddy cocktail of fear and relief welled up in Suzy's chest. "You see?" she said, pulling Frederick from her pocket so he could see the statue, the H. E. C., and the sorting car behind it, dwindling into the distance. "We've got a smaller mass now that we've lost the carriages, which means we've got greater acceleration. They'll never catch us now."

Dozens more statues had emerged from the city, but they, too, were receding into the distance, unable to match the *Belle de Loin*'s remarkable speed.

"I'll admit, that's pretty clever," he said.

"That's physics," she said. "It's what I do."

"Well done, that postie!" cried Stonker as Suzy re-entered the cab. "Now, brace yourselves, both of you. It's almost tunnel time."

Suzy ran to the front window and looked out. They were fast approaching the fringes of the city, where the Fourth Bridge completed its span of the canyon below and anchored itself in solid ground. The foothills of the mountains reared up less than a mile ahead of them, and the tracks ran up to a sheer cliff face, hundreds of feet high, with a row of tunnel mouths across it. She traced the rails of their own track to a large tunnel in the middle of the row. The signal above it was green. The way was clear. They were going to make it.

And then the roof of the cab exploded, raining chunks of burning timber down on them. They threw themselves flat, and Suzy looked up through her fingers, through the smoking hole in the roof tiles, and into the hateful eyes of Crepuscula.

She was flying high above the locomotive, suspended in the claws of her monstrous gargoyle, whose wings blotted out the sun like dark sails. The creature swooped down on them, while Crepuscula took aim with her cane.

There was a flash, and Suzy just had time to see something like lightning jump from its tip before the cab's rear door and windows blew in and a flare of blue light engulfed everything around her.

"What the devil?" she heard Stonker exclaim.

Suzy's vision swam back into focus. Apart from her injured paw, Ursel appeared unharmed, and Stonker was still at the controls. But behind the cab, the tender was a bonfire of blue flame, full of hissing, popping bananas.

"She's going to blow us to pieces!" Stonker cried.

The gargoyle sailed a short way above the cab, close enough for Crepuscula to shout down to them. "Halt!" she shrieked. "If Frederick reaches the Ivory Tower, it's all over. What he knows is too important."

There was an explosion in the depths of the tender, sending a fresh gout of fire into the sky, and the gargoyle banked to avoid it. Crepuscula called out again as it did so, and Suzy couldn't be sure what she said over the roar of the locomotive, but it sounded like, "The fate of the Impossible Places depends on it!" Crepuscula raised her cane and loosed another bolt of magic, which missed. Then the gargoyle peeled away and she was gone.

"Disaster!" cried Stonker, pointing ahead of them through the front window. Suzy looked. Crepuscula's magic hadn't missed its mark at all—she had been aiming at the tunnel. The stone archway, barely a few hundred yards ahead, was crumbling, and the darkness inside it flickered like the image on an old TV set.

Stonker threw himself at the brake lever, but Suzy pushed him back.

"We have to go through," she said.

"The tunnel's collapsing. You'll kill us!"

"Crepuscula will kill us if we stay here."

They locked eyes as they both struggled for purchase on the lever, neither one of them gaining control. And then it was too late, as a rattling rain of stone dust struck the body of the locomotive, the world went dark, and the *Belle de Loin* plunged through the falling masonry into the tunnel, taking Stonker, Ursel, and Suzy with it.

25

Bad News Travels Fast

"Are you all ready?" Captain Neoma surveyed her platoon. She had assembled twelve of her most capable guards in the briefing bunker outside the Observatory, and they stood to rigid attention, their plate armor polished, their plasma rifles charged and ready.

"Yes, Captain!" they chorused.

"I won't lie to you," she said. "This is a dangerous mission against a powerful foe. We'll be outnumbered, but we'll have the element of surprise, and we need to use it to our advantage. In and out quickly, grab the snow globe, and go. Do I make myself clear?"

"Yes, Captain!"

One side of Neoma's mouth curled into a satisfied little

smile. "It certainly beats babysitting. Am I right?" She saw the smile reflected in the other women's faces. After all the intrigue and uncertainty, it felt good to be on the brink of a proper fight again. "Then why are we still standing here?" she barked. "Let's move out!"

She turned to lead them out of the bunker, only to find Lord Meridian standing in the doorway. "I'm afraid that won't be necessary, Captain," he said. "We no longer need to worry about the snow globe falling into the wrong hands. Or any hands, come to that."

"Sir?" Captain Neoma could already feel her pent-up excitement turning to agitation. From the shuffling of feet behind her, the guards felt the same. "Why not?"

"Because he's been destroyed, along with the Impossible Postal Express and its crew." He gave a resigned shrug. "It's a shame, I suppose. I had been rather looking forward to meeting them."

Neoma's excitement nosedived straight through agitation and into dejection. As much as she had grown to dislike that little brat Frederick in his absence, she hadn't wanted to see him dead. But Lord Meridian already seemed to have moved on.

"We'll have to recruit a replacement, of course," he said. "We can't afford to let the project fall behind. Have someone start canvassing the better schools in the Western Fenlands, would you?"

"But, sir," said Neoma. "What about Crepuscula?"

"What about her?" he said. "She's got no prize left to fight for. She'll return to the Obsidian Tower and sulk." He chuckled at the thought. "Now, if you wouldn't mind, I'd like you all back at your posts, please."

At a nod from Neoma, the guards trooped out, but with a fraction of their former enthusiasm. She followed them, trying to ignore her own disappointment. Not only had she been denied a fair fight with Crepuscula, but she would also never really know why Frederick had fled the Observatory.

She had been counting on him for some answers.

26

BLASTOFF!

The gargoyle set Crepuscula down in front of the row of tunnels, then launched itself back into the air with a snap of its wings. Cupping her chin in her hand, Crepuscula watched with resignation as the last of the broken tunnel mouth fell in. The flickering blackness flared bright purple for a second, there was a sudden inrush of air that sucked in clouds of dust like a huge vacuum cleaner, and then, with an anticlimactic fizz, the light was gone, leaving just the bare rock of the cliff face inside the shattered arch.

She was still standing there a minute later when, with a pounding of granite feet, the statues finally caught up with her. Having no breath to be short of, they simply stood and waited, following her half-vacant gaze and awaiting new orders. None came. She didn't even seem to have noticed their arrival.

"What have you done?"

Finally jogged out of her reverie, she looked around into the scowling features of Fletch. Unlike the statues, he was very much out of breath, red-faced and sweating from the long run from the post office. He braced his hands on his knees and pointed at the ruined tunnel mouth. "You've killed them."

"Yes, almost certainly." There was no triumph in her voice. "It's really quite unfortunate."

"Unfortunate? You've brought the tunnel down on them. It's a death sentence!"

"They were supposed to stop," she said. "But it seems I miscalculated."

"You're a monster," he said, plunging his hands into his pockets and turning his back on her. "And I'm sorry I ever set eyes on you. Do what you want, but I'm not helping you anymore."

"Have it your way," she said, and he flinched, expecting a blast of magic to strike him at any second. But when he looked back, she was still watching the tunnel mouth, as though expecting it to do something.

"Evil witch," he muttered to himself as he stalked quickly away. "If there were any justice, she'd have gone in with them." He sniffed. "And so would I, fool that I am." His hands were shaking, from shock and anger and grief, but he refused to let any of it show while he was still in sight of her.

He had only gone a small distance, picking his way along the tracks toward the center of town, when he heard her speak again.

"Boys? I want you to run along to the Ivory Tower and see if our friends on the train made it through. I'm not expecting good news, but it's better than not knowing." She clapped her hands, and the statues took off at a run, each heading for a different tunnel. Fletch watched them go with a mixture of awe and disgust. No living thing would ever dare set foot in a tunnel without a vehicle to see them safely through, but he supposed the statues were made of stronger stuff.

"No respect for the dead," he spat. "Or anyone else."

But watching the statues vanish into the tunnels stirred something else in him as well. It wasn't hope—he knew better than to hope for the impossible—but it felt a bit like it. It was adjacent to hope. It was uncertainty, in the face of insurmountable facts.

Stonker, Ursel, and the girl couldn't have survived the cave-in. It was impossible. And yet...

And yet Crepuscula had her doubts, small though they

may be. Enough doubts to send her army through to finish the job, in case it needed finishing.

Which it didn't. It couldn't.

Could it?

Fletch had wandered as far as the H. E. C. and sorting carriage, which stood, abandoned, on the main line where they had come to rest after being uncoupled from the *Belle de Loin.* They were all that remained of the Impossible Postal Express.

He rested a hand against the pitted iron hull of the H. E. C. It still trembled with life, thanks to the myriad machines inside it. He had worked on a few of them himself: machines to go anywhere, from the depths of the oceans to the farthest reaches of space.

And just like that, he knew what he had to do.

Crepuscula turned from the tunnels when a sudden flash of light temporarily lit the bridge like a second sun. She shielded her eyes from the glare and from the clouds of dust that billowed into the air.

Beyond her remaining guard of statues, some way back across the bridge, the H. E. C. rose into the air on a column of fire. It rose slowly at first, but gathered speed with an earsplitting roar, until it was a vanishing speck in the tan sky.

"What's that disagreeable creature doing now?"

Crepuscula said. "These trolls always find the most ridiculous means of hurling themselves about." She traced the capsule's trajectory until it disappeared from her sight completely. Then she turned back to the tunnels, and waited.

Fletch sat at the H. E. C.'s control panel and allowed himself a smile as the carriage rocketed through the cloud layer into a clear blue sky. He hadn't been sure the old crate would even make it off the chassis, it had been so long since it had flown, but everything was working as though it had been built yesterday.

"Made to last," he said, giving the panel an affectionate stroke. "Of course, they say the landing is the tricky bit."

He craned his neck, fighting against the g-forces that pinned him to the seat, and looked out of the starboard porthole. The curvature of the world was visible outside, and the blue sky was darkening to black as he left the atmosphere behind. His body relaxed a little as the g-forces began to slacken, and gravity released its hold on him. Soon, he would be completely weightless. "Good thing I skipped breakfast," he mused, making sure his seat belt was secured.

He made a few course adjustments and brought the H. E. C.'s nose around. Over the rim of the horizon, the moon was just rising.

27
TUNNEL TROUBLE

There was a noise like a thunderclap as the tunnel mouth fell in behind them. But unlike a thunderclap, the sound didn't fade away—it swallowed itself, turning into a sucking absence of noise that somehow felt every bit as loud.

Suzy suffered a moment of disorientation as her brain tried to process the sound that wasn't really there. She staggered, and Ursel caught her.

"Hrunk?"

"I'm okay," she said. "How's your arm?"

Ursel shrugged and hooked a claw in the direction of the fallen tunnel mouth. As if on cue, a burst of gray light

split the darkness in a web of fractures, reaching out from a ghostly furnace glow directly behind the train.

"What's going on?" screeched Frederick from her pocket. "What's all that noise? Somebody tell me what's happening!"

Ursel growled, her fur standing on end.

"Who said that?" yelled Stonker.

"Just pretend you didn't hear it," said Suzy, stuffing her hand into her pocket to muffle Frederick's voice. "And tell me how much trouble we're in."

"The tunnel's rolling up like a tube of toothpaste," said Stonker, who was welded so tightly to the controls they might have been a part of him. "We'll never make it through!"

"Can't we outrun it?" Suzy shouted, joining him and trying to make sense of the various dials and readouts.

"We're already at full speed," he shouted. "Everything's wide open—our pressure's in the red. It won't be enough!"

Suzy swallowed a lump of raw terror; she simply didn't have time to be scared right now. "What if we lost more mass?" she said, thinking aloud.

"What?" bellowed Stonker. "I can't hear you!"

Without wasting any more time on words, Suzy turned and raced to the ruined rear doorway. "Ursel! Help me!" She lay on her front and reached down out of the cab to the chain that coupled them to the still-blazing tender.

The pin locking it in place was even harder to remove than the one behind the tender had been and only started to give when Ursel leaned out and closed her teeth around it. They pulled together, and with much effort, it slid free. Suzy tossed it aside as Ursel unhooked the chain. Then, together, they put their weight against the tender and gave it a shove.

It separated from the cab and had only fallen a few feet behind them when the cave-in claimed it. Suzy, who had been expecting an explosion of debris, stared in fascination as the tender unfolded into a neat little fractal pattern of cubes and squares. Like crystals in a kaleidoscope, the shapes multiplied and folded in on themselves, smaller and smaller, until they formed a single point of matter, which was swallowed by the glare. Then it was simply ... gone.

Suzy stared into the gray fire, hypnotized. Just as she could sense the noise it made without actually hearing it, so she realized she couldn't actually see the cave-in properly. The light wasn't really light. If she turned her head just a little and looked at it from the corner of her eye, it strobed in and out of vision. She didn't understand it—this was something that even Einstein would have struggled with—but it was here. And it was getting closer.

"Did that help?" she yelled, retreating to Stonker's side.

The troll set his mouth in a hard line and glared at his instruments.

"We're lighter," he barked. "Might have bought us a few seconds."

"Is that enough?"

Stonker pressed his lips together until they almost disappeared. He gripped the controls so hard his knuckles glowed white. Then there was a *pop!* and one of the pipes beside the mantelpiece split, venting steam. Stonker flinched.

"We're pushing her too hard. She can't keep this up for long."

As if in confirmation, the glass in one of the pressure gauges shattered, and the needle inside it went flying past them, out of the back of the cab, straight into the maw of the cave-in.

"But we can't slow down," she said.

"I know."

Suzy watched the firestorm sucking up the rails like steel spaghetti just a few feet behind them, inching ever closer. "We can make it," she said.

He shook his head, as though it weighed more than he could bear. "Nobody's ever beaten a cave-in."

"Because nobody's ever tried it with the *Belle de Loin*," she said.

His answering smile was weak, but it lit a fire in her.

She reached out and placed a hand over his. Then she reached out to Ursel, who wrapped one huge paw around both their hands, locking them together.

Suzy didn't feel brave—not really—but pretending she did felt surprisingly close to the real thing.

"If we were about to die, you'd tell me, right?"

Suzy blushed as Frederick spoke up, and Stonker and Ursel both looked sideways at her.

"I'm trying to pretend I didn't hear it," said Stonker, "but he's making it rather difficult."

They all turned at a dull, metallic note behind them and immediately shrank back against the fireplace. The gray fire of the cave-in was pressing right up against the back of the cab now. Through the empty doorway they could see it unraveling the loose coupling chain into a dizzying series of loops that stretched out to impossible distances before being compressed into nothing. Within a few seconds, half the chain had gone and the rear wall of the cab began to stretch and distort.

"It's got us!" said Stonker. "Once it reaches the wheels, we're done for."

Brick by brick, the rear wall began unraveling, breaking into strings of two-dimensional matter. Inch by inch, the *Belle de Loin* was being devoured.

"All hands to the gangway!" ordered Stonker. "We've got to stay ahead of it."

Suzy pulled the door open, and Ursel scooped her and Stonker up under one arm, loping along the gangway in huge, swinging strides. "I'm afraid this is it," said Stonker as Ursel set them both down at the far end of the gangway. The fractures were all around the train now, huge and jagged and inescapable. "May I just say, it's been an honor serving with you both." He adjusted his jacket and snapped off a salute.

"What?" screamed Frederick. "This can't be right! You're supposed to protect me. You promised!"

Suzy barely noticed. In fact, she hardly felt anything, not even fear. There was no use for it anymore—the worst was happening. They had lost, and her heart felt like it was breaking. "I didn't want it to be like this," she sobbed. "It's all my fault. I'm sorry, I'm so sorry. I thought I was doing the right thing." Tears started from her eyes, breaking Ursel, Stonker, and the glaring tunnel into a blurry mess of colors. "We were so close! It almost worked! It almost—"

"Hurk!"

Ursel grabbed Suzy again, and she thought that Stonker thrust his hand out in front of her face, pointing wildly at something. She turned to look, but everything was a kaleidoscope of black and gray. And then, suddenly, shining white, and a blast of new air that tasted like copper and dust and furniture polish.

Stonker burst out laughing in her ear, and she pressed her palms to her face, forcing the tears away. She opened her eyes to another world.

The *Belle de Loin* raced along beneath a milky-white sky, crisscrossed with glittering trails of silver. There were hundreds of them, like a giant spider's web, and it was only when Suzy saw other trains hurrying along them that she realized they were rails. They hung unsupported in the air, as though weightless, each of them ending in a tunnel mouth that seemed to be set into the very sky itself.

Suzy leaned out over the handrail, the wind whipping at her hair, and saw that, sure enough, the rails beneath the *Belle*'s wheels were floating in the air like all the others. That wasn't too surprising. What was surprising was that there was no ground in sight below them, just more sky. It surrounded them in every direction for as far as she could see—flat, white, and featureless except for the tunnel mouths.

The final death of their own tunnel was audible as a muffled explosion behind them. The cave-in had done its work, leaving nothing inside the archway but an expanse of fractured white rock.

Suzy looked again and finally realized, with a shock

of revelation that left her breathless, that they weren't surrounded by sky at all; they were inside a gargantuan sphere of white stone, perhaps a hundred miles across, glowing softly with its own inner light. They had emerged through one of its walls and were racing toward the center.

The *Belle*'s wheels were screaming in triumph. Suzy, Stonker, and Ursel screamed with them, hugging each other and letting the wind carry away their tears of relief and elation.

"We made it!" Stonker clapped Suzy on the shoulder and jumped up and down with excitement. "I can hardly believe it, but we made it. Look!" He pointed ahead of them, and Suzy squinted into the onrushing wind.

An immense column of white stone stood in the center of the sphere, running from top to bottom like the core of an apple.

"The Ivory Tower!" said Suzy.

"So we're *not* going to die now?" said Frederick. "Honestly, why can't you people keep me up to date?" She ignored him.

"How do we get inside it?" she said.

"Through Center Point Station," Stonker said, jabbing a finger toward a ring of sleek white buildings surrounding the center of the tower.

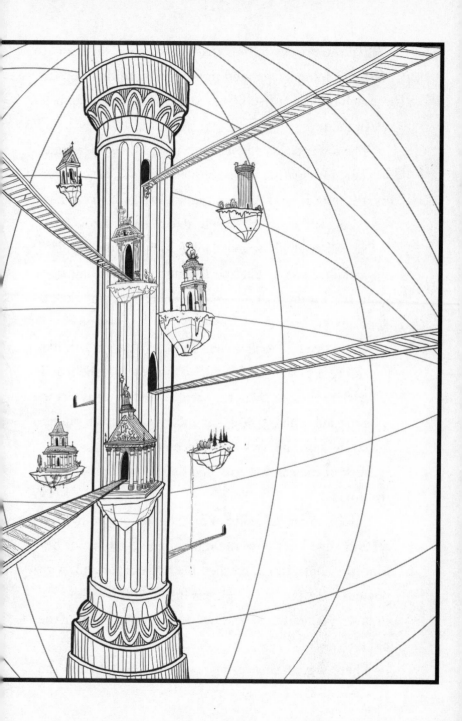

Like the dozens of rails that led to them, the station buildings hung suspended in the air and didn't appear to touch the tower itself. Suzy could see a large gap between them.

"The tower doesn't let just anyone in, remember," said Stonker, anticipating her next question. "We have to get off at Center Point and show them a Fact of Entry. Then the tower will lower the drawbridge to let us across."

She followed his finger, looking for the drawbridge. She couldn't see it, but she did notice something else about the tower. "Uh . . . ," she said. "It's getting closer. Very quickly."

"Good grief!" Stonker went rigid. "What am I thinking? I forgot to slow us down!" He pushed past them and ran back to the cab. Suzy ran after him, so she was just in time to catch him by the collar and save him from plunging straight off the back of the locomotive.

Most of the cab was missing: Barely two feet of floor remained.

"It took so much," said Suzy as Stonker dusted himself off and edged out onto the remaining stub of floor behind the controls. He reached the brake lever and, with obvious care, put his weight against it. "I'll have to slow us down gradually, or the shock will tear what's left of the old girl apart."

There was an answering screech of metal from the

chassis, and the brake lever began to vibrate like a tuning fork. Stonker vibrated with it.

"Come on!" he grunted. He pushed the lever over harder. The screech of the brake blocks grew louder.

And then the lever broke. It came up out of the floor with a short, sharp *snap!* and Suzy had to grab Stonker again to stop him from pitching over the edge and onto the track. He held up the severed lever and stared at it in horrified wonder.

"Oh dear," he said.

Suzy looked from his wide, scared eyes to the useless length of lever. "What do we do now?" she said.

"Frumf," said Ursel, sticking her head in through the door.

"I'm afraid she's right," said Stonker. "There's nothing we can do. We're a runaway train."

28

BREAKING AND ENTERING

"Maybe we could jump," said Stonker.

Suzy took one look at the blur of track racing past just beneath their feet. "At this speed?" she said. "We'd be smashed to pieces." She buried her fingers in her hair and clenched them into fists, willing her brain to work more quickly. It refused. "I'm out of ideas," she said.

"So am I," said Stonker. "At least we'll go out with our boots on."

"I'm not wearing boots," said Suzy. "And I refuse to die in my slippers. There must be something we can do."

"There isn't," he said, calmer now. She could tell he was already preparing himself for the inevitable and wanted to remain dignified to the last. "We're going to hit Center Point like a sledgehammer."

She fought her way past Ursel and onto the gangway, suddenly desperate to see the final, fatal end of their journey.

Center Point raced toward them, a yawning mouth with a curved glass roof, already close enough for her to see the busy platforms inside. Their track dead-ended in heavy buffers, beyond which was a large concourse filled with people. Behind that, the station's rear glass wall offered a spectacular view of the Ivory Tower. She supposed she might appreciate it more if it wasn't about to kill them.

"Just so I'm clear," said Frederick, "we're about to die again?"

"Shut up," she said.

"This is it," said Stonker. "Brace yourselves." He let a long, screaming note out of the *Belle*'s whistle as they rocketed into the station. Heads turned. People ran.

Suzy threw herself back into the cab and wrapped her arms around as much of the pipework as she could, a second before the *Belle* hit the buffers with a crash and jumped free of the tracks. Suzy's feet left the ground. She caught glimpses of people leaping clear as the *Belle* slammed back down, barely slowing as it plowed a screeching furrow of sparks and shrapnel across the concourse. Ursel howled, and even Stonker cried out as they smashed pastry stands and ticket barriers to scrap beneath their wheels.

Suzy tightened her grip on the pipes and turned her face away from the flying debris outside. And there, right in front of her, was the dial with the words THIS WAY UP. A sudden, desperate idea flared in her mind. "Is gravity really negotiable?" she shouted.

"Usually!" Stonker yelled back. "But why do you want to—"

Then, with an almighty crash, the locomotive smashed through the station's rear glass wall and flung itself off into the gulf between the station and the tower. There was a horrible moment of weightlessness as the *Belle*'s forward momentum fought to stave off the pull of gravity. Suzy felt her feet leave the floor again, but this time they didn't come back down, as they began their fatal plunge toward the bottom of the sphere, so many miles below.

She twisted the dial.

For a second, she was afraid her idea had failed. They were still falling. But as she looked out of the cab, she realized they weren't falling *down* anymore. The dial had done its job—she had shifted the pull of gravity on the train, and they were falling *sideways*. Straight toward the tower.

"Hang on!" she shouted as the huge wall of white stone

filled the view through the front windows. It was massive, maybe even bigger than the Obsidian Tower, and as it grew closer she could see stained glass windows blazing in a rainbow of colors in its sides.

"Are you mad?" Stonker cried in her ear. He was hanging on to her arm with both hands, the rest of his body suspended in the air behind her. Ursel, who was gripping the mantelpiece with her uninjured paw, looked equally unhappy.

"I know what I'm doing!" Suzy cried, praying that it was true.

Ursel grunted and pointed through the front window. They were heading straight for one of the stained glass windows.

"Hold on!" Stonker shouted, and ducked his head against Suzy's shoulder. Ursel wrapped the two of them in her huge arms, and Suzy buried her face in the bear's warm fur.

Glass smashed. Then there was a jarring shock, a dull explosion, and everything went dark.

"Are we alive? Did we make it?"

Frederick's voice reached Suzy through roiling clouds of dust and smoke. She sat up and waited for everything to stop spinning.

The *Belle de Loin* lay at a drunken angle, surrounded by the wreckage of the stained glass window. A few embers guttered in the cab's fireplace, and the cooling metal of the boiler ticked and pinged. Otherwise, the great locomotive was finally silent and still.

"I think we did," she said, her voice jittery with adrenaline. "Is everyone all right?"

The floor stirred underneath her, and she realized that she was sitting on top of a tangle of yellow fur and oversized mustache. She rolled aside as Ursel and Stonker both sat up.

"Grunk," said the bear, rubbing herself on the head.

"Yes," said Stonker. "It's not quite how I would have chosen to get here, but we all seem to be in one piece. How's our mystery guest?" He nodded at the bulge in Suzy's pocket.

"I'm fine, no thanks to you lot," said Frederick. "Now let's go before something even worse happens."

"Go?" Stonker raised his eyebrows, unleashing a puff of dust from each of them. "Go where?"

"We've got to find the library," said Suzy. "We're looking for a book."

"Then you're in luck," said Stonker. "Look around you."

The last of the dust had settled, and Suzy was finally able to see the space they had invaded. A great many old wooden bookcases lay strewn around like toppled dominoes, and the walls were lined from floor to ceiling with yet more shelves. Books lay in piles amid the debris, their pages torn and dirtied.

"Oh dear," she said. What if *Harmful Spells and How to Break Them* was among the wreckage?

Stonker climbed to his feet and inspected the controls. Every single one of them was dead: the glass in the panels cracked, the mantelpiece broken, the carriage clock smashed to fragments on the floor. He prodded the embers in the fireplace with his toe. They let out a weak cough of sparks and died. He rested his forehead against the ruined pipework and drew in a shuddering breath. "I hope this is worth it," he said with a quaver in his voice.

As she looked around at the devastation, Suzy wasn't at all sure that it was. The damage to the library was bad, but the damage to the *Belle* was even worse. Suzy wasn't sure the old locomotive would ever run again, and the thought brought a lump to her throat. She wanted to say something to Stonker and Ursel, to reassure them, but knew she didn't have the words.

"Don't just stand there gawking!" said Frederick. "We need to get to the advanced magical practice section, and the guard will be here any minute."

"You do what you must," said Stonker, sounding old and tired all of a sudden. "We'll stay here with the..." He patted the mantelpiece, and a chunk of it came away in his hand. "...with the wreck. I can't just abandon her here. Besides, I expect we'll have some explaining to do once the authorities arrive."

The sound of many running boots reached them from the depths of the library.

"I didn't want any of this to happen," she said, backing away. "But it really is for the best." *Is it, though?* The treacherous little itch in her brain wasn't so certain, but she chose to ignore it. She didn't want to imagine what it would mean to discover she was wrong, after everything that had happened. "Crepuscula wants to take control of the Union. If I can find the right book, I can use it to help expose her plan and stop her. I know it sounds crazy, but I'll explain it all properly when I get back. I promise."

Stonker nodded, and Ursel put a comforting arm around him. Then, with the sound of boots growing closer, Suzy turned and ran.

29

In Pursuit of Knowledge

The library was big. Suzy had assumed the *Belle* had crashed into its main hall, but she quickly realized that it was just a side room. As she scrambled over the fallen bookcases and around the locomotive's crumpled boiler, she passed through an ornate wooden archway into an even larger space. This one reached up several stories, with a broad spiral staircase wrapping around it and several landings on which she could see countless rows of shelves all stuffed to bursting with more books.

"Where do we start?" she said, pulling Frederick out of her pocket.

"Third floor," he said. "Second room on your right. The advanced magical practice section."

She pressed her nose against the snow globe and glared in at him. "How do you know that?"

He hesitated, but only for a second. "I'm a genius, remember? Now come on!"

Before she could argue, there were signs of movement at the top of the staircase, and the sound of more boots arriving at a run.

"The Lunar Guard!" he hissed. "Hide!"

Suzy dashed for cover behind one of the large, free-standing bookcases in the center of the room. It was tall enough to screen her from sight from the landing above, but faced the bottom of the stairs so, by removing a couple of the books and peering through the gap, she had a perfect view of the guards as they clattered down the final flight, weapons at the ready.

She frowned. They were all young women, wearing matching silver jumpsuits beneath plate armor and heavy utility belts. They all wore their hair in a pageboy cut, each dyed a different color—she saw acid green, fire-engine red, and neon blue jog past. Each of them carried a chunky silver rifle, and Suzy got the distinct impression they knew how to use them.

"Look alive, ladies," their sergeant barked. "Secure the

crash site and check for any wounded. And stay frosty—you know how important this is."

Suzy shrank back as the sergeant took a last look around the room before jogging after her squad.

"What happens if they find us?" Suzy whispered.

"Nothing good," Frederick said. "So please, let's get a move on before reinforcements arrive." It was enough to stir Suzy to her feet.

"Third floor?" she said.

"Second room on the right. And quickly!"

She padded as quickly and quietly as she could up the stairs, aware that she had nowhere to hide should anyone step out onto one of the landings above them. It was a long climb, which gave her time to pick at the stray thread of another unanswered question. "Why are they called the Lunar Guard?" she whispered.

"Why do you think?" said Frederick.

"Well, *lunar* means anything to do with the moon," she said, trying to keep one eye on the room below them, in case any of the guards reappeared. "But we're not...oh."

And suddenly it all clicked into place. Everything she had seen since she had jumped aboard the Impossible

Postal Express, all the places she had been, all the things she had learned: There was one thing connecting them all.

"We're on the moon," she said. "We're *inside* the moon. It's hollow!"

"Of course we're inside it," said Frederick. "Where else would we be?"

She almost laughed at the realization. It had been there in the nebulous sky above the Obsidian Tower. The sailors of the *La Rouquine* had used it to navigate by and had put it on their rum bottles. And she had seen it in Trollville, carved above the entrance to the post office. Three different Impossible Places, all with the same moon.

"But it's *my* moon," she said, reaching the first landing. "I mean, the actual *moon* moon. The one that orbits Earth."

"So? It orbits everywhere."

But how was such a thing possible? She was tempted to duck through an archway to another room, labeled LUNAR HISTORY, but crept on past it.

"Center Point Station..." She thought aloud as she started up the next flight of stairs. "It's not just a name, is it. The moon is the center of the Union."

"The one point where it all meets and overlaps, yes," said Frederick. "It's the Meridian. Like the hub in the middle of a wheel, showing its face into each Impossible Place equally. Honestly, this is the most basic geography."

But there was still something wrong. Something that didn't fit. "Then why can I see it from Earth?" she said. "Earth isn't part of the Union."

"How should I know?" he said. "Just hurry up before our luck changes."

Too late. There were the sounds of more footsteps from downstairs, and the voice of the sergeant reached them.

"Secure this floor. Backup's on the way."

Suzy scampered up the remaining stairs to the next landing, thankful that her slippers muffled her footsteps. She was halfway up the third and final flight when a door banged open somewhere above her, and the sound of more heavy boots reverberated through the library.

"Quickly!" hissed Frederick.

She clutched him to her chest and ran, mounting the top of the stairs and sprinting along the landing to the second archway. Sure enough, the sign above it read ADVANCED MAGICAL PRACTICE, and as she ducked through it she caught a brief glimpse of the first reinforcements clattering out onto the landings above. There were a lot of them.

Suzy huddled against the wall just inside the arch and listened to the new squads thunder past outside, so close they made the floor quake beneath her. Over the noise, a voice from the landing called out, "Sergeant Mona, what's the situation down there?"

"Crash site secured," came the sergeant's distant reply. "Two crew, one with an injured arm. We're tending to her now."

"Do either of them have the snow globe?"

Suzy tensed.

"No," said the sergeant. "They claim to know nothing about it, but the human girl is missing. We've started a search."

"We're here to assist you," said the speaker on the landing. "Lord Meridian wants that snow globe at all costs."

The hairs stood up on the back of Suzy's neck. *They know all about us!* Her hiding place, already precarious, suddenly seemed even more exposed.

"We'll take each floor in turn," said the speaker, her voice starting to fade as she descended the stairs. "Work our way up."

"Did you hear that?" hissed Frederick as the woman's footsteps receded. "You really need to hurry."

But Suzy didn't move and instead tightened her grip on him until his glass squeaked between her palms. "They know who we are," she said.

"Can't we worry about it later?"

"No." She gave him a hard look. "You've been lying to me again."

"I haven't, I promise!"

"You know your way around the library. The guards

knew we were coming. Lord Meridian is looking for you! You've been here before."

She heard him swallow, although he had no throat to do it with. "Maybe."

Suzy screwed her eyes shut—she was so furious, she couldn't even bear to look at him. "I've risked my life— I've risked other people's lives—to help you. Wilmot died saving us, and you still can't tell me the truth." She swallowed a lump of rage. "I'm going to hand you over."

"You wouldn't!"

His challenge was all she needed, and a calm determination filled her as she stepped out onto the landing. She was going to do it. She didn't doubt herself.

"You've come too far to give it all up now!" he whispered, his voice tight with fear. "You don't know what you're doing!"

"Watch me." She could hear the guards tramping to and fro below them. It would only be a few seconds before one of them looked up and saw her.

"I work here," he said, the words almost falling over one another, he spat them out so quickly. "At least, I did until I ran away. There. Are you happy now?"

She wasn't, but she brought him back to eye level. "Tell me why," she said. "And make it good."

"I'm a spy," Frederick said. "There are hundreds of us here. We're called observers."

"Do you really expect me to believe that?" she snapped. "Why would a library need spies?"

She had retreated with him through the archway to the cover of the shelves again and was backing along the aisles, keeping one eye on the titles she passed. *The Joys of Levitation*; *You'll Believe a Man Can Fly*; *Gravity Is for Wimps*...

"Because it's not just a library anymore. Lord Meridian changed all that."

"The keeper of the tower?"

"He's obsessed with knowledge," he said. "Hungry for it. The tower's collection isn't enough for him. He wants more, and faster. He wants to know *everything*."

"That's ridiculous," she chided. "No one can know everything. It's impossible."

"You haven't met him," he said. "He's not like you or me. Once he learns a fact, he never forgets it. They say he can recite every book in this library, word for word, from memory. And when he ran out of books, he set up the Observatory."

Suzy frowned. "He wants to study astronomy?"

"No," he said. "He wants to study the Union. It's a magical observatory, staffed with observers like me, and each of us is assigned an Impossible Place to watch over. We record everything we see and hear."

Suzy paused to pull a book down from the nearest shelf: *VWORP, VWORP—Advanced Dematerialization*. She replaced it and hurried on. "So what were you spying on?"

"The Western Fenlands," he grumbled.

"You mean that country you're definitely not the prince of?"

"I was born there," he muttered. "I hated it."

"So I guessed," said Suzy. "But you said you grew up on a farm. So how on earth did you end up here?"

"I got a letter one day," he said. "A handwritten invitation from Lord Meridian himself. He said word had reached him about how clever I was, and he wanted me to work on his new 'research project.' All top secret stuff. He offered me room and board here in the tower, access to the library, and a full education at the end of it. It was like a dream come true. At first."

"What changed?"

"Crepuscula." An edge of fear crept back into his voice. "I don't know how she found me, but I looked through my spyglass one morning and she was just standing there, staring back at me. Like she knew I'd be watching." Suzy felt a little thrill of fear and shivered on his behalf. "She told me she knew Lord Meridian was working on something big, and she offered to make me a very rich young man if I could get her proof of it. I had to gather as much information as I could on the Observatory—who we were watching, how we were doing it, and why—and put it all in a NeuroGlobe she'd send me."

Suzy stared at him in horror. "And you agreed?" she said. "After everything Lord Meridian had done for you!"

"It's not as simple as that," he replied, although the shame in his voice was palpable. "I thought if I went home with a fortune, my parents would be pleased to see me. We could leave the farm and buy a proper house somewhere that didn't stink of cows all the time. And I'd finally have somewhere I wanted to stay, with a family that wanted me."

Suzy still wasn't sure whether or not to believe him, but part of her half hoped this story was a lie. Because it was a very sad story, and, if true, she would have to feel sorry for him. And she was still too angry with him to want to do that.

She turned the corner into the next aisle, and the first book she picked off the shelf was called *Spells of Transformation*. A quick flip through the pages told her it was mostly concerned with changing base metals into gold, but they were definitely getting closer.

"Why didn't you want to stay here?" she said. "I thought this was your dream job."

"It turned out to be really, really dull," said Frederick. "Lord Meridian had me watch the Fenlands parliament building for a whole year. Everyone from the premier and his advisers down to the cleaning ladies. I assumed the other observers were studying really fun stuff, but we're not allowed to discuss our findings with each other, so I never knew what any of them were looking at until I started gathering evidence for Crepuscula. I had to ask a few leading questions here, eavesdrop on a few sneaky conversations there. It took me months, but I finally started putting the pieces together."

"And? What did you find?"

"That the 'research project' wasn't what Lord Meridian said it was," he said. "We were supposed to be studying everything from crop rotation to animal migrations, but really we were all looking at the same thing—people of influence. Monarchs, politicians, generals, and business people all across the Union."

"But why?"

"Have you ever heard that expression 'Knowledge is power'?"

Suzy frowned as she considered the implications. She was beginning to have a very bad feeling indeed. "Spying on that many powerful people," she said. "If he knows everything they know, he'd be more powerful than any of them."

"Exactly," said Frederick. "No one would be able to stand against him, except maybe for Crepuscula, and that's only because she's even worse than he is. She's already one of the most dangerous people in the Union, and if she ever finds out just how big the Observatory project really is, and decides to get her hands on it...no one would be safe from her."

Suzy shuddered at the thought. "We can't let that happen."

"Agreed," he said. "This should be the place. Check the shelf."

She stopped and scanned the spines. "I don't see it," she said. "But I think there's one missing. Look." She held him up so he could see the one empty space on the shelf. "Someone must have taken it."

"Who?" He was starting to sound frantic.

"Who do you think, Frederick?" said a woman's voice, a second before a figure stepped out from the shadows in front of them.

"Oh no!" he squealed. "Not her! Run, Suzy!"

But Suzy couldn't run. She was frozen to the spot by the sight of the rifle pointing straight at her.

30

MEETING MERIDIAN

Suzy stared at the white-hot energy crackling deep within the barrel of the rifle, which was held by one of the Lunar Guard. Her bubble-gum pink hair fell to her shoulders, which bore a captain's insignia, and Suzy caught the flash of a gold tooth as the woman gave a triumphant sneer.

"Captain Neoma," said Frederick, his voice cracking with fear. "What are you doing here?"

"Waiting for you," she said. "Lord Meridian has the book you're looking for and invites you to join him in his study for a little chat. Probably about why you slipped past my guards and blew a smoking hole in my otherwise flawless career."

Without taking her eyes from Suzy, she unclipped a small radio from her belt and spoke into it. "Sergeant Mona? I've apprehended the fugitives. Inform His Lordship, and bring the other intruders up to the advanced magical practice section."

"Wait," said Suzy. "You don't know what you're doing."

"I know exactly what I'm doing," said Neoma, replacing the radio. "Frederick here tried to sell us all out to Crepuscula, and now he's going to pay the price. A few decades in a prison cell ought to do it."

"No!" they both chorused.

Sergeant Mona's squad thundered into the room in two neat rows, with Stonker and Ursel between them. Ursel wore a field dressing on her arm. They both had their arms cuffed in front of them.

"Hello, Suzy," said Stonker, out of breath from the forced march. "I'm afraid it's not going terribly well."

"Quiet," snapped Neoma, ignoring Ursel's answering growl. "Sergeant, I need you to stay here and get this library secure. The rest of you, come with me. Let's not keep His Lordship waiting."

A large, rattling antique lift carried them from the library to the heights of the tower, where they stepped out into a short length of corridor. A reinforced door at the

opposite end was labeled OBSERVATORY. NO ENTRY WITH-
OUT PERMISSION.

"House rules," said Neoma, pausing outside it. "You
will not speak to any of the personnel on the other side
of this door. You will not touch or otherwise interfere with
any of the equipment you see. We take our security very
seriously."

"Then why are we allowed in at all?" said Suzy.

"A good question," said Neoma. "But I don't second-
guess His Lordship's orders. I just follow them."

They all fell into step behind her as the door swung
open, and she marched them inside.

"Wow," Suzy breathed, staring around at the rows of
desks, the elaborate domed ceiling, and the Great Spyglass on its dais in the center. "It really does look like an
observatory."

The observers had all turned from their desks to watch
the group's progress as Neoma cut across the center of
the room, around the base of the Great Spyglass, to the
curator's office. She knocked and waited for the muffled "Come in," before ushering Suzy, Stonker, and
Ursel inside. The rest of the guards took up positions
outside the door.

"Lord Meridian," Neoma said, saluting. "As per your
orders, I have—"

"Suzy Smith." A small old man in a gray suit rose from

the leather armchair in which he had been sitting. Ignoring Neoma, he took Suzy by the hand and shook it. His skin felt cool and dry as old paper. "It's so nice to see you in the flesh. You've had quite a time of it, my dear, quite a time, but here you are at last. Welcome." He released her. "And J. F. Stonker, driver of the Impossible Postal Express." He shook Stonker's shackled hand as well. "Congratulations on outrunning that cave-in. A first for any locomotive, unless I'm very much mistaken. Which I'm not."

"Oh," said Stonker, pleasantly perplexed by the whole experience. "Thank you very much."

"Perhaps now you can let go of the guilt of your rather shabby past." Lord Meridian smiled and released Stonker's hand, letting the troll recoil, open-mouthed with shock.

"How do you know...?" Stonker croaked. But Lord Meridian had already moved on to Ursel, resting a hand on her uninjured paw.

"And a locomotive is nothing without its firewoman, of course," he said. "You're a credit to your species, and your employer, Ursel. And doing it all with a broken heart, no less."

Ursel shook herself free of the old man's touch and bared her fangs in a snarl.

"Please don't think me discourteous," said Lord

Meridian, turning his back on her. "But I've been admiring the efforts of the Impossible Postal Express from afar for quite some time now, and I feel as though I know you all rather well. Better than you know one another, perhaps."

He perched on the edge of his desk. "Of course, I've spent so much time looking out into the Union when I should probably have paid closer attention to what was happening right under my nose. Isn't that right, Frederick?"

Frederick gave an anxious little squeak as Neoma plucked him from Suzy's grasp and handed him over.

"Please, sir," he cried. "I'll give you the information back. Just let me go. I'll do anything!"

"I don't doubt it." Meridian set Frederick down on the desk. "That's the trouble with hiring the morally flexible. They make excellent observers, but incorrigible traitors. I really should have seen it coming." He chuckled at his own joke.

"So it's true?" said Suzy. "You've been spying on the Union?"

"I've been observing it," said Meridian. "You see, as keeper of the Ivory Tower, I have an obligation to gather knowledge for the improvement of the Impossible Places, and what better way to gather that knowledge than to study them directly? The more I know, the more improvements I can make, and I know more than anyone. I alone can see the big picture." He raised his cane and pointed past them, through the window overlooking the Observatory. "That's what all this is for—amassing the pieces of the big picture and putting them together, in here." He tapped himself on the forehead. "Speaking of which, I believe you brought a piece of it for me yourself. Captain?"

Neoma had confiscated Fletch's wand and the Fact of Entry in the elevator, and now handed them over. Meridian took the wand between a finger and thumb.

"You were planning to restore Frederick with this?" he said, wrinkling his nose. "Dear me, no. It's not compatible with a transfiguration spell at all. It would be like playing the violin with a hammer." He gave an exaggerated shudder at the prospect and tossed the wand onto his desk before turning his attention to the Fact of Entry.

"Ah yes," he said. "Mr. Trellis's encounter at the Mountains of Madness. Very intriguing." He pressed the Neuro-Globe to his forehead and closed his eyes. Suzy watched as the clockwork inside the glass began turning more quickly, and the ribbon of red energy zipped around between them. There was a quick pulse of red light from the depths of the globe, and Lord Meridian smiled. "Very intriguing indeed," he said. "I can see why he was so tempted to accept the offer."

The clockwork slowed, and he opened his eyes again

before dropping the sphere into his jacket pocket. "Excellent. We don't have this in the archive, and a new fact is always to be welcomed. My thanks."

"I don't want your thanks," said Suzy.

"Of course not. You want something in return." He crossed to the bookcase behind his desk and pulled down a large, leather-bound volume. Suzy didn't have to read the gold-embossed title to know what it said: *Harmful Spells and How to Break Them.* "I have very few moral obligations as keeper of the tower, but fair exchange of knowledge is one of them. It's something of a sacred duty."

"Please, Suzy," piped up Frederick. "Just do as he says. I want to be me again."

"You'll find everything you need on page seventy-six," said Meridian, passing her the book. "I'll even lend you my own wand, as a favor." Suzy ran her fingers over the cover, but some instinct warned her not to open it. "Go on," prompted Meridian. "You did make the boy a promise, after all."

Suzy felt a cold chill steal over her skin. "You've been watching me, too?"

"Of course. You've been caring for Frederick, and I didn't dare let him out of my sight once I'd found him again. He knows too much."

"You mean he knows what you're really doing here," said Suzy.

311

Meridian fixed her with eyes as cold as moonlight. "Does he, now?"

"No, I don't!" said Frederick. "Don't listen to her!"

Suzy glared at him. Why was he trying to lie again now? "He told me everything," she said. "You're not watching the Impossible Places. You're just watching their leaders. And I think I know why."

"She doesn't!" said Frederick. "Honest. She doesn't know what she's saying!"

"Do tell," said Meridian, ignoring him.

"I think you're doing it to take control," she said. "You can make the leaders do anything you like—because you know their most valuable secrets, all their plans and weaknesses. You don't even need an army, because you can control everything from here. The leaders will work for you in secret, and nobody will even realize it."

For a moment, the room was silent. Then Neoma spoke, very quietly.

"My lord, is this true?"

"Of course not, Captain." He dismissed the notion with a wave of his hand. "You should know better than to believe such nonsense."

This did nothing to remove the troubled look from Neoma's face, however. Her eyes strayed to the window and the desks outside it. "Yes, sir, but maybe we need more transparency. We're watching five hundred Impossible

Places at once, and nobody but you really knows what we're learning. And then there's all the meetings you've been holding. What if we—"

She was interrupted by a squeal from her radio, and a panicked voice broke out of it. *"Intruders in the library! We're under attack! I repeat, we're under—"* The voice was lost amid a rending of wood, which was itself drowned out by a deep, unearthly bellow that Suzy knew all too well and that set the hairs on her arms on end.

"Oh no," she murmured. "They followed us."

Captain Neoma, meanwhile, unshouldered her rifle. "Looks like I'm going to get that fight after all," she said with a grim smile. "Crepuscula's here."

31

A TRUTH FOR A TRUTH

Lord Meridian's face darkened as a distant explosion rocked the tower, shaking a fall of dust from the ceiling. "Captain? I thought you'd tripled the perimeter patrols."

"I did, sir. Right up until you told me we had nothing left to worry about."

More sounds of destruction crackled through the radio, and another explosion shook books from the shelves.

"A rare miscalculation on my part," he said. "I didn't think Crepuscula would continue her pursuit once the tunnel collapsed."

"Your orders, sir?" Neoma sounded impatient.

"Fight her off, of course," he said. "She clearly wants

control of the Observatory. She cannot be allowed to have it."

Neoma gave him an appraising stare, and for a second Suzy thought she might refuse the order. But then Neoma flicked a switch on the side of her rifle, and it hummed to life with a buzz of energy. "Yes, sir." She kicked the office door open and led the waiting guards away at a run, although she spared a second to glance back at Suzy. Her look of doubt hadn't fled entirely, and Suzy now felt it reflected in her own face. Something was wrong. Not the secret dictator and his insidious spy program, or the army of evil statues that was probably about to kill them all. This was something else, something that didn't quite fit with what she already knew. That itch in her brain was back again.

Meridian made a quick gesture in the air with his cane, and the door swung shut by itself. "This really is very troubling," he said.

"Why?" said Frederick. "Don't you think the Lunar Guard can win?"

"I was talking about the four of you," said Meridian. "You're far too well informed, despite young Frederick's best efforts to keep the whole truth to himself." He looked to Suzy. "You really should have believed him when he told you some things are too dangerous to know. Now something will have to be done about it."

"Wait," said Stonker, looking the old man in the face for the first time since they had shaken hands. "D'you mean to say that Suzy's story is true? You're going to take control of the Union's leaders?"

"Not 'going to,'" Lord Meridian said. "I already control them."

"But that's appalling!"

Meridian shrugged. "Somebody has to do it."

"No, they don't," said Stonker. "And even if they did, why should it be you?"

"Oh, that's easy," said Meridian. "I know best."

Suzy couldn't detect any hint of malice or mockery in his voice, but it didn't make his words any less disturbing. Stonker looked equally horrified.

"You've really no need to worry," Meridian said. "Letting people choose their own leaders is wonderful in theory, but they keep making the *wrong* choices. Better to have someone in charge who knows what they're doing, wouldn't you say? And I really am doing a lot of good."

"Like what?" said Suzy.

"Reforming things," said Meridian. "Building up those things that deserve their place, and pruning those that don't. Take the Ether Web, for instance."

Stonker gawked at him. "You're behind that?"

"Unofficially. But yes, it's one of my proudest achievements. Instant transfer of information across the Union, and all of it filtered and managed by me. If there's something I want the people of the Union to know, I can tell them in a heartbeat. And if there's something I think they're better off not knowing, well…" He smiled. "I can see that it's lost. The Web has changed everything."

"It's put a lot of good trolls out of work for one thing," said Stonker, starting to flush red at the tips of his ears.

"Yes." Meridian adopted a look of studious solemnity. "The Troll Post network is an unfortunate but necessary casualty of progress, I'm afraid. You were revolutionary in your day, but it's time to yield to the future." He nodded, as though confirming his own conclusion. "And the same is true for troll technology in general, wouldn't you agree? It might be entertaining, but it's rarely efficient, and never consistent. No two machines are ever alike! We deserve better."

"It gets the job done," said Stonker, the angry blush creeping down his ears to his cheeks. "And it's made with real heart."

"The troll elders told me much the same thing," said Meridian. "Until I threatened to stage a hostile takeover of Trollville by the Vampire Kings of Chiroptera. They've had their beady, night-vision eyes on the Fourth Bridge for years. Ideal for roosting under, apparently."

"I refuse to stand here and take this!" said Stonker.

"But you already have," said Meridian. "I've been

diverting funds and resources away from Troll Territory and toward other, more promising projects for over a year now. When there's nothing left worth keeping, I'll have your elders sell the land to someone who can put it to better use. It's sad in many ways, I know, but I can hardly reshape the Union without cutting away the dead wood, now, can I?"

Stonker was positively apoplectic now. "Trolls are not 'dead wood'!"

Meridian shrugged again. "We'll have to agree to disagree. Of course, the great irony is that all this power is only effective as long as nobody suspects it exists. The leaders will all keep my secret to protect their own secrets, but if the Impossible Places at large ever find out about it, the game's up. People are harder to manipulate when they know they're being manipulated. That's why I can't afford any loose ends."

The words shook Suzy out of her reverie. "What are you going to do to us?" she asked.

"I was considering an amnesia spell," he said. "But one only has to overlook a single detail among all those tangled memories and emotions and everything comes flooding back." He made a clucking sound with his tongue as he thought. "No, it will have to be a complete mind wipe, I'm afraid."

"A what?" she said, backing away.

"That's monstrous," said Stonker. "Not to mention illegal."

"Nothing is illegal for me anymore," said Meridian. "But for what it's worth, I am sorry it's come to this. You're all very fine people, and it's a pity there won't be any 'you' left after the wipe. You'll have to spend a few years relearning basic skills like talking, eating, and dressing yourselves. But try to look on the bright side." He turned a sympathetic smile on them. "You all get a fresh start."

"What about me?" said Frederick.

"It's the cells for you, I'm afraid," said Meridian. "At least you won't take up much room."

Another explosion shook the building, strong enough to set the glitter swirling in Frederick's globe, and Meridian had to steady himself against the desk to avoid falling. "That infernal woman," he muttered. "As if I didn't have enough to deal with." He flourished his cane. "Right. Who'd like to go first?"

Maybe it was the jolt of adrenaline to her brain as he turned to her, but Suzy was suddenly able to put the first pieces of the puzzle together. *It's Crepuscula. Meridian's surprised she followed us, but why? If she wants to take control of the Observatory, shouldn't he have been expecting an attack? And why now? She could have attacked ages ago, but she didn't. Because she was following us. She was following Frederick.*

Suzy didn't have the answers she needed, but these felt like the right questions.

"Wait!" she said, playing for time. "I still haven't read the spell you gave me."

Meridian paused, clearly displeased. "Must we do this now?"

"Yes," she said. "I won't be able to do it once you wipe my brain, will I?"

Meridian looked from her to Frederick and back again. He sighed. "Very well," he said. "But be quick about it."

She hurried to the desk and picked up Frederick. The spell book lay beside him, but her hand passed over it and closed around Fletch's wand instead.

"I've already told you," said Meridian, "that wand won't work with that spell. You'll kill him."

"I know," she said.

Frederick squeaked. "What are you doing?"

"Trust me," she whispered, and turned back to face Meridian. "I've changed my mind," she told him. "I don't want the spell anymore."

"What?" said Frederick. "Suzy, you promised!"

"We had an understanding," said Meridian, his voice clipped. "The spell in return for the Fact of Entry. I've discharged my duty to you."

"I'm entitled to any piece of information in exchange for my Fact of Entry," said Suzy. "I haven't looked at the spell yet, so I'm asking for something else instead. That's allowed, right?"

Meridian let out a long, whistling breath through his nose. "Technically, yes. But you are trying my patience."

"This won't take long," she said. "Just tell me—does Crepuscula really want to take over the Union?"

"Are you serious?" Frederick cried. "Why do you need to know that?" But to Suzy's immense satisfaction, Meridian's face had drawn into a scowl so deep she thought his eyebrows might collide.

"That's confidential," he said through lips pressed into a thin white line.

"So you *do* know," she said. "Which means it's your sacred duty to tell me. Does she want to conquer the Union or not?"

She watched his face twist, as though he was trying to keep the words locked up inside his mouth. His cheeks went red, then white with the effort. He started to sweat. But whatever the weight of his obligation to her, it was too great for him to bear. Like a balloon bursting, he opened his mouth and let out a gasping rush of air, with one word on it.

"No!"

Suzy smiled. "Thank you," she said. "You've been very helpful. And I'm sorry about your head."

Confusion overtook Meridian's anger. "What about my head?"

"My friend Ursel is about to hit you on it."

Meridian spun around, raising his wand to defend himself, but as Suzy had hoped, Ursel's reflexes were quicker. She raised her great paws, still in their cuffs, and brought them around as one in a wide arc, catching Meridian on the side of the head and lifting him off his feet. He sailed through the air and collided with a book-case.

"Run!" shouted Suzy, already making for the door. Meridian's answer rang in her head, and she could already feel a host of others clicking into place around it. She hoped they were the right answers. Because everything depended on them.

32

The Liar, the Witch, and the War Zone

Suzy, Stonker, Ursel, and Frederick made it to the exit before Meridian staggered out of his office, shouting orders at the observers, some of whom rose from their seats but were otherwise too surprised or timid to act. Suzy locked eyes with Meridian for a second before the door swung shut behind her, and felt very glad of the distance between them; his face was set in a look of stern fury that sent a shiver of dread right through her.

"Where are we going?" wailed Frederick as she hammered the button to call the elevator. She heard it clanking up the shaft toward them and hoped it would be quick enough.

"I'm sorry," she said. "We'll find another way of

changing you back, I promise. But I had to find out what Meridian knew."

"You promised the last time," he muttered.

"It's better than getting your brain wiped clean, m'boy," said Stonker, casting anxious glances back over his shoulder toward the Observatory door. "At least you're still you. After a fashion."

The elevator arrived, and Ursel bundled them all in through the doors before they were even fully open. Suzy thumbed the button to take them back down to the library. At the other end of the corridor, the Observatory door swung open to reveal Meridian, his cane raised and its tip fizzing with magic.

"Get back!" shouted Stonker. They pressed themselves to the walls as the blast from Meridian's cane struck the back of the elevator, missing the end of Suzy's nose by inches and leaving a smoldering mark that smelled of wet garbage.

"I demand that you stop this!" barked Meridian. They heard his footsteps approaching up the corridor at a run, but the doors slid shut and the elevator jerked into motion. Suzy wiped a bead of sweat from her brow.

"Well, I can't say I think much of his hospitality," said Stonker. "Chap like that should be able to afford a few more manners." Ursel growled in agreement.

"You still haven't told me where we're going," said

Frederick. "And why did you ask him about Crepuscula? What's she got to do with anything?"

"You tell me," said Suzy. "You told me she was planning to conquer the Impossible Places."

"No, I told you *someone* was planning to conquer them. You're the one who assumed it was Crepuscula. I just didn't correct you."

"Why on earth not?" she said.

"Because I knew Meridian might be watching us," he said. "And the less you knew about his plans, the less reason he'd have to hurt you. It might have worked, too, if you hadn't just blurted everything out right in front of him."

"How was I supposed to know that?" she said, although the flush in her cheeks was as much due to embarrassment as anger. She'd never even suspected he'd been trying to protect her. "And anyway," she said, wanting to get past the feeling, "I still don't really know how you ended up inside that snow globe."

"Or on the Express, for that matter," said Stonker. "Not that it's any of my business what people put in the mail, but you're at the unusual end of the scale."

"It wasn't my fault," Frederick said. "Crepuscula sent me a NeuroGlobe to store all the information I was gathering for her on the Observatory project. I was supposed to fill it up and send it back to her, but once I realized what was really going on here, I didn't dare. If the Observatory was a tool for controlling the Impossible Places, she could never be allowed to find out about it. If she took power, she'd be an even worse ruler than Meridian."

"So what did you do instead?" said Suzy.

"I told you," he said. "I ran away. I couldn't stay here, and I couldn't go to Crepuscula, so I decided to take care of things myself. You remember what Meridian said about people being harder to manipulate if they know they're being manipulated? I thought that if I could tell the whole Union what was going on, the people would rise up together and throw Meridian out of power. Then I'd be a hero, and my parents would *have* to welcome me back. 'Our son, Freddie, he saved the Union, you know.' All I needed was somewhere safe to hide while I figured out how to open the NeuroGlobe, so I slipped out through the garbage chute one night and stowed away on a train home."

"Why did you need to open the NeuroGlobe?" she said. "You'd already been using it."

"Crepuscula had put a lock spell on it," he said. "I could put things into it, but I couldn't get them out again. Not without the correct incantation, anyway. I should have guessed she'd add a few other security measures as well."

"Like what?"

"Like the curse," he said sadly. "When I couldn't

unlock the globe, I tried smashing it open with a hammer. The next thing I knew I was inside it, looking out."

Suzy looked at him with fresh understanding. "You mean *you're* the NeuroGlobe?"

"Sort of. It trapped me inside and then disguised itself. Crepuscula's little joke."

"But that still doesn't explain how you ended up on our train," said Stonker.

Suzy got the sense that Frederick was gathering himself for something difficult. "My parents," he said at last, very quietly. "They boxed me up and mailed me to Crepuscula. I begged them not to, but she'd already offered them the reward money she'd promised me. I suppose they wanted to be rich, too."

Suzy didn't know what to say. She still wasn't sure whether she liked Frederick much, but she was certainly starting to feel sorry for him. After all, he had tried to do the right thing in keeping the NeuroGlobe from Crepuscula, even if it had all really been to impress his parents. Perhaps that had been selfish in a way, but then she thought of her own parents. They had never made her feel worthless or unwelcome and would certainly never try to *sell* her. Frederick wasn't so lucky, and she vowed that if she ever made it back, she would never do anything to annoy them ever again. Probably.

A dull boom somewhere close by shook the elevator in

its shaft, and they could hear a fizz and crackle of what sounded like lightning. The smell of smoke reached them from somewhere.

"Hold on," said Suzy. "This is it."

The elevator bounced to a stop, the doors opened, and they stepped out into a war zone.

❧

The Lunar Guard were arranged in a line across the nearest side of the library's central reading room, their plasma rifles blasting streams of white-hot energy into the phalanx of statues bearing down on them.

The statues boiled into magma where the energy hit them, and the air was filled with foul-smelling steam. Every few seconds one of the statues stumbled and fell, shattering to rubble, only for another to step forward and fill the gap. And so their line advanced, inexorably, one thudding step after another.

"If anyone's got any Pop Bottles left, use them now!" shouted Neoma. She was in the center of the guards' line, her gold tooth flashing as she blew a statue's head to slush.

Suzy and the others ducked as a handful of small glass bottles filled with bright green liquid arced through the air, detonating in bursts of vivid fire as they struck the statues. Half a dozen of the stone figures were blown to pieces, and the rest were thrown to the ground by the force of the explosions.

The guns fell silent as the guards ducked and covered, and for a second the only sound Suzy could hear through the ringing of her ears was the whir of shrapnel ricocheting off the wall behind her.

"Wish me luck," she whispered to the others. Then, before they could stop her, she dashed past Neoma and into the battle-scarred no-man's-land between the opposing forces. "Stop!" Suzy shouted.

"Help!" yelled Frederick. "She's trying to get me killed!"

Nobody listened. The surviving statues were already climbing to their feet, their line closing up once more. Suzy heard the hum of the guards' rifles behind her, ready for the last stand.

"Ready!" barked Neoma. "Take aim!"

She never got any farther. Before she could give the order to fire, something quick and black raced out from between the statues' feet, slipping across the floor in dark tendrils that seized three of the guards in quick succession. They fell, screaming, into darkness, leaving nothing behind, and Suzy was momentarily overcome by the memory of Wilmot's last moments.

"Fall back!" shouted Neoma.

"Suzy! Get away from there!" Stonker yelled. Ursel roared.

Suzy screwed her eyes shut. If her plan was going to work, it had to work *now*.

"Crepuscula!" she shouted at the top of her lungs. Frederick whimpered.

"Well?" came the too-familiar voice. "I'm waiting."

Suzy opened her eyes.

Crepuscula stood there, hands folded over the head of her cane. The sight of her banished Suzy's fear in an instant, replacing it with a burning hatred that she found much harder to control—here was the woman who had killed Wilmot. Suzy wanted to scream at her, to charge at her with Fletch's wand, but she bit her tongue and planted her feet more firmly among the rubble. "I'm here to return your NeuroGlobe," she said.

Crepuscula eyed the snow globe with guarded interest. "As simple as that?"

"No," said Suzy. "Once you've changed him back, you're going to let Frederick, me, Ursel, and Stonker go unharmed. Promise me that, and all the evidence that Frederick collected is yours."

"Perhaps I don't want it anymore," said Crepuscula. "I've already seized the Tower, after all."

"Not yet, you haven't," Neoma growled. Crepuscula gave her a pitying look.

"If all you wanted was the Ivory Tower, you would have brought your army here ages ago," said Suzy. "But you didn't, which means you're here for the NeuroGlobe instead."

Crepuscula raised an eyebrow, and then her cane, pointing the tip at Suzy's forehead. "You've tried so hard to keep him from me. What's changed?"

"I learned the truth," said Suzy. "Lord Meridian is controlling the Union. I thought you wanted to as well, but he says that's not why you're here."

"And why do you believe him?"

"Because he didn't want to tell me," said Suzy. "I think that means you're trying to stop him."

A little smile of satisfaction teased the corners of Crepuscula's mouth, though the tip of the cane didn't waver. "Of course I am, you silly girl. Did you think I'd been trying to get Frederick back for the pleasure of his company?"

Suzy heard the guards fanning out behind her, taking up better positions. The skin on her back began to crawl; if they opened fire, she would be caught between them and their target. If they hit her, there wouldn't be much of her left. "You need the evidence he gathered," she said. "But why? How is it going to help you?"

"Because this isn't an attack." It was Lord Meridian's voice, and everyone turned as he made his way into the reading room, stepping between the guards and coming to a halt beside Suzy. "It's an arrest. She wants to lock me away, but she knows she can't do it without evidence, don't you, Selena?"

Suzy started. She hadn't considered that Crepuscula might have a first name, nor that anyone would ever dare use it to her face, but Crepuscula seemed unfazed.

"You've gone too far, Aybek," Crepuscula said. "Mother always warned me you would. As keeper of the Obsidian Tower, it's my duty to intervene."

"Duty," he scoffed. "You couldn't wait to come crashing in here. You've always been the same, ever since we were children. Whatever I do, you have to best it or destroy it. Well, it stops today."

"Wait." Suzy looked between them in astonishment. "Are you two . . . brother and sister?"

"Twins," said Crepuscula. "Non-identical."

"Thank goodness," said Meridian. "Imagine sharing that face." Crepuscula gave him a mocking smile in return.

"But you've got different names," said Suzy.

"Different titles," said Crepuscula. "They come with the towers. Along with certain *responsibilities*." She directed this last word at Meridian.

"My responsibility is to improve the Impossible Places," said Meridian. "Which is precisely what I'm doing."

"He means he's been watching people," said Suzy.

"Spying on their leaders, so he can make them do what he wants."

Crepuscula nodded. "I thought it might be something like that. Did you really think I wouldn't notice when you turned your spyglasses on me, Aybek? My fillings vibrated."

Meridian frowned. "The result of bad dentistry, no doubt."

"Spare me," she said. "Magic of that strength is difficult to hide from an expert, even from a distance. And I started to notice it everywhere I went, from one Place to another. That's why I was able to make contact with young Frederick. He turned his attentions on his parents' farm so often I could smell the residual magic a mile away. All I had to do was stand there in the yard and wait for him to spot me." She spared Frederick a withering glance. "And if he hadn't had ideas above his station, I would have already put a stop to all this nonsense."

"I'm sorry," Frederick said in a low moan. "I thought you were going to take the Observatory for yourself. Just please let me go and I'll never break a promise again. I promise!" This prompted a derisive snort from Neoma.

"Your word isn't worth much," said Crepuscula. Her glare slipped from Frederick to Suzy. "Yours, on the other hand . . ."

Suzy bristled—she could see the old woman's thoughts slotting into place behind those lilac eyes.

"I may be prepared to accept your proposal," said Crepuscula, "on one condition."

"What?" said Suzy.

"I will let your friends go," she said, "if you take Frederick's place inside the snow globe."

Suzy heard the others gasp, and Ursel growl, but it all seemed very far away. This one huge horrible thought rang in her mind like a bell, drowning out everything else.

"A few years on my mantelpiece might do you good," Crepuscula continued. "Or maybe the boiler room, if I get tired of you. It might just teach you to respect your elders and betters."

At this, a tiny voice cut through the din in Suzy's mind. It belonged to the fury she had been keeping in check throughout the confrontation, and it had lots of things to say. She knew that saying them would be a *very bad idea*, but she no longer cared. What else could Crepuscula do to her?

"Betters?" she said, feeling the blood rushing to her cheeks. "What makes you think you're better than anyone?"

"I'm not a thief, for one thing," said Crepuscula.

"No," said Suzy. "You're a monster."

Crepuscula didn't react, but her shadow did. It

darkened and flexed, drawing other shadows to it until the floor was black with them. Meridian leveled his wand at Crepuscula, prompting the statues to take a crashing step forward, swords raised. The guards braced themselves. But Suzy persisted.

"I don't care if you're here to do the right thing—you don't want to be respected. You just want to be feared. You bully people, threaten them, and leave a trail of destruction wherever you go. You don't deserve my respect, and I'll never give it to you. Not after what you did to Wilmot."

Crepuscula's brow furrowed. "Wil-what?"

"The Postmaster," said Suzy. "In Trollville. Do you even remember him?"

For a few seconds, it was clear that she didn't. "Do you mean that fussy little boy with the complaint form?"

"He was my friend," said Suzy. "And you killed him."

"I did nothing of the sort."

"You did," said Suzy, her eyes pricking with angry tears. "I saw you."

"Did you?" Crepuscula raised her free hand and clicked her fingers. Everyone flinched, expecting some outburst of magic, but instead they heard a distant cry of alarm. Suzy and the others looked around, trying to pinpoint the source of the noise, but it seemed to come from nowhere. It grew rapidly louder, and closer, until the shadow on the floor shivered, heaved, and spat something large and flailing straight up into the air. The thing crashed back down to earth at Suzy's feet, and she looked down into Wilmot's startled face.

"Hello," he said, rubbing his head. "Could someone tell me what's happening?"

"Wilmot!" Suzy fell to her knees and threw her arms around him, almost dropping Frederick in her haste.

"I see you looked after my hat," he said.

"I thought you were dead!" she exclaimed. "What happened to you?"

"I just slipped him into a spare pocket dimension I like to carry with me," said Crepuscula. "It seemed quicker than dealing with all that paperwork. Honestly, I don't know what all the fuss is about."

"Postmaster!" Stonker arrived at a run, quickly followed by Ursel, and tried to clap Wilmot on the shoulder. His hands were still fastened together, though, so the gesture was more like a clumsy karate chop, which almost sent the young troll sprawling. "I never thought I'd set eyes on you again."

Ursel had just enough freedom with her handcuffs to slip her huge arms over the crew and squash them together in the most literal bear hug Suzy had ever experienced.

"Delightful," said Crepuscula. "Now hurry up and make your choice, girl. You've wasted enough of my day as it is." The air between her cane and Meridian's fizzed with suppressed magic.

"Suzy?" Wilmot looked at her in confusion. "What is she talking about?"

Suzy gave him her bravest smile, then extracted herself from Ursel's embrace. "I'm sorry," she said. Ursel tried to catch hold of her again, but Suzy stepped back out of reach. "It's the only way she'll let you all go."

Meridian cleared his throat. "I may have another solution," he said.

"What?" said Suzy hotly. She didn't want to hope that the old man might actually be able to help her.

"It's very simple, really," he said. "Guards? Shoot her. Shoot them all."

Suzy went cold, and Ursel drew the others closer to her chest, ready to shield them from harm. But the guards just shuffled their feet and looked to Captain Neoma for confirmation.

"My lord," Neoma said. "Our job is to protect you and this tower from harm, not to act as your personal assassins, and definitely not to help you hold the Union for ransom. So with all due respect, I think it's time you took your orders and shoved them somewhere." She turned her plasma rifle on him, and the other guards followed suit.

"Treachery, Captain?" He gave a bitter little smile. "I'll see you banished for this."

"Try it," she said, flashing him a golden smile. "Old man."

"Do stop being such a sore loser, Aybek," said Crepuscula. "It's over. Accept it." She held a hand out to Suzy, who flinched. There was a weight of fear on her chest, and she could feel it growing as she thought about everything she was giving up—not just her freedom, but her dignity, her body, her future. She almost sobbed out loud as she thought of her mom and dad, waking up and finding her gone. They would never know what had happened to her...

Frederick, still cupped in Suzy's hands, spoke up. "I'm sorry, Suzy," he said. "I didn't mean for any of this to happen."

"Neither did I," she replied, her voice shaking.

She took a deep breath. Then she smoothed her bathrobe out, picked a stray hair from her face, and handed Frederick to Crepuscula.

33

A Promise to Be Kept

Suzy had expected the old woman to gloat, but Crepuscula just grunted in acknowledgment.

"So that's it, then?" said Meridian. "I'm expected to just surrender?"

"Yes," said Crepuscula. "Once the formalities are out of the way." Keeping her eyes and wand on her brother, she raised the snow globe to her lips and whispered something to it. Then she tossed it into the air, as though she had simply discarded it.

Horrified, Suzy started forward, hands outstretched to catch it before it hit the ground and burst. But she was too slow, and it dropped out of reach. She screwed her eyes shut.

The *pop!* of breaking glass never came, and when she opened her eyes again there was no sign of the snow globe at all. Instead, a small, pale boy with ash-blond hair and a pinched face stood on the spot where it should have hit. He wore the same plain gray uniform as the other observers and held a NeuroGlobe in one hand.

"Frederick?" she said. "Is that you?"

The boy looked down at his own body in surprise, then back up with a smile. "Yes!" he said in Frederick's voice. "It worked! I'm me again!"

"That's one promise fulfilled," said Crepuscula. "Time for another."

Suzy's heart gave a painful lurch as Crepuscula beckoned to her, but she refused to let the sorceress see her fear. Nevertheless, her breathing quickened as she approached Crepuscula and her ears filled with a piercing whine that grew louder by the second.

It was only when Crepuscula looked past her that Suzy realized she could hear it, too. Meridian, Frederick, the guards, Ursel, and the trolls all looked toward a large stained glass window in one wall. The sound was coming from outside it, and a dark shape was growing in size beyond the glass.

"What—?" Suzy began, but that was all she had time to say before the window exploded inward, and the dark shape smashed through it, trailing fire.

People scattered as it plowed across the room with a scream of metal, leaving a wake of flaming books and splintered shelves behind it. Suzy threw herself backward and felt a blast of heat wash over her as the thing raced past. She thought she saw Crepuscula, caught right in the thing's path, throw her hands up in front of her face, but then Suzy hit the ground, and the object struck the opposite wall with a blow that threw everybody still standing to the floor.

Suzy sat up, spitting dust from her mouth. The room was full of smoke, and everything around her had been reduced to a shifting vortex of vague shapes. "Frederick?" she called. "Wilmot? Is everyone all right?"

There was an answering chorus of coughs and splutters.

"I'm fine," called Frederick from somewhere to her left.

"So are we," came Wilmot's voice.

"Grunf!" confirmed Ursel.

"Good grief!" Stonker staggered toward her out of the haze, his uniform white with dust. "Did you see what that was?"

"No," said Suzy. "I was too busy trying not to die."

He caught her by the shoulders, pulled her to her feet, and turned her to face the smoldering object. It was as big as a bus and lay at a drunken angle, surrounded by blackened books. "Don't you see?" he said. "It's the H. E. C."

Its paintwork had charred and blistered, it was missing

its wheels, and its front end was a concertina of twisted metal, but she realized with astonishment that he was right. And as they watched, the hatch on its side popped open and a figure stumbled out, clad in the silver space suit she had seen hanging on the rack inside. The figure groped its way clear of the wreckage before raising the helmet's reflective visor. "Whoops."

"As I live and breathe," exclaimed Stonker. "Fletch!"

The engineer turned to them in surprise, still a little unsteady on his feet. "It's true what they say, Stonks. The landing really is the tricky part."

The smoke and dust began to settle, and Suzy was able to see the extent of the damage. Neoma and her guards had already taken up fire extinguishers and were tackling the small fires that had sprung up in the H. E. C.'s wake, while Ursel, Wilmot, and Frederick picked their way over the wreckage to rejoin her and Stonker. It was only when she saw Meridian that she realized everything had gone wrong.

He stood among the rubble, his suit scorched and his hair in disarray, but with a look of triumph on his face. Crepuscula lay on the floor at his feet, glaring up at him as he pressed the tip of his cane into her forehead. In his other hand, raised high above his head, he held the NeuroGlobe.

"Not another step," he warned as the statues advanced.

"Unless you want me to turn her into something resembling wallpaper paste." Crepuscula tried to prop herself up on her elbows, but he pressed down harder, forcing her flat. The statues lowered their swords.

"This won't help you, Aybek," Crepuscula said. "You've got no friends left, and I've got too many witnesses. Not to mention more statues on the way."

He laughed. "And I have every army in the Union to command," he said. "Why, just today I struck a deal with the Berserker Chief to rally his people to my cause should I ever need them."

"The Berserkers don't take orders," she said, "and they don't answer to *anybody*."

"They do now," Meridian said imperiously. "They will reduce your statues to dust, and I will declare you an outlaw, banished for the rest of your days."

"The people of the Union will never stand for it," she said.

"But they will." He grinned. "You may have inherited some nostalgic sense of justice along with your tower, but your bedside manner is awful. As long as people think you're a monster, you won't be missed."

Crepuscula grimaced, and her shadow writhed beneath her. It had shrunk to a smudge, its edges badly frayed, and Suzy wondered if it had somehow absorbed the bulk of the H. E. C.'s impact on Crepuscula's behalf.

"What are we going to do?" whispered Frederick.

"I don't know," Suzy said. Her head was reeling, as though she were still on the *Belle de Loin*—everything felt out of control, careering toward disaster. She hated feeling so helpless.

Defeated, she let her hands fall to her sides, where one of them brushed against something heavy in her pocket: Fletch's wand. She took it out, not knowing what to do, but unable to just stand there empty-handed. There had to be *something*...

"With you gone, I'll be able to step up my restructuring program," Meridian went on. "I'll dispense with whole worlds. Why, I could put Troll Territory out of its misery in weeks, rather than years."

"Don't you dare!" said Stonker.

"But I do dare," said Meridian. "I'm the only one with the capacity to imagine a greater future, so only I can hold the strength to realize it."

Suzy stared at the wand in her hand, feeling so angry with herself she could have cried. She had carried it so far with her, she had thought it was the key to saving Frederick, but she still didn't even know how to use it. It might as well just be a stick of metal.

...not much more than a blunt instrument, really... Frederick's words resurfaced in her memory, dislodging others.

...like playing the violin with a hammer...

… when I couldn't unlock the globe, I tried smashing it open …

A hammer.

The wand twitched in her hand, as though in answer to her thoughts, and suddenly, inexplicably, it felt different. Not just an awkward length of metal anymore, but a tool. A tool with a purpose.

She moved quickly, before Meridian could react. Aiming at the NeuroGlobe in his hand, she pointed the wand and felt the truth of its purpose. It wanted to smash things. To shatter great big holes in reality.

So she let it, and it twitched again as a bolt of invisible, silent magic leaped from its tip toward the globe. *Go on*, she thought. *Smash it wide open.*

There was no sound of breaking glass—just a moment of connection in which she knew without a doubt that the wand had done its job: It had struck the NeuroGlobe with all its might.

With a dull thud, the globe dropped to the carpet where, a second before, Lord Meridian had been standing. Suzy stepped forward very cautiously and looked down at it. It was no longer full of shifting energy and clockwork, but had regained its gaudy ceramic base. A storm of neon glitter was just settling on the familiar form of the little frog inside it, which blinked up at her and spoke with Lord Meridian's voice.

"What happened?" it said. "Why is everything so big?"

It blinked again as understanding dawned. "No!" it raged. "You did this? I demand you let me out this instant!"

Suzy picked up the snow globe and gave it a vigorous shake. "I don't think so," she said. "I think you deserve this."

"Never a truer word spoken." Panting with effort, Crepuscula finally regained her feet. "Hand him over." Suzy was only too happy to comply. Crepuscula looked in at her brother and gave a weary cackle. "Whatever else happens, Aybek, this is how I'll always remember you."

"Oh, shut up," he said. "Just hurry up and lock me away, so I don't have to look at you anymore."

"Gladly," she said. "But not before I've seen one last promise kept. There's room for two in this snow globe, you know."

Suzy went cold as the old woman turned her eyes on her, but before she could react further, she found Ursel's arms locked around her body, holding her back.

"We will not let you do this, madam," said Stonker, putting himself between Suzy and Crepuscula. "It's not right."

Suzy put a hand on his shoulder. "It's okay," she said, although she certainly didn't feel it. "I have to do this. Please. I gave my word." The truth was that, if she waited any longer, she knew she wouldn't have the courage to go through with it.

Stonker looked shocked, then sad. His mustache drooped. But he stepped aside and nodded at Ursel who, after a moment's indecision, released her hold. Suzy stepped forward, eye to eye with Crepuscula.

"I'm ready," she lied.

Crepuscula grunted. "I wasn't sure you'd keep your word."

Her dismissive tone stoked the last of Suzy's anger, though she was too tired to retaliate now. "Just get it over with."

Crepuscula studied her closely, as though looking for something. "Very well," she said. "Apologize for stealing from me, and we'll call it even."

Suzy thought she had misheard. "Sorry?"

"Close enough." Crepuscula dropped the snow globe into her pocket.

"What?"

"I wanted to be certain you could really be trusted when it counts," Crepuscula said. "And now I am."

Suzy gaped at her, relief and anger fighting for control of her feelings. "How dare you put me through all that!" she said. "I thought I was giving up my life!"

"And it was very noble of you," said Crepuscula. "Perhaps you'd like a sticker, or a lollipop or something?"

Suzy was about to tell her exactly what she would have liked, but Wilmot caught her by the arm.

"Don't push your luck," he said. "We're all still in one piece. Let's leave it at that, shall we?"

"No, let's not," said Neoma, cutting in. "Someone needs to take responsibility for this mess, and it's not going to be me." She indicated the rows of ruined bookshelves and the smoking wreck of the H. E. C.

"Why not?" said Crepuscula. "The tower needs a new keeper. Someone who knows the ropes. Someone trustworthy."

"I'm a guard, not an academic," said Neoma. "I don't want the job."

"Which makes you the perfect person to take it," said Crepuscula. "You'll be less tempted to abuse your privilege. But perhaps you'd rather trust someone else with it?" She raised her eyebrows ever so slightly, while a flurry of emotions swept across Neoma's face.

"No," she growled at last. "If anyone's going to make a mess of this, I'd rather it be me. But this is only until I can find a proper replacement—is that understood? I can probably handle the fallout from the Union leaders, but I don't know how to run a library."

"No, you don't," said Crepuscula. "But he might." She turned to Frederick, who flinched.

"Out of the question," said Neoma. "I wouldn't trust that little sneak as far as I can throw him, though I'd like to throw him a very long way. Preferably off the top of the tower."

"It's up to you, of course," said Crepuscula, "but he has a reasonably sharp mind. Perhaps an honest job will be enough to keep him out of trouble."

Neoma gave Frederick a look that suggested she doubted this very much. Frederick, for his part, didn't dare say a word, although Suzy could see the eager spark of hope in his eyes.

"You know your way around the shelves, I suppose," Neoma said.

"I do!" said Frederick, springing forward. "I'll take care of everything down here for you. Shelving, research, the archives. You name it!"

Neoma surveyed the ruined shelves again, clearly weighing the amount of work involved in restoring them. "If you do anything to annoy me *in the slightest*, I'll let you live just long enough to regret it. Is that understood?"

Frederick nodded, half scared, half excited. "So is that a yes?"

"Against my better judgment," said Neoma. "Don't make me regret it."

"Splendid," said Crepuscula. "I'll leave a few of my boys to help clean up." She rapped her cane against the floor, and ten of the statues lumbered over. "Do whatever the new Lady Meridian tells you to do," she said. "Within reason, of course."

The statues turned as one to face Neoma, who grimaced.

"'Lady Meridian' is going to take some getting used to," she said. Then, addressing the statues, "You're going to help my new librarian here tidy up. Is that understood?"

The statues bowed, and she smiled, despite herself.

"And if you so much as misfile a book," she went on, "I'm going to blast you all into gravel."

They bowed again.

"Might I recommend dismantling the Observatory while you're at it?" said Crepuscula. "I'll share the contents of Frederick's NeuroGlobe with the public. It will let the leaders know they've nothing to fear from the Ivory Tower any longer, but they'll want to make sure such a thing can't happen again. A pile of broken spyglasses might just keep the mobs from your door."

"I never liked the place anyway," said Neoma. "Sergeant Mona? We're redecorating the Observatory. Break out the explosives."

"What about the observers?" said Frederick as Sergeant Mona and her squad jogged away. "They're all out of a job now."

"They can find better ones," said Neoma.

"What if we make them library assistants?" he mused. "I could use the help."

"You're the head librarian," said Neoma. "It's up to you."

"Head librarian!" he said, beaming. "Let's see what Mom and Dad make of *that*."

The last Suzy saw of him, he was hurrying away among the rubble, arguing with Neoma.

"This is someone else's problem now," said Crepuscula. "So if you'll excuse me, I'm going to put my brother somewhere safe."

"Not on your mantelpiece, I hope," said Meridian from her pocket.

"I was thinking of a prison cell," she said. "For a very long time." He made a noise of disgust.

She gathered her shawl around her shoulders and began stirring the air with her cane.

"Wait!" said Suzy as a cold wind with no apparent source began to circulate around the old woman. "There's something I forgot to ask."

"Make it quick," said Crepuscula, still working her spell.

"The moon," said Suzy. "Why can I see it from Earth if Earth's not part of the Union?"

"I've no idea," said Crepuscula. "Aybek? Do you know?" She pulled him out of her pocket.

"Of course I do," he said. "I can remember every fact I've ever learned. But I don't see why I should tell her anything." Crepuscula gave him a quick, hard shake, but he remained stubbornly silent.

"He'll probably sulk for a few years," she said, dropping him back in her pocket. "But you're friends with a librarian now. Try asking him." The wind was whipping Crepuscula away, along with her words. She started to be there, and not there, flitting in and out of vision, along with her remaining statues. Before she vanished completely, Suzy heard her parting words strung out on the wind. "And stay out of trouble."

34

FINAL DESTINATIONS

Having assigned her guards to their duties, Neoma accompanied Suzy, Ursel, and the trolls back to Center Point Station, where she set about haranguing the staff into commissioning a train to take them home. This gave Suzy ample time to sit down with the others on the terrace of a ruined sandwich stall, in the furrow of destruction plowed by the *Belle*, and tell them everything that had happened since her first encounter with Frederick at the Obsidian Tower.

Her cheeks burned with embarrassment as she revealed just how much she had lied and hidden from them, but they seemed too fascinated to be angry, and when she finally finished, Stonker slapped his knee and said,

"Remarkable! I doubt the Old Guard have got a story half as good among them. Eh, Postmaster?"

Only then did they realize that Wilmot's seat was empty. At some point during her story, he had slipped away.

She found him kicking a paper cup along the concourse, his head bowed in thought.

"Hey," she said, falling into step beside him. He didn't look up, and her insides stung with shame. They had to walk a little farther before she finally gathered the courage to speak again. "I'm really sorry, Wilmot," she said. "If I hadn't broken my promise, none of this would have happened. You wouldn't have been swallowed by the shadow, the Express would still be in one piece..." With awkward fingers, she unpinned the badge from her bathrobe and handed it to him. "I wasn't a very good postie."

He took the badge and ran his thumbs across its raised surface. "Maybe not," he said, "but that's not your fault. It's mine."

She looked at him in surprise. "What?"

"I was too eager to have a postie on the staff. I just handed you the badge and a parcel and pushed you out the door to fend for yourself. It was irresponsible of me. I'm sorry."

The idea of him needing to apologize was so ludicrous she almost laughed. "I volunteered, remember?"

"I know," he said. "But as Postmaster, I should have refused your offer and delivered the package myself. I was a bit of a coward."

With a shock, she realized he was angrier with himself than with her. She threw an arm around his shoulder and pulled him into a sideways hug. "You stood up for me in the post office vault. It was the bravest thing I've ever seen."

He blushed. "Not really. I was just doing my job at last."

"And doing it brilliantly," she said. "You're the best Postmaster in the business."

"Thank you." His lips flickered into a nervous smile. "And you'd probably be a very good postie, with a bit of practice. After all, most people never get to see inside the Ivory Tower, and you helped overthrow its curator. That's quite an accomplishment. I think."

It was her turn to blush now. "I'm just glad we're all safe."

"Me too."

They grinned at each other until Neoma's voice cut through the station's PA system. "Train for Trollville departing from Platform 3 in five minutes," she barked. "I want every troublemaker on it, and out of my moon."

They arrived in Trollville to a heroes' welcome; it seemed that every troll in the city, young and old, had assembled to greet the passenger train that dropped them off. The crew of the Impossible Postal Express stepped down onto the platform, and the crowd surged forward.

And ran right past them.

"What's going on?" said Suzy. Everyone in the crowd had their hands full: oilcans, hammers, drills, sheets of scrap metal, a large brass door knocker... It looked like they had raided a scrap yard on their way to the station.

Then she saw where they were heading and let out a gasp of sorrow.

Six of Crepuscula's statues were advancing up the tracks behind their train like pallbearers, carrying something huge on their shoulders. It was the wreck of the *Belle de Loin*, and as they set it down, the crowd swarmed over it and the sound of heavy work began immediately.

"What are they doing?" Suzy shouted over the cacophony of hammering and welding.

"What trolls always do," said Stonker, puffing his chest out. "Taking what they have and making something with it."

"Do you really think they can fix the *Belle*?" she asked.

"Certainly," he said. "She won't be quite the same *Belle*

de Loin, of course. She'll be something new, but she'll have the same heart. And she'll have something of every troll in Trollville in her." His eyes sparkled. "The rest of the Express will need rebuilding as well. The sorting car may have survived, but we'll need a new tender and a new H. E. C. I'm rather looking forward to it."

Suzy watched the work progress and felt her tired spirits lift a little.

Just then, a fresh chorus of voices sounded from the far end of the platform. It was the Old Guard, with Gertrude and Dorothy in the lead, and they bore down on the crew like a tidal wave. Gertrude gave Suzy a hard stare as she swept past, before snatching up Wilmot and pulling him to her bosom in a viselike grip.

"Oh, my boy, I thought you were gone forever!" she sobbed. Dorothy had locked her arms around the pair of them and was wailing freely, while the members of the Old Guard pressed in on all sides, clapping them all on the shoulders, offering handkerchiefs, and congratulating Wilmot on what they had clearly already agreed was a miraculous resurrection.

Mr. Trellis, meanwhile, skipped over to Suzy and prodded her square in the chest. "Well?" he said. "Did my Fact of Entry come in handy?"

Suzy laughed and hugged him. "It got me exactly what I needed to know," she said.

"Good." He winked. "You've been places I haven't, and you'll see plenty more, I'll wager."

"I'd like that," she said. Before she could expand on the thought, a hand rested on her shoulder, and she turned to find herself face-to-face with Fletch.

"Time to go, my girl," said Fletch. "Time's a-wastin'."

"Already?" she said.

But of course it was. All the peril and excitement had almost driven the problem of getting home clean out of her mind, but now she remembered that her parents would almost certainly be awake, and frantic with worry. The police might even be waiting for her.

Ursel leaned down and wrapped both her and Stonker up in a crushing hug. Wilmot finally managed to free himself from Gertrude's embrace and squeezed in beside them.

"Thank you," Suzy said as she pressed her cheek into the bear's warm fur for the last time. "All of you. For everything. I think you're the best train crew in the Impossible Places."

"Very kind of you to say so, m'dear," said Stonker. "It's been an experience having you aboard."

"I'm sorry for all the trouble."

"Nonsense," said Stonker. "We'll be back on the rails in no time. Isn't that right, Postmaster?"

"Indeed," said Wilmot. "Although this might be my

358

opportunity to finally reorganize the indexing system in the sorting car."

Ursel made a guttural noise that sounded a lot like laughter before she finally released her hold on them.

Suzy took a last look at her friends. What would her old life be like now that she knew all this was possible? She tried to picture herself going to school every day, doing her homework, watching TV...but couldn't even imagine it.

"All right," she said, fighting back a stray tear as she turned to Fletch. "Let's go."

The train emerged in Suzy's hallway and eased to a whistling halt. The room was still abnormally huge, and to her alarm, daylight streamed in through the windows.

"What time is it?" she said, climbing down from the carriage.

Fletch sprang down after her and consulted his pocket watch. "Half past five," he said.

Suzy almost sat down, the shock was so great. "I've missed the whole day!" she said. "Mom and Dad'll be frantic!"

"They don't look bothered." He hooked a thumb in the direction of the living room door, which still stood ajar. Suzy got that queasy feeling of vertigo again as she looked through it, but Fletch was right—her parents were exactly where she had left them, sprawled on the sofa, snoring steadily. "The spell doesn't just wear off," said Fletch. "You've got to remove it. Like that princess in that castle, slept for a hundred years before some prince woke 'er up. Poor bloke. He didn't stand a chance against 'er morning breath." He looked around again and smacked his lips. "I can have this done in five minutes, and then I'll break the spell. Sound good?"

"I think so," she said. "It's Saturday, so they haven't missed work or anything, and I'll just tell them I had a pajama day. But what happens after that? Are you still planning to scramble my brain?"

He squinted down his nose at her. "The way I see it, people on much better pay grades than me haven't bothered, so I don't see why I should."

He cried out in shock as she threw her arms around him. "Thank you, Fletch," she said, the bristly hair of his ears catching her tears. "I don't want to forget any of it."

"Gerroff," he grumbled, but he didn't actually make any move to dislodge her. "Besides, I can't do much of anything without my wand, can I?"

"Oh yes, of course." She released him and reached into her pocket. "Here."

The old troll's face brightened as she handed it over.

"That's more like it," he said. He ran his fingers along its length and gave it a little twirl.

"I'm sorry I took it," she said.

"At least you got some use out of it. Now stand aside. There's work to be done."

It took him barely two minutes, in the end. With a final tap on the kitchen door, he returned the wand to his tool belt and strolled back to the waiting train.

"All done," he said with obvious pleasure. "The room'll snap back into shape once the train's out of the way, and the tunnels will seal behind it. Are you ready for me to wake those two up?"

She nodded. He pulled a small pouch from one of his pockets and reached into it with his finger and thumb, withdrawing a pinch of what looked like sand. But when he raised it to his lips and blew it in the direction of the living room, it seemed to dissolve into the air itself. "That should do it." Fletch returned the pouch to his pocket, signaled to the engine driver, and jogged to the waiting carriage, scrambling aboard.

"Take care, Fletch," she called after him. "Give my love to the others. And if you ever need another shortcut . . ."

He made some reply, but the engine's whistle drowned him out. She just had time to see him wave before the train disappeared into the tunnel mouth. Then, in an instant, both train and tunnel were gone, the kitchen door was just a door, and the hall was back to normal. It was over.

Suzy shut her eyes and let the comforting mundanity of home wash over her. She was truly, deeply happy to be back, safe and secure in a place she understood, and yet the feeling was tinged with a vague sadness—for the first time, she realized she hadn't wanted her adventure to end.

Her parents woke feeling groggy and more than a little alarmed at having missed almost an entire day.

"We must have been overdoing it," said her mother, rubbing the sleep from her eyes. "I'm so sorry, sweetheart. You should have woken us."

"I've kept busy," she said, and then surprised them both by throwing her arms around them and hugging them close. "I missed you, though."

"It's all right, Suzy," said her dad, returning the hug. Then, after a little thought, "Have you dyed your hair?"

❧

The next day dragged by. Then the next week. Suzy ate her breakfasts, went to school, did her homework, brushed her teeth, went to bed, and did all the dozens of little things she knew she was supposed to, day in, day out. Even the blond in her hair faded away. She barely noticed any of it.

She found herself looking at the moon a lot each night and wondering...

And then, on a Sunday morning, as she was lying awake in bed and trying to understand how she could possibly hope to fill another day of empty hours, she heard her dad call from downstairs.

"Suzy? There's a parcel for you."

He sounded confused, and she wasn't sure why until she remembered that the mailman didn't deliver on Sundays.

She came down to find him holding a brown paper parcel. "I don't recognize the stamp," he said. "It must be from abroad." He handed it over.

It didn't have her address on it, just the words SUZY SMITH in large, blocky handwriting on the front. And the stamp... It was printed on blue paper instead of gold leaf, but there was no mistaking the profile of Queen Borax the First.

Suzy gasped. "Thanks, Dad!" She turned and ran upstairs, where she threw herself down on her bed and tore the parcel open. A bundle of red-and-gold cloth fell out—a Troll Post uniform. She held it up to herself in the mirror. It was a good fit and looked brand-new. Her deputy's badge was pinned to the lapel and had been polished to a shine.

She returned to the parcel, where she found a single

363

sheet of note paper. The heading read, FROM THE OFFICES
OF THE IMPOSSIBLE POSTAL SERVICE. Beneath that, in the
same square handwriting as the envelope, were the words
Practice makes perfect. See you soon.

It was signed, simply, *Wilmot.*

ACKNOWLEDGMENTS

Just as no train can run without its crew, so this book would never have got under way without the help and influence of a great many people.

First and foremost, Claire Fayers, who for years has patiently read my unpublished (and unpublishable) manuscripts, and always offered me keen insight and encouragement. Without your friendship, enthusiasm, and coffee, this story might never have made it farther than my laptop.

Gemma Cooper, the greatest agent a writer could possibly wish for. Not only did you help me turn my truncated first draft into a fully functional story, you worked minor miracles to find it the best possible homes. It's a tremendous comfort to know you've got my back.

My fantastic editors: Anna Poon and Holly West at Feiwel and Friends, Rebecca Hill and Becky Walker at Usborne, and the wonderful teams at both houses. Thanks, all of you, for making me, Suzy, and the crew feel so welcome. I knew from the start that we were in the right hands, and your passion and insight have made this an unforgettable ride. I can't thank you enough.

All the many people who have supported and encouraged my reading and writing over the years. You are legion, but special mention goes to Miss Joyce of Newport Libraries, who always knew which books I'd like (and who lent me her VHS recording of the final episode of classic *Doctor Who* when I missed the original broadcast); Patrick Jones and Lloyd Robson, for having faith that a handful of teenagers could take on the world; Tim Lebbon and Gary Greenwood, who didn't laugh at my very first handwritten attempt at a novel, but took me to the pub and told me to keep at it; Aurélien Lainé, Caleb Woodbridge, David Williamson, and Kieran Mathers for their unwavering friendship and feedback; the Team Cooper brain trust, but especially Paul Gamble, who gave this book its subtitle.

My family. Mum, Dad, Chris, and Grandma: You always made sure there were good books at hand, and encouraged me to read them. I would never have wanted to write this story if I hadn't learned to love all those others first.

Aurelien and Théo: for keeping me busier, happier and prouder than I would ever have imagined possible. Please keep at it.

And finally, for Anna: You've always been far more patient with me than I deserve, and none of this would have been possible without your love, advice, and support. Thank you, and I love you.